The Land and People of
SOUTH AFRICA

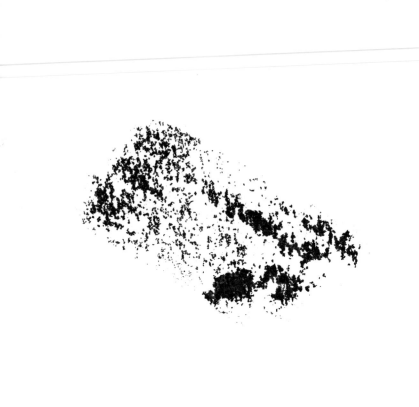

The Land and People of
SOUTH AFRICA

by Jonathan Paton

J. B. LIPPINCOTT   NEW YORK

Country maps by Philip Stickler/Stickler Cartography

Every effort has been made to locate the copyright holders
of all copyrighted materials and to secure the necessary
permission to reproduce them. In the event of any questions
arising as to their use, the publisher will be glad to make
necessary changes in future editions.

The Jane Gregory Agency has extended permission to reprint the
poem "Alexandra" on pages 55–57 from *Selected Poems*
by Mongane Serote (A. D. Donker, 1982).

THE LAND AND PEOPLE OF
is a registered trademark of
Harper & Row, Publishers, Inc.

The Land and People of South Africa
Copyright © 1990 by Jonathan Paton
Printed in the U.S.A. All rights reserved.

Library of Congress Cataloging-in-Publication Data

Paton, Jonathan.
    The land and people of South Africa / by Jonathan Paton.
        p.   cm. — (Portraits of the nations)
    Bibliography: p.
    Includes index.
    Summary: An introduction to the history, economy, geography,
politics, art, and culture of South Africa.
    ISBN 0-397-32361-1 : $. — ISBN 0-397-32362-X (lib. bdg.) :
$
    1. South Africa—Juvenile literature.   [1. South Africa.]
I. Title.   II. Series: Portraits of the nations series.
DT753.P39   1990   89-2477
968—dc19   CIP
                                                        AC

10 9 8 7 6 5 4 3 2 1
First Edition

To Margaret, Nic, Anty, and Pam,
who have always supported me
with encouragement and love

ACKNOWLEDGMENTS

I owe thanks to many people who have encouraged me and offered me expert advice in the writing of this book. Regrettably I cannot mention every name, but I would in particular like to thank the following for their help, which in some cases has been listed after the name: Fay Byrne, Luli Callinicos, John Earle, Ingrid Hudson (photographs), Guy Leadbeater (economic trends), Lisa Martus, Gail Mortinson, Denise Newfield, Anthony Paton (art), Nic Paton (music), Malcolm Purkey (theater), Peter Randall (Beyers Naude, religion, Namibia and Angola, Gandhi, Archbishop Tutu, literature), Mallory Saleson (role of women), Walter Saunders (van Riebeeck, Mosheshwe, Shaka), Phillip Stickler (maps), Mike Taylor, Tony Traill (click languages), Viv van der Sandt, Elito Viglieno, Lyn Wadley, Eddie Webster (trade unions). Finally I would like to thank my editor, Marc Aronson, for the invaluable help and advice he has given me throughout the writing of this book, as well as for his enthusiasm and encouragement in times of stress.

Contents

THE WORLD

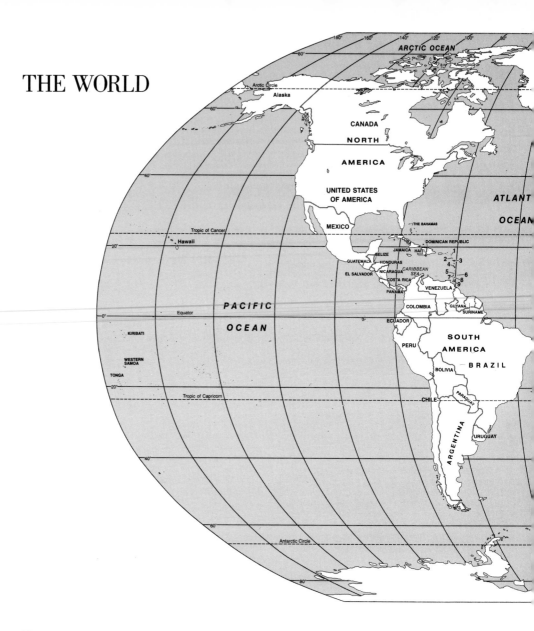

This world map is based on a projection developed by Arthur H. Robinson. The shape of each country and its size, relative to other countries, are more accurately expressed here than in previous maps. The map also gives equal importance to all of the continents, instead of placing North America at the center of the world. *Used by permission of the Foreign Policy Association.*

Legend

———— International boundaries

-------- Disputed or undefined boundaries

Projection: Robinson

0	1000	2000	3000 Miles

0	1000	2000	3000 Kilometers

Caribbean Nations

1. Anguilla
2. St. Christopher and Nevis
3. Antigua and Barbuda
4. Dominica
5. St. Lucia
6. Barbados
7. St. Vincent
8. Grenada
9. Trinidad and Tobago

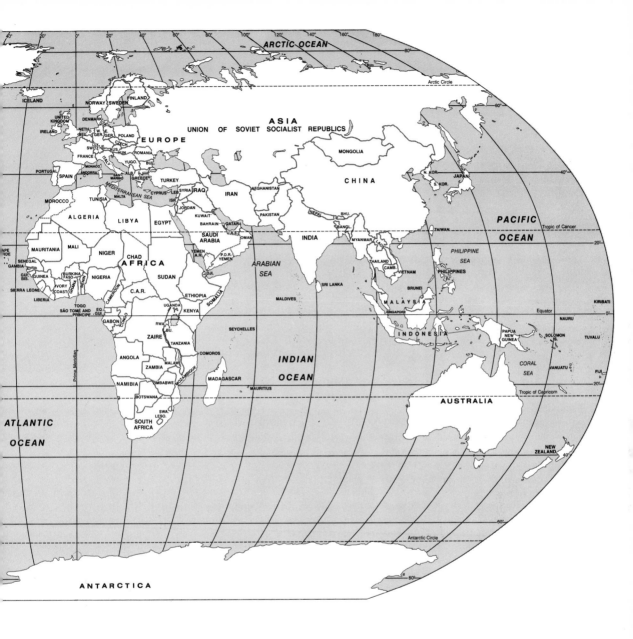

Abbreviations

ALB.	—Albania	C.A.R.	—Central African Republic
AUS.	—Austria	CZECH.	—Czechoslovakia
BANGL.	—Bangladesh	DJI.	—Djibouti
BEL.	—Belgium	E.GER.	—East Germany
BHU.	—Bhutan	EQ. GUI.	—Equatorial Guinea
BU.	—Burundi	GUI. BIS.	—Guinea Bissau
BUL.	—Bulgaria	HUN.	—Hungary
CAMB.	—Cambodia	ISR.	—Israel

LEB.	—Lebanon
LESO.	—Lesotho
LIE.	—Liechtenstein
LUX.	—Luxemburg
NETH.	—Netherlands
N. KOR.	—North Korea
P.D.R.–YEMEN	—People's Democratic Republic of Yemen

RWA.	—Rwanda
S. KOR.	—South Korea
SWA.	—Swaziland
SWITZ.	—Switzerland
U.A.E.	—United Arab Emirates
W. GER.	—West Germany
YEMEN A.R.	—Yemen Arab Republic
YUGO.	—Yugoslavia

Mini Facts

OFFICIAL NAME: Republic of South Africa

LOCATION: Southern extremity of Africa, bordering on the Indian Ocean on the east and south and the Atlantic Ocean on the west. Traversed by the Tropic of Capricorn. To the northwest are Botswana and Namibia, to the north Zimbabwe, to the east Mozambique and Swaziland. Lesotho is completely surrounded by South Africa.

AREA: 473,000 square miles (1.25 million sq. km.), larger than Texas and California combined

POPULATION: 34 million (in the mid-1980's)

CAPITALS: Administrative capital: Pretoria
Legislative capital: Cape Town
Judicial capital: Bloemfontein

TYPE OF GOVERNMENT: Republic

LANGUAGES: Official: English and Afrikaans.
Many other languages are spoken, including Zulu, Sotho, and Xhosa.

OFFICIAL RELIGIONS: 72 percent of South Africa's population is Christian, including 12.5 percent in the Dutch Reformed Church and 9.2

percent in the Catholic Church; 20 percent of the black population belongs to the African Independent Churches, which are Christian; 1.2 percent of the total population is Muslim; there are 120,000 Jews

HEAD OF STATE (AND HEAD OF GOVERNMENT): State-President (five-year term)

NATIONAL ASSEMBLY: The tricameral Parliament that came into existence in 1985 includes three houses: a house for whites (178 members), known as the House of Assembly; a house for coloureds (85 members), known as the House of Representatives; and a house for Indians (45 members), known as the House of Delegates. Elections are held every five years. Blacks are not represented in Parliament and may vote for homeland governments or local councils only.

ADULT LITERACY: Progressive organizations claim that over 9 million South African blacks are illiterate. 55 percent of adult blacks have less than four years of schooling. The government defines literacy as the successful completion of four years of education.

LIFE EXPECTANCY: Males: white, 67; coloured, 56; Indian, 62; black, 58 Females: white, 76; coloured, 62; Indian, 68; black, 62

MAIN SOURCES OF INCOME: Manufacturing and mining

MONETARY UNIT: Rand

South Africa:
The Southern Tip
of Africa

Sea and Sand

Sea and sand
My love
My land,
God bless Africa
Sea and sand
My love
My land,
God bless Africa
But more the South of Africa
Where we live. . . .
Bless the angry mountains
And the smiling hills
Where the cool water spills
To heal the earth's brow

Bless the children of South Africa
The white children
And the black children
But more the black children
Who lost the sea and the sand
That they may not lose love
For white children
Whose fathers raped the land. . . .

Sea and sand
My love
My land,
God bless Africa

This poem was written by Don Mattera, a black South African poet and journalist. Officially he is classified as a "coloured" person. His grandfather was Italian and his grandmother was part black. His poem tells of the pain and the suffering that lie beneath the beauty of his country, South Africa.

South Africa is today the only remaining white-ruled country in sub-Saharan Africa. The overwhelming majority of the population is black. A significant proportion of the black population is engaged in a bitter struggle for majority rule in the country. The white government of South Africa, on the other hand, is determined to preserve white culture and identity and fiercely opposes supporters of majority rule. This growing conflict will be a central focus of this book. But first attention will be given to South Africa's place on the continent of Africa.

The Republic of South Africa and the neighboring countries of Namibia, Botswana, Zimbabwe, Mozambique, Swaziland and Lesotho
Inset: The location of South Africa on the continent of Africa

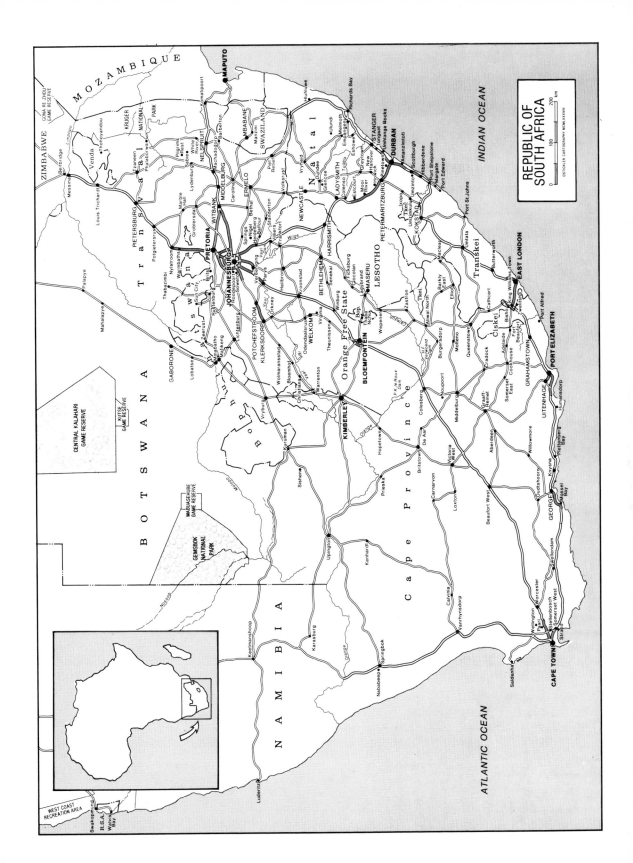

MOZAMBIQUE

ZIMBABWE

GONA RE ZHOU
GAME RESERVE

INDIAN OCEAN

MAPUTO

REPUBLIC OF
SOUTH AFRICA

OSTKLIER CARTOGRAPHY MCMLXXXVII

0   100   200   km

KRUGER
NATIONAL
PARK

Venda

Beitbridge

Messina

Louis Trichardt

Thohoyandou

PIETERSBURG

T r a n s v a a l

Komatipoort

MBABANE

Manzini

SWAZILAND

Pilgrims
Rest

White
River
Sabie

NELSPRUIT

Machadodorp

Carolina

ERMELO

Piet
Retief

Vryheid

Hluhluwe

Richards Bay

Umhlanga Rocks

STANGER
Tongaat

DURBAN

Amanzimtoti

Scottburgh

Hibberdene

Margate

Port Edward

Port St Johns

N a t a l

Melmoth

Ulundi

Empangeni

Eshowe

New
Hanover
Howick

PIETERMARITZBURG

Pinetown

Umkomaas

LADYSMITH

Estcourt

Mooi
River

Colenso
Glencoe

Dundee

NEWCASTLE

Volksrust

Standerton

Frankfort

Bethal

BETHLEHEM

HARRISMITH

Reitz

Vrede

Villiers

Heidelberg

Nigel
Springs

PRETORIA

WITBANK
MIDDELBURG

Nylstroom

Warmbaths

Thabazimbi

Marble
Hall

Lydenburg

Groblersdal

Balfour

Potgietersrus

Rustenburg

JOHANNESBURG
Roodepoort
Soweto

Krugersdorp

Brits

Sun City

Vereeniging
Vaal

Parys

Sasolburg

Heilbron

Bop.

Frankfort

Pietermaritzburg

Ixopo

Kokstad

KOKSTAD

Umtata

Transkei

Butterworth

EAST LONDON

King William's Town

Zwelitsha

Bisho

Fort
Beaufort

Ciskei

GRAHAMSTOWN

Port Alfred

UITENHAGE

PORT ELIZABETH

Humansdorp

Jeffreys
Bay

George

Knysna
Plettenberg
Bay

Mossel
Bay

Oudtshoorn

Swellendam
Somerset West

Strand

Worcester
Wellington
Paarl
Stellenbosch

CAPE TOWN

Saldanha

BOTSWANA

CENTRAL KALAHARI
GAME RESERVE

KUTSE
GAME RESERVE

Palapye

Mahalapye

GABORONE

Lobatse

B o p h u t h a t s w a n a

Mmabatho

Malikeng

MAFIKENG

Zeerust

GEMSBOK
NATIONAL
PARK

MABUASEHUBE
GAME RESERVE

NAMIBIA

Keetmanshoop

Karasburg

Springbok

Nababeeps

Luderitz

Kuruman

Vryburg

Christiana

Sishene

Hotazel

Postmasburg

Kenhardt

Upington

Calvinia

Van Rhynsdorp

Kimberley

KIMBERLEY

Warrenton

Bloemhof

Wolmaransstad

Orkney

KLERKSDORP

POTCHEFSTROOM

WELKOM

Virginia

Odendaalsrus

Theunissen

Winburg

Senekal

Ficksburg

Clocolan

Ladybrand

MASERU

LESOTHO

Wepener

Zastron

Aliwal North

Barkly
East

Lady Grey

Elliot

Maclear

Dordrecht

Queenstown

Molteno

Burgersdorp

Steynsburg

Orange Free State

BLOEMFONTEIN

Brandfort

Edenburg

Trompsburg

Reddersburg

Smithfield

Colesberg

Noupoort

Middelburg

Cradock

Graaff-
Reinet

Somerset
East

Adelaide

Cookhouse

Willowmore

Aberdeen

Beaufort West

Loxton

Victoria
West

Carnarvon

De Aar

Hanover

Britstown

Hopetown

Prieska

Preaska

Kenhardt

C a p e   P r o v i n c e

ATLANTIC OCEAN

R.S.A.

Walvis
Bay

Swakopmund

WEST COAST
RECREATION AREA

The Continent of Africa

The Republic of South Africa, situated at the southernmost tip of the continent of Africa, occupies an area about one twenty-third of the size of the whole. Africa is the world's second-largest continent, after Asia, with an area of 11,680,360 square miles (19,739,808 square kilometers). It contains one quarter of the world's habitable surface. From Algiers in the north to Cape Town in the south in a direct line is about 5,000 miles (8,450 kilometers). From Cape Verde in the west to Cape Guardafui in the east is almost the same distance. The continent of Africa is over three times as large as the United States.

The African coast is almost unbroken. It has very few bays and inlets, and is therefore poor in harbors. The continent also has few navigable rivers. This is because the interior of Africa is primarily a raised

Downtown Cape Town backed by Table Mountain.

plateau, and the coastal regions drop sharply to the sea. As a result there is much scenic beauty, especially on the eastern coast, where the drop is steeper than in the west. The rivers run through panoramas of mountains, hills, cliffs, and valleys, and are full of waterfalls and rapids. After the rains these rivers are swift and turbulent, but they are very uneven in flow, especially in South Africa, which for the greater part receives very little winter rain.

The lack of harbors and navigable rivers was one of the reasons why Africa was largely unknown to the people of Europe, who called it the "Dark Continent." But, others, such as the Arab traders who had easy access to Africa because prevailing winds in the Indian Ocean took them down the continent, linked East Africa with China and India. The darkness lay in the minds of the Europeans, not in Africa itself.

Colonization and the Slave Trade

By the end of the fifteenth century Europeans had finally "discovered" Africa. The first Europeans came seeking a route to the east, and in search of Christian allies against the Moslems. But, sadly, as more and more Europeans came to Africa from the seventeenth century onward, it was primarily to conquer, and later to colonize, the continent. The slave trade prospered, and it is estimated that until slavery was abolished, twenty million Africans were seized and taken from western and central Africa to the Americas, half of whom would die on the voyage. The renowned explorer / missionary David Livingstone estimated that for every slave taken, ten other Africans lost their lives, but there is no way of verifying these figures. By the beginning of the nineteenth century the life of the slave trade was drawing to its end, though slavery continued in Southern Africa for a few decades. During the nineteenth century great regions of Africa were becoming parts of European empires, and the practice of segregation and racial discrimination was universal. Both slavery and colonialism had catastrophic effects on Africa south of the Sahara.

Yet it would be too simplistic to say that colonization was purely evil. It was a complex and contradictory process. Certainly in terms of Western medicine, literacy, and efficient governments, the colonists had much to offer Africa. But they also inflicted deep wounds on the soul of the continent. The practice of segregation, the vast and visible difference between white wealth and black poverty, the contemptuous attitude of many colonists toward the indigenous people, the callous and sometimes cruel treatment of people as things rather than as persons, all these things left ugly scars.

South Africa

South Africa today is characterized by many of the marks of colonialism, but it would be unfair to compare it with the colonies of Africa. The Europeans went to countries like Ghana, Nigeria, French Africa, and Uganda to rule, not to settle. There was some settlement in Kenya, Tanzania, Angola, and Zaire, but with the coming of independence and the passing of authority to African majorities, white settlers left these countries in large numbers, many of them going to Zimbabwe (formerly Rhodesia) and others to South Africa. After the independence of Zimbabwe in 1980 many white Rhodesians left their country and settled in South Africa, although in recent times some have returned to Zimbabwe. There was also considerable white immigration to South Africa from Mozambique after that country's independence from Portugal in 1975.

The five million whites who live in the Republic of South Africa today are *not* colonists who plan to return to Europe in due course. The majority of whites—the Afrikaners—are descended from the Dutch who first arrived in South Africa in 1652 and from other European settlers who came to the Cape before 1795. The ancestors of many English-speaking whites came to settle in South Africa in the first half of the nineteenth century. The vast majority of the country's 29 million blacks, Indians, and coloureds accept the fact that the whites are in South Africa to stay. They do *not*, however, accept the fact that they should be ruled by the whites, whom they outnumber by more than five to one.

South Africa is one of the most complex countries in the world. It is a country of wealth and poverty, of technology and tradition, of beauty and terror. This book will attempt to describe the many contradictions in a country that is today the focus of world attention. If certain sections of the book dwell on the scenic beauty of the land, it is not because the ugliness and suffering are being ignored. There *is* beauty in the mountains and forests and coastlines and in the spirit of the people. But ugliness and pain and suffering are also to be found in the ghettos of the urban poor and in the red, barren soil of the rural peasant.

Don Mattera, whose poem "Sea and Sand" is quoted at the beginning of this chapter, has poignantly captured some of the beauty and the pain and the suffering of South Africa in another poem, "Expectation":

> *Many sunsets*
> *Gold and crimson*
> *Have dripped on the horizon,*
> *Weeping for the dying day.*
> *Many dawns*
> *Have risen*
> *In timely resurrection*
> *From their cradles of light.*

Sunsets and dawns
Dawns and sunsets.
I have seen them all
But when,
Oh when will I see that day
When love will walk the common way
To heal my wounded people
And break the shackles around their hearts?

The Republic of South Africa: Land and People

Although not the largest country in Africa, South Africa remains a large country by world standards. Its land area is about 473,000 square miles (1.25 million square kilometers), which makes it somewhat larger than Texas and California combined and more than twice as large as France. The distance from the largest city, Johannesburg, to the second-largest city, Cape Town, is 840 miles (1400 km.). Cape Town and the third-largest city, Durban, southern Africa's busiest seaport, are about 1,100 miles (1,800 km.) apart. Johannesburg and Durban are separated by 360 miles (600 km.). Estimating the population in South Africa is a complex matter, and some experts have argued that Durban's rapidly growing shack settlements occupied by black people have made the city considerably larger than Cape Town.

South Africa and Her Neighbors

The Republic of South Africa is made up of four provinces and a number of black "homelands." The four provinces came together to form the Union of South Africa in 1910. They were the Cape Province, the Orange Free State, the Transvaal, and Natal. Certain areas in each province were set aside by the government for the various black inhabitants. These were originally called "Native reserves" but today are referred to as "homelands." Four of these homelands have been granted independence, but South Africa is the only country in the world that has embassies in these countries. They are Transkei, Ciskei, Bophuthatswana, and Venda. These are not easy to locate on a map. Bophuthatswana, for example, consists of several pieces, and these are scattered throughout the provinces of the Cape, the Transvaal, and the Orange Free State. Two small countries on the map of South Africa *appear* to be part of the Republic of South Africa but are not. One is the Kingdom of Lesotho, which is completely surrounded by South Africa. The other is the Kingdom of Swaziland, which is *almost* surrounded by South Africa. Both Lesotho and Swaziland are independent countries, though not long ago they were ruled directly from Britain. South Africa's other neighbors are Botswana, Zimbabwe, and Mozambique. Namibia is a country that was under South African administration but which, according to an agreement signed on April 1, 1989, is supposed to become independent. It is a country that has been the subject of much controversy.

South Africa: The Land

South African landscapes are wide and sweeping. Much of the interior of the country is high plateau that falls away to the east, south, and west. This interior plain bears a resemblance to Texas, Arizona, and New

Mexico. The drop on the eastern side of the plateau is the most dramatic. This area is referred to as the "escarpment." The peaks of the Drakensberg Mountains in Natal are well over 10,000 feet (3,000 meters) above sea level. These mountains stand 5,000 feet (1,500 meters) above the surrounding country. Beneath them a series of hills and valleys stretches out like an irregular undulating staircase leading down to the sea. Many rivers flow swiftly from the Drakensberg Mountains to the Indian Ocean just over 100 miles (about 170 km.) away as the crow flies.

There is also an escarpment in the eastern Transvaal. Here the drop is also dramatic, but it differs from the Natal escarpment in that the surrounding country at the bottom of the drop is at a much lower altitude than its counterpart in Natal. This low-lying area, only a few miles from the top of the plateau, is known as the Lowveld. Veld is the name for southern African grassland with scattered trees and shrubs. The Lowveld is less than 2,000 feet (600 meters) above sea level. Here the largest game reserve in South Africa—the Kruger National Park— is situated.

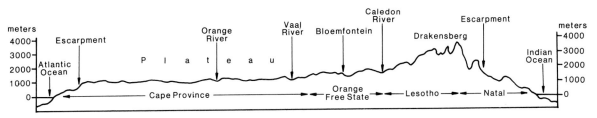

Section across South Africa along Latitude 29° S

The region of South Africa situated on the vast high plateau is known as the Highveld. This consists largely of an almost treeless plain, but in the more inhabited sections trees have been planted in the last 150 years. The largest city on the Highveld is Johannesburg, which is at an

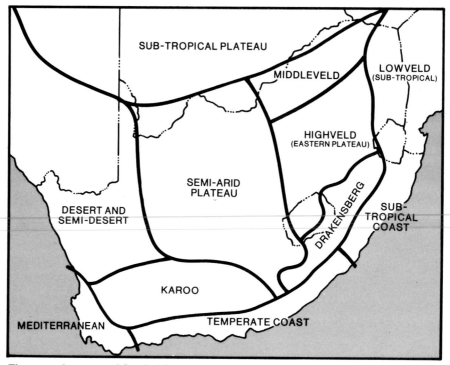

SUB-TROPICAL PLATEAU

MIDDLEVELD

LOWVELD
(SUB-TROPICAL)

HIGHVELD
(EASTERN PLATEAU)

SEMI-ARID
PLATEAU

DESERT AND
SEMI-DESERT

DRAKENSBERG

SUB-
TROPICAL
COAST

KAROO

MEDITERRANEAN

TEMPERATE COAST

The natural regions of South Africa

altitude of 5,800 feet (1,750 meters) above sea level. An American city situated at a similar altitude is Denver, Colorado.

The coastline of South Africa stretches for 2,760 miles (4,600 km.). Several bustling harbor cities are located on this coast, as well as many superb beaches. The Atlantic and Indian Oceans meet at the southernmost tip of Cape Province. Many visitors feel that the Cape Peninsula, with its Table Mountain, is the most majestic part of South Africa. The scenery here is certainly grand, but the grandeur is found throughout the mountain ranges of the Cape Province. Behind the mountains of the southern Cape lies the vast and arid Great Karoo, an area which many travelers prefer to avoid.

Buffels Bay in the Cape Peninsula. Sea and land meet in a wide variety of outcroppings, coves, and beaches along South Africa's long coastline.

The Natal coast runs north and south from Durban, South Africa's premier vacation city. The Natal coastal belt has a subtropical climate. The summers are wet, hot, and humid. This region reminds some people of the coastline of Florida.

South Africa: The People

From the description of South African scenery above, the reader will no doubt be struck by the wide range of contrasts in the landscape. There is also an exciting diversity among the people of South Africa, where more than a dozen languages are spoken. This rich cultural diversity is superbly captured in the following poem by Jeremy Cronin. Written as much for *sound* as *meaning*, the poem can be read quickly to hear the words and voices; translations for a second, slower, reading follow.

To Learn How to Speak

To learn how to speak
With the voices of the land,
To parse the speech in its rivers,
To catch in the inarticulate grunt,
Stammer, call, cry, babble, tongue's knot
A sense of the stoneness of these stones
From which all words are cut.
To trace with the tongue wagon-trails
Saying the suffix of their aches in -kuil, -pan, -fontein,
In watery names that confirm
The dryness of their ways.
To visit the places of occlusion, or the lick
In a vlei-bank dawn.
To bury my mouth in the pit of your arm,
In that planetarium,
Pectoral beginning to the nub of time
Down there close to the water-table, to feel
The full moon as it drums
At the back of my throat
Its cow-skinned vowel.
To write a poem with words like:
I'm telling you,
Stompie, stickfast, golovan,
Songololo, just boombang, just

To understand the least inflections,
To voice without swallowing
Syllables born in tin shacks, or catch
The 5.15 ikwata bust fife
Chwannisberg train, to reach
The low chant of the mine gang's
Mineral glow of our people's unbreakable resolve.

To learn how to speak
With the voices of this land.

Notes on "To Learn How to Speak" by Jeremy Cronin

KUIL:

Afrikaans word meaning "pool." Near Cape Town is a river called Kuilsrivier in Afrikaans, meaning "river of pools."

PAN:

Afrikaans word (also used in English) meaning depression or hollow ground in which water accumulates after rain. Near Johannesburg is a town called Brakpan named after a pan of brackish water on the outskirts of the town. *Brak* is an Afrikaans word meaning "brackish."

FONTEIN:

Afrikaans word meaning "spring." The judicial capital of South Africa is Bloemfontein, an Afrikaans word meaning "flower spring."

VLEI:

Afrikaans word meaning "lake" or "swamp."

STOMPIE:

A word of Afrikaans origin meaning "cigarette butt."

STICKFAST:

To stick fast is to "get stuck," a literal translation of an Afrikaans word.

GOLOVAN:

A word invented by black miners (derived from an African language) to refer to a dump truck used in gold mines for the transportation of gold-bearing ore.

SONGOLOLO:

A word of Nguni origin that refers to any of the so-called "pill" millipedes with hard shiny exterior armor, which roll into a flat, springlike coil if touched or alarmed (definition taken from *A Dictionary of South African English* by Jean Branford).

IKWATA BUST FIFE:

The way some Africans would pronounce "a quarter past five."

CHWANNISBERG:

The way some Africans would pronounce "Johannesburg."

Population

The population of the Republic of South Africa in the mid-1980's was about 34 million. This population was made up of the following groups:

BLACKS:	25 million
WHITES:	5 million
COLOUREDS:	3 million
ASIANS:	1 million

In 1989 an unofficial estimate put South Africa's population at 40 million, with the black population approaching 30 million.

Estimating the Population

The population figures given in this book are a combination of official Government estimates and educated guesses by the author. Official estimates are nearly always underestimates, particularly of the black population.

In estimating the population of South Africa as a whole, officials exclude the population figures of the four independent homelands, Transkei, Ciskei, Bophuthatswana, and Venda. Thus the Government gives the impression to the outside world that the black population of South Africa is much smaller than it is. In the author's opinion these four homelands are an integral part of South Africa, and their populations should be included in the total population of the country, as has been done here.

The government policy of "apartheid" (pronounced apart-hate), or segregation, has ensured that these four groups are separated from each other residentially, educationally, and in many other ways.

Explanation of South Africa's Racial Groups

The black group is by far the largest. The blacks are descended from many ethnic groups and consequently they speak a wide variety of languages. The large language groups are the Zulu speakers (8 million), the Xhosa speakers (4 million), the Tswana speakers (2 million), and the Sotho speakers (4 million) (1985 figures). The National Party government in South Africa has argued that each group constitutes a separate "nation" and has urged various ethnic groups to accept independence in the "homelands" that have been created by the state. It

Residents of a village near Estcourt, Natal, stage a protest meeting in November 1988. They are threatened with removal from their land, which they have occupied since 1910.
Gill de Vlieg, Impact Visuals

White schoolchildren relax in a Johannesburg shopping mall during their vacation.
Ansell Horn, Impact Visuals

is true that many black people who live in the rural areas are aware and to some extent proud of their ethnic affiliations, but increasingly millions of blacks, especially those who live in the cities, are demanding majority rule in South Africa. A large proportion of urban blacks totally rejects the homeland policy of the government.

The whites consist largely of two subgroups—the English-speaking South Africans and the Afrikaners. The Afrikaners, who speak a language called Afrikaans (very closely related to Dutch), are descended from the Dutch settlers who came to the Cape with Jan van Riebeeck in 1652, from French Huguenots who settled in the Cape later in the seventeenth century, and from other cultural/ethnic groups. Many thousands of British settlers came to the Cape and Natal in the nineteenth century, and many English-speaking South Africans are descended from these settlers. In addition there are thousands of immigrants from Britain who have come to live in South Africa in the last thirty or forty years. Other groups of European settlers in South Africa include Portuguese, Greeks, Italians, and Germans.

Most South Africans of Asian descent are still referred to as "Indians." For convenience it is the term that is used in this book. Indians were first brought to the colony of Natal by the British in the 1860's to work on the newly established sugar plantations. After the contracts had expired, the Indian laborers were given the option of settling in Natal. Many did so and became market gardeners, hawkers (a South African word meaning "street sellers"), and servants. Indian traders followed them and opened businesses in the growing town of Durban. Today most of South Africa's Indians still live in Natal, particularly in the cities of Durban and Pietermaritzburg. But there are also smaller groups of Indians living in the Transvaal and the Cape. Until recently no Indians were allowed to live in the Orange Free State. The first language of most Indians today is English, although a number of Indian languages and dialects are still spoken.

The "coloured" population (often referred to outside South Africa as people of "mixed race") is much larger than the Indian one. Many coloured people do not like the label "coloured" and prefer to think of themselves as "black." Some use the terms "so-called coloured" or "classified coloured." For the sake of convenience, the word "coloured" will be used in this book. The coloured people are a blend of various groups, of slaves from Malaya, of white settlers and sailors, of the Khoikhoi people, and of various black peoples. When the Dutch first came to the Cape in 1652, they found it inhabited by one such group, the Khoikhoi. The latter were soon conquered. Some Khoikhoi fled

A Muslim family eat a meal in their Hillbrow apartment.   The Star, Johannesburg.

inland. Others stayed to work for the white settlers. Today most of the coloured people of South Africa live in the Cape Province. But there are also coloured communities in other parts of South Africa. Most of the coloured people of South Africa speak Afrikaans, or dialects of it, though many also speak English.

A Multicultural Country

South Africa is indeed a country of many tongues and voices. All the groups discussed in this chapter constitute the people of South Africa.

They are *all* South Africans: blacks and Indians, English-speaking South Africans and Afrikaners and coloureds. Very few black people speak English or Afrikaans as a first language. Their mother tongue may be Zulu or Xhosa or Tswana or Sotho or Venda, to mention only a few. Many urban blacks are excellent linguists who can speak English and/or Afrikaans as well as two or three or four black languages.

The official languages—English and Afrikaans—are displayed on buildings, on notice boards, and on signs throughout the country. Sometimes English appears above and Afrikaans below, and sometimes the order is reversed. Sometimes one language is on the left and the other on the right. On recent postage stamps the language alternates from stamp to stamp.

Languages and Peoples of South Africa

One of the reasons South Africa is a puzzle to the outside world is that such a rich variety of people lives there, and they speak such a variety of languages. Further, certain groups of people have been called by different names in the course of their history—for example, Dutch, Voortrekker, Boer, Afrikaner all refer to the same group. Here is a list of the main languages and peoples of South Africa followed by a brief definition of each. There are many more groups, languages, and terms, but the major groups have been included. Some definitions are based on those in the 1987 edition of *A Dictionary of South African English* by Jean Branford.

AFRICAN:

A black inhabitant of South Africa. At one stage the South African government used the word "Bantu" instead of African. The term "native" was used widely at one stage but is considered derogatory today. The term "African" has, on the whole, been replaced by "black."

AFRIKAANS:

The language of the Afrikaner people, which evolved as a distinct language from what was formerly known as Cape Dutch. One of the two official languages of South Africa, English being the other. It is the first language of about sixty percent of the white population and a majority of the coloured population.

AFRIKANER:

A white South African who speaks Afrikaans, though many coloured South Africans also speak Afrikaans and are sometimes referred to as "brown Afrikaners." The word means "African." Most Afrikaners are descended from the early Dutch settlers. More and more of these settlers became farmers and were known as "Boers." "Boer" is a word of Dutch origin meaning "farmer." Those farmers who moved from place to place became known as "trekboers." Today the term "Boer" when applied to an Afrikaner is considered derogatory, unless that person is a genuine farmer. The Boers who trekked into the interior of the country toward the middle of the nineteenth century were called "Voortrekkers." In many ways they were the equivalent of the American pioneers. Then they became farmers again and established their "Boer" republics. Towards the end of the nineteenth century the language called

Afrikaans was taking the place of Dutch and more and more Boers were calling themselves "Afrikaners."

ASIAN:

A term applied to most people of Asian origin living in South Africa. The majority of these people are of Indian origin. The term "Indian" is still used extensively in South Africa, though some people used the term "Asian" when referring to Indians. There are also several thousand people of Chinese origin living in South Africa.

BANTU:

A term literally meaning "people." The term is disliked by black people in South Africa partly on political and partly on linguistic grounds: "Bantu" may also refer to an extensive group of Negroid peoples of southern and central Africa, or to any of the languages spoken by these peoples.

BLACK:

A word sometimes used to mean the same as "African." However, since the rise of the black consciousness movement the term has also been used to refer to all groups that are "not white," i.e. to Africans, coloureds, and Asians.

BOER:

See Afrikaner. An Afrikaans word meaning "farmer" but at one stage used to refer to an Afrikaner.

COLOURED:

A term disliked by many "coloured" and black people. Used officially to refer to people of "mixed race." The term does *not* refer to the African people of South Africa. Many coloured people sometimes refer to themselves as "so-called coloureds" or "classified coloureds" but some also consider themselves as "blacks."

ENGLISH:

One of the two official languages of South Africa, Afrikaans being the other. It is the first language of about forty percent of white South Africans, who are sometimes referred to as "English-speaking South Africans" and occasionally as "the English." It is also the first language of nearly all Indian South Africans as well as of a minority of the coloured population. It is the language of commerce and industry and is the language that is used in several black schools in preference to a black language.

GRIQUAS:

The Griquas are a people who are neither Sotho nor Nguni speakers. They are of Khoikhoi origin and are descended from ex-slaves, Tswanas, and whites.

INDIAN:

A member of the Asian racial group of Indian descent or birth.

KAFFIR:

An abusive term for a black person, still used by some racist white South Africans to insult black people but one that can result in legal action. The word is of Arabic origin and means "infidel" or "unbeliever." Its equivalent in the United States is "nigger."

KHOIKHOI:

A term meaning "men of men" and used to refer to people sometimes called "Hottentots." They were an indigenous people in South Africa at the time of the arrival of the first white settlers.

NATIVE:

A term used at one stage to mean "African." Now seldom used and considered a pejorative term by many South Africans.

NDEBELE:

A people of Zulu stock now living in the northeastern Transvaal and Zimbabwe. It also refers to their language, a dialect of Zulu.

NGUNI:

A group of Bantu peoples comprising Zulu, Xhosa, and Swazi speakers. The term also refers to the languages spoken by these people.

NONWHITE:

A term used to refer collectively to Africans, Asians, and coloureds, but considered a pejorative term by many South Africans.

PEDI:

A North Sotho people.

SAN:

A term used to refer to people sometimes called "bushmen."

SOTHO:

A language spoken by the Basotho people, sometimes also called the Sotho people. There are two dialects of this language: North Sotho, or Pedi, and South Sotho. Most of the inhabitants of the country called Lesotho speak South Sotho.

TSWANA:

The Tswana are also a Sotho people, and their language, Tswana or Setswana, bears some resemblance to the two other Sotho languages. The people of the homeland Bophuthatswana, and of South Africa's northwestern neighbor, Botswana, are mainly Tswana-speaking.

VENDA:

A Bantu people of the northern Transvaal and their language. Venda is also the name of the homeland where most of the Venda people live.

VOORTREKKERS:

Dutch-speaking pioneers who joined the Great Trek in the 1830's. They quit the Cape Colony because they were dissatisfied with British rule and the abolition of slavery and moved into the interior of the country, where they claimed large tracts of land. After the trek they were referred to as "Boers."

XHOSA:

The African people of the Transkei and the Ciskei. Many Xhosa people also live in other parts of the country. Also the language of the Xhosa people, related to Zulu and to Swazi, all of which form the Nguni group of languages.

ZULU:

An Nguni people who live mainly in the homeland of KwaZulu and in Natal. But there are also many Zulus in other parts of the country, particularly on the Witwatersrand. The term also refers to their language.

Shared Words, Shared Lives

It is not only languages that are shared by the various groups in South Africa. Some languages have borrowed words from others, words that are now used by all South Africans. Perhaps the most common of these is the Afrikaans word *veld* (pronounced "felt"), which describes in general terms the South African countryside and may be compared to the Australian "bush" or the North American "prairie." Some foods of the various cultures have become the favorite foods of South Africans of all races. The *mealie* (also *mielie*), a variety of corn, is a common vegetable. Finely ground *mealie meal* is the staple food of many South Africans. Also popular are *mealies* boiled and eaten on the cob as Americans sometimes eat corn. *Putu* (pronounced "poo-too") is a traditional African preparation of *mealie meal* that is cooked until it forms into dry crumbs and is eaten with meat and gravy. Many white South Africans also enjoy *putu*, a word of Nguni origin. Very popular with South Africans is *biltong* (too expensive for poor people today). *Biltong* consists of air-dried salted strips of boneless meat. The word is of Dutch origin. Also very popular with many South Africans, particularly whites, is the *braaivleis* (pronounced "bry-flace") or barbecue. *Braaivleis* is an Afrikaans word often abbreviated by both English and Afrikaans-speakers to *braai*. *Braai* means "grill" and *vleis* means "meat". *Boerewors*, Afrikaans for "farmer's sausage," is also popular at a *braaivleis*. A Zulu word used by many South Africans is *muti*, a term describing African medicines. (The word means "tree" or "shrub" in Zulu.) Whites will sometimes say, "I must take my *muti*," when they are referring to western medicines.

Race Classification

The absurdity of race classification in South Africa is shown in this report, which appeared in the Johannesburg *Star* on March 21, 1986:

1985 had at least 1000 'chameleons'

by Political Staff

PARLIAMENT—More than 1,000 people officially changed colour last year.

They were reclassified from one race group to another by the stroke of a Government pen.

Details of what is dubbed "the chameleon dance" were given in reply to Opposition questions in Parliament.

The Minister of Home Affairs, Mr. Stoffel Botha, disclosed that during 1985:

· 702 coloured people turned white.
· 19 whites became coloured.
· One Indian became white.
· Three Chinese became white.
· 50 Indians became coloured.
· 43 coloureds became Indians.
· 21 Indians became Malay.
· 30 Malays went Indian.
· 249 blacks became coloured.
· 20 coloureds became black.
· Two blacks became "other Asians."
· One black was classified Griqua.
· 11 coloureds became Chinese.
· Three coloureds went Malay.
· One Chinese became coloured.
· Eight Malays became coloured.
· Three blacks were classed as Malay.
· No blacks became white and no whites became black.

Fun run spectators, Johannesburg.   Anna Zieminski, Afrapix

South Africa is a country in which the majority of the citizens are not allowed to vote for the Parliament that governs the country. However, it seems inevitable that one day the present voteless black majority will have the vote. (At present blacks may vote for representatives in certain black areas only, not for representatives in Parliament.) In a new, free South Africa what will the official language be? Possibly English. Not that Afrikaans will disappear, for it is spoken by millions of people of all races. But whether Zulu or Sotho or some other black language will become an official language remains to be seen.

In the chapters that follow discussion will at first center on the land of South Africa, on its mountains and rivers, its landscapes and seascapes, its cities and villages. Then the clock will be turned back and the focus will be on the complicated history of this beautiful and strife-torn land.

The Western Cape

Cape Town, often referred to as the Mother City of South Africa, lies at the foot of the spectacular Table Mountain. This setting is one of the most dramatic in the world. Table Mountain rises 3,563 feet (1,086 meters) out of the sea, and has a long flat top like a table. On its northern face is a precipice nearly two miles (three kilometers) in length. Sometimes, when the sky is otherwise clear, a thin layer of dense white cloud lies on top of the mountain, and this is called the Tablecloth. On either side of Table Mountain lie two smaller but also impressive mountains. To the east is Devil's Peak, 3,280 feet (1,000 meters) high, and sometimes also covered by the Tablecloth. To the west is Lion's Head, 2,198 feet (670 meters) high. From the various mountaintops there are panoramic views of the city and of its busy harbor.

Before the seventeenth century many sailors had sailed around the Cape of Storms, or the Cape of Good Hope, as it came to be called. But it was in 1652 that Jan van Riebeeck landed on the site of present-day Cape Town and planted the flag of the Dutch East India Company.

The Mother City is officially the second-largest city of South Africa. The estimated population of greater Cape Town in 1985 was 1,960,000, which was made up of 1,100,000 coloureds, 540,000 whites, 300,000 blacks, and 20,000 Indians and other Asians. The different racial groups live in separate areas of the city, but Cape Town is not unique in this regard. The Group Areas Act prevents the various races of South Africa from living in the same area.

The statue of Jan van Riebeeck stands in downtown Cape Town, Table Mountain rising in the background. South African Tourism Board

Cape Town is rich in history and culture. Its castle, built on the site of van Riebeeck's fort, was constructed between 1666 and 1679 and is the oldest building in South Africa. Many famous old Dutch houses have been preserved, and today one can still see their white walls, their gables, their shuttered windows, their oaks, and their vineyards. They rejoice in names like Vergelegen, Meerlust, and La Gratitude. One of the best known is Groot Constantia which was completed in 1685 and was the home of Governor Simon van der Stel. Most of these old houses had slave quarters, and these can still be seen.

Another old house in Cape Town is Groote Schuur, which means "Great Barn." This was the home of Cecil John Rhodes, millionaire Prime Minister of the Cape Colony in the latter part of the nineteenth century. Rhodes bequeathed Groote Schuur to the South African nation on his death in 1902, and it subsequently became the home of the Prime Ministers of South Africa.

Two well-known institutions are situated in the grounds of the Groote Schuur estate. The first is the University of Cape Town, one of the universities that has taken a lead in resisting government interference in university education. The other is Groote Schuur hospital, where Professor Christiaan Barnard performed the world's first human heart transplant in 1967.

South Africa's Houses of Parliament stand in the center of Cape Town. Here the laws of the Republic of South Africa are made. Lying a half mile offshore in Table Bay is bleak Robben Island, 1.86 miles (3 km.) long and almost a mile (1.5 km.) wide. The first sailors found the tiny island covered with birds and seals (*robben* is a Dutch word meaning seals). However, soon after van Riebeeck's arrival, convicts were sent there, and today the island houses a maximum-security prison. For many years political prisoners have been sent here, the most famous being Nelson Mandela, who has since been transferred to the mainland.

The Cape Peninsula

The lonely and beautiful tongue of the Cape Peninsula extends southward for about 40 miles (70 km.) from Cape Town. The mountains along the peninsula fall straight into the sea, and the road on the western side runs high above the Atlantic Ocean. Small wonder Sir Francis Drake called this area "the fairest Cape in the whole circumference of the earth." The southernmost part of the peninsula is called Cape Point. To the west lies the cold Atlantic Ocean, the ocean that washes the shores of Cape Town itself. To the east is the warmer Indian Ocean, which stretches eastward to the west coast of Australia.

Typical Cape Dutch homestead in the Western Cape.   South African Tourism Board

The western Cape enjoys a Mediterranean climate. The winters are cold and wet, the summers hot and dry. Strong winds blow for much of the year, and in winter the nearby mountains are snow-capped. It is an ideal climate for growing grapes, and in this area they grow in abundance. In addition to grapes a great variety of other fruit is grown in the western Cape—apricots, peaches, apples. The traveler journeying northeast from Cape Town, whether by road or rail, passes through valley after valley of orchards and vineyards.

Stellenbosch

In the heart of the winelands lies a charming university town named Stellenbosch, South Africa's second-oldest town. It is a town of beautiful old homes and streets lined with oak trees. The University of Stellenbosch was established in 1918, and its staff and students are predominantly Afrikaans-speaking. For miles around Stellenbosch many fine wine estates are found. The Cape produces some of the best wines in the world. To the east the majestic peaks of the Drakenstein mountains dominate the horizon, and to the north a major road and a railway line prepare for their dramatic ascent into the interior of the country, which in many places is at an altitude of 6,000 feet (1,800 meters) or more.

The "Other" Cape Town

In the first chapter both the beauty and the tragedy of South Africa were mentioned. The white traveler is often so overwhelmed by the beauty of the land that he or she disregards the pain and the suffering.

Away from the oak-lined suburbs and fashionable beaches of Cape Town live thousands of the poorer citizens. Many of them are coloured or black. Thousands of poor people live in an area called the Cape Flats,

Laundry day in a black township near Worcester, western Cape. Orde Eliason, Impact Visuals

a sandy tract that connects the Cape Peninsula with the mainland. In recent times a great deal of unrest has taken place in areas where black people live. A squatter town called Crossroads has been much in the news, for it is here that the government has tried to prevent black migrant workers from building shacks and settling down with their families. The homes of many Crossroads inhabitants have been destroyed and their occupants have been "removed" to distant homelands.

Tent town near Cape Town, a temporary home for many Crossroads refugees. Guy Tillim, Impact Visuals

In another part of Cape Town called District Six the homes of thousands of coloured people were destroyed some twenty years ago. The inhabitants were forced to move to "coloured" areas. District Six was near the heart of "white" Cape Town, and therefore according to government policy had to be destroyed. The reasons for these harsh actions will become clearer when the policy of apartheid is discussed. Today District Six is a derelict wasteland which, at some time in the future, will be "redeveloped."

Here is another poem, also by a coloured poet, this time from Cape Town. It deals with the problem of whether to focus on the beauty or the pain of South Africa. The poet's name is James Matthews.

It is said
that poets write of beauty
of form, of flowers and of love
but the words I write
are of pain and of rage

I am no minstrel
who sings songs of joy
mine a lament

I wail of a land
hideous with open graves
waiting for the slaughtered ones

Balladeers strum their lutes and sing tunes of happy times
I cannot join in their merriment
my heart drowned in bitterness
with the agony of what white man's law has done.

The Cape Interior and Garden Route

The Cape Province is the biggest of South Africa's four provinces, though the Transvaal has the largest population. The distance from Cape Town to Kimberley, on the northeastern boundary of the Province, is 605 miles (975 kilometers).

In the heart of the Cape Province lies the mighty Great Karoo, stretching from the Swartberg range in the southwest to the escarpment in the east. In fact there are three Karoos—the Little Karoo, a smaller region lying to the south of the Great Karoo; the Great Karoo, an area of relatively flat plains broken every now and then by strangely shaped hillocks; and the Northern Karoo, the largest region, stretching from the escarpment to the Orange River.

The Great Karoo

The Karoo is a semiarid area, the landscape stretching endlessly from one horizon to another. The word "karoo" (also spelled karroo) is of Khoikhoi origin and means "land of thirst." The traveler journeying by road or rail from Cape Town to Johannesburg passes through this vast, desertlike plain for hour after hour. Nothing could be more different from the fertile valleys of the western Cape. Yet the inhabitants of the Karoo go into raptures over its beauty. The traveler who sees it for the first time is soon fascinated by its solitude, by its stony flat-topped hillocks known in Afrikaans as "koppies," by the colors of its fantastic rocks. The plain is seemingly barren, and yet these desolate wastes can be transformed by one good rain. Much of the Karoo is covered by short

A sheep farm in the Karoo.   Jason Laure

tough scrub that withstands drought. This scrub country is one of the best areas in the world for sheep farming.

The Karoo can be very hot in summer, and afternoon temperatures often reach peaks of well above 86° F (30° C). Temperatures of over 104° F (40° C) have been recorded. Winters are cool, and there is often frost to be seen on early winter mornings. Sunrises and sunsets are spectacular as dust particles in the atmosphere refract the sun's rays and splash the skies with splendid red and orange hues.

One of South Africa's best-known novels is *The Story of an African Farm* by Olive Schreiner, first published in 1883. Schreiner spent many years as a governess on isolated Karoo farms, and her novel is set on one of them. Here is the opening paragraph of the book:

The full African moon poured down its light from the blue sky into the wide, lonely plain. The dry, sandy earth, with its coating of stunted "Karroo" bushes a few inches high, the low hills that skirted the plain, the milk-bushes with their long, finger-like leaves, all were touched by a weird and an almost oppressive beauty as they lay in the white light.

The Northern Karoo

The Northern Karoo lies on the high plateau that stretches vast distances across the interior of South Africa. It is the most barren part of the Karoo and has a tiny population living in scattered and isolated villages. In the northern section of this area flows the Orange River, South Africa's largest river. The distance from its source in the mountains of Lesotho to its mouth in the Atlantic Ocean is about 1,300 miles (2,200 km.). It is an erratic river, sometimes a raging flood over 5 miles (8.5 km.) wide while in the dry season sections of it are no more than a chain of stagnant pools. It contains a spectacular waterfall known as

The Kalahari Desert. National Parks Board

Augrabies Falls. The name Augrabies is taken from the Khoikhoi word *aukoerebis*, probably meaning either "place of great noise" or "hollow place." To the north of the Orange River, and still in the Cape Province, the great Kalahari Desert (strictly speaking a semidesert) begins. The largest section of this semidesert is in neighboring Botswana.

The Little Karoo

The Little Karoo is a valley lying between the Swartberg range to the north and the Langeberg and Outeniqua mountains to the south. It is an area well-known for ostrich farming, which is mainly centered around the town of Oudtshoorn, the ostrich-feather capital of the world.

Not far from Oudtshoorn are the Cango Caves, a network of underground caves that are among the finest caverns in the world. The vast entrance to the caves was first occupied by the San many centuries ago. Some of their paintings have been discovered on the walls. But the San were unable to explore the inner treasures of the caves because they had no portable light.

The first white person to discover the caves was a farmer whose herdsman had pursued a wounded buck into a small opening in the mountainside. Today one can be guided on a 1.86-mile (3-km.) journey through innumerable chambers and corridors, containing some fearful tunnellike ascents.

Stalactites and stalagmites in the Cango Caves, near Oudtshoorn. South African Tourism Board

The water seeps down continually through the earth and rocks and, laden with carbonates, reaches the roof of some tremendous chamber, where it falls drop by drop, leaving at its point of fall and at its point of arrival on the stony floor a microscopic deposit of carbonate. One pillar, called a stalactite, grows from the ceiling, and another, called a stalagmite, grows to meet it from the floor until, after centuries, they meet, forming organ pipes, canopied beds, pillared temples, statues, and bridal chambers, forms of animals and men and demons, some white, some tinted with colors from who knows where; all of them fantastic. Needless to say, the caves are a great tourist attraction.

To many the Little Karoo is more appealing than the Great Karoo. For in this world of thorn and rock and stone, there are green trees and fields and pleasant farmhouses. The most striking tree is the Lombardy poplar, planted in straight lines, an inescapable feature of the pattern that human beings have imprinted on this area.

The Cape Mountain Passes

Between the Great Karoo, the Little Karoo, and the coast are a number of mountain ranges. Skilled engineers have built a number of spectacular passes between these heights. The builders of the Swartberg Pass were forced to go almost to the very summit of the Swartberg in order to construct a road across it. But in other places rivers run in gorges right through the mountain mass, and engineers have made roads along their beds, as they did through Meiring's Poort, which is also in the Swartberg range. *Poort* is an Afrikaans word and, like the English word "portal," means a gateway or opening.

The Cape mountain passes are of every kind. The Tradouw Pass crosses the Langeberg range. The name "Tradouw" is of Khoikhoi origin and means "woman's pass." The pass is noted for its lushness of vegetation and the profusion of wildflowers in spring. The Swartberg

Pass, built by convict labor at the end of the nineteenth century, is magnificent but also harsh and somber. Perhaps the most spectacular is Prince Alfred's Pass, crossing the Outeniqua Mountains and linking the Little Karoo with the coastal town of Knysna.

The Garden Route

Knysna is situated halfway along a scenic coastal road called the Garden Route, which runs for about 143 miles (230 km.) from Mossel Bay in the west to Storms River in the east. Many magnificent coastal resorts lie along this route, and huge forests stretch into the interior. The Knysna Forest contains hundreds of giant trees, including many yellowwoods, relatives of the American redwoods. The best known is King Edward's tree. It is 151 feet (46 meters) high, has a girth of 31 feet (9.5 meters), and is thought to be nearly a thousand years old. Yellowwood trees and many other rare trees are protected in South Africa and may not be cut down except in special circumstances.

Two striking sandstone cliffs that guard the entrance to Knysna harbor are known as the Knysna Heads. The waves of the Indian Ocean enter the harbor through this gateway, and hundreds of sea and water birds are to be seen.

East of Knysna is the impressive Tsitsikamma Forest. Under the huge trees there is a carpet of ferns, bracken, and arum lilies. The giants of this forest are also yellowwoods. Another fine tree is called the stinkwood, whose finished timber is very striking and is much used for making furniture.

Much of the Garden Route lies to the south of the Outeniqua Mountains. "Outeniqua" is a Khoikhoi name meaning "the carrier of honey," a fine image to apply to the lush vegetation. The Outeniqua Mountains catch the moisture-laden winds from the ocean, and the whole coastal belt abounds in rivers, streams, forests, and ferns. In the spring the area is rich in wildflowers of every kind, small lakes and pools covered with water lilies, and meadows ablaze with watsonias of every color.

Port Elizabeth

East of the Garden Route lies the city of Port Elizabeth, the fifth-largest city in South Africa and the third-largest port. The estimated population of greater Port Elizabeth in 1985 was 650,000. The city was founded by the British in 1799 on a site overlooking Algoa Bay. It was here that the first large group of British settlers arrived in 1820. Port Elizabeth is an important industrial center. There are large automobile factories in the city and in Uitenhage, only 12 miles (20 km.) inland. Many other industries have also been established around the automobile factories. From the busy harbor, products such as wool, mohair, and citrus fruits are exported. Port Elizabeth is also a vacation city with many fine beaches.

"Beauty and tragedy"—this is a phrase that will often come to mind in this book. The beautiful eastern Cape was the birthplace of Steve Biko, one of South Africa's most important black leaders. He was detained in 1977 under the Terrorism Act and kept naked and mana-cled in a prison in Port Elizabeth. He died in detention on September 12, 1977. The circumstances of his death will be discussed more fully in the chapter entitled "Resistance."

About 200 miles (320 km.) northeast of Port Elizabeth lies East London, another important port city. Many citizens of the Ciskei seek work there.

Grahamstown

Grahamstown, a small but attractive city, is situated 80 miles (130 km.) inland from Port Elizabeth. Grahamstown is often called "the city of saints," for in spite of its relative smallness, it contains over forty churches. Many of the 1820 settlers were given farms in the vicinity of Grahamstown, and the city became their market town. Grahamstown is an educational center, with several excellent schools and a university, Rhodes University. But close by "white" Grahamstown is the black township where many poor and unemployed people live.

Kimberley

Another Cape Province city is Kimberley, nearly 620 miles (1,000 km.) northeast of Cape Town. Diamonds were first discovered in the area that came to be called Kimberley, and by the 1870's a busy little town had sprung up in the barren landscape. The early days of Kimberley were rough and exciting. Fortune seekers streamed into the diggings, with a generous proportion of crooks and scoundrels. It was not an easy life, but there was always the hope of a big discovery. Men worked hard, gambled hard, drank hard, lived hard. By law all racial groups were entitled to seek their fortune, but in practice whites made it almost impossible for blacks to share in the wealth.

The area where the diamonds were found was easy to work at first. But the diggings grew deeper and deeper. Soon there were ten thousand men working there, looking feverishly for the small hard stones that could make a person's fortune. Quickly, the area of their activities began to look like a great crater in the ground; it was roughly circular, and had a circumference of about a mile and a diameter of 1,500 feet (450 meters). By 1889 the hole was 1,500 feet (450 meters) deep and very dangerous.

This hole came to be called the Big Hole, and thousands of men searched for diamonds in the small piece of ground they had claimed. Each bucket of earth and stone had to be carried by wires out of the hole. Every now and then parts of the hole collapsed. Men lost their claims, and many were killed. At times rain fell and the hole was flooded. Men fought and quarreled. There was near chaos.

Some kind of order was finally brought about by Cecil John Rhodes, who came from Britain to Kimberley at the age of eighteen. In a short time he controlled the whole venture and founded the company of De Beers. To this day opinions are divided over whether he should be admired for stabilizing the mine or condemned for his methods and his other political schemes.

The Highveld

The Highveld occupies about 17 percent of South Africa's total land area. It is the largest of the country's natural regions. Virtually the whole of the Orange Free State is on the Highveld, as is most of the southern Transvaal. Much of it is open prairieland, gently undulating, but with many scattered low hills. The highest parts are in the east near the Drakensberg escarpment. Consequently the rivers of the Highveld flow westward. The Highveld enjoys a summer rainfall, and the vast grasslands are beautifully green in summer. But in the cold, dry winters the grass is dead and brown. Very few trees grow on their own on the Highveld, though clusters of eucalyptus and other trees planted by settlers are to be found at irregular intervals. Willow trees grow along the banks of many rivers. Highveld summers are often hot, and dra-

A waterfall in the Drakensberg. This river arises on the high plateau and continues to drop several thousand feet on its way to the Indian Ocean.

matic thunderstorms are frequent. The winter nights are crisp and clear but bitterly cold, with the temperature often dropping below freezing point.

The Highveld is good farming country and produces much of South Africa's corn, wheat, meat, and dairy produce. It is also rich in mineral wealth, and its many mines produce gold, diamonds, and coal. There are several mining and industrial towns on the Highveld, most of them in the southern Transvaal. More than one third of all South Africa's citizens live in the towns and cities of the southern Transvaal, and most of these live in greater Johannesburg.

Johannesburg

Johannesburg, at 5,740 thousand feet (1,750 meters) above sea level, is by far the largest city in South Africa and is the industrial heart of the country. It is very difficult to give an accurate assessment of its population, because surrounding metropolitan Johannesburg is a densely populated region of satellite suburbs, towns, and cities. Johannesburg's biggest satellite is the twin city of Soweto (*South Western Township*), a vast, sprawling complex of "matchbox" houses where about two million black people live. When the census is taken, many people are afraid to say how many people live in a house for fear that some of them may be arrested for being there illegally. Official estimates are always considerably lower than the actual population. It was unofficially estimated that in 1988 over 4 million people lived in greater Johannesburg (including Soweto).

It is strange to think that just over a hundred years ago Johannesburg did not exist. Then, after the discovery of gold in the area in 1886, a shantytown grew up on the empty grassland and continued to grow. People from all over the country and from many other parts of the world flocked there to seek their fortunes. The city took its name from two officials connected with the administration of the Transvaal Republic, one named Johannes Rissik and the other Johannes Joubert.

Today Johannesburg stands at the center of the most important gold-producing area in the world. In the city are found the head offices

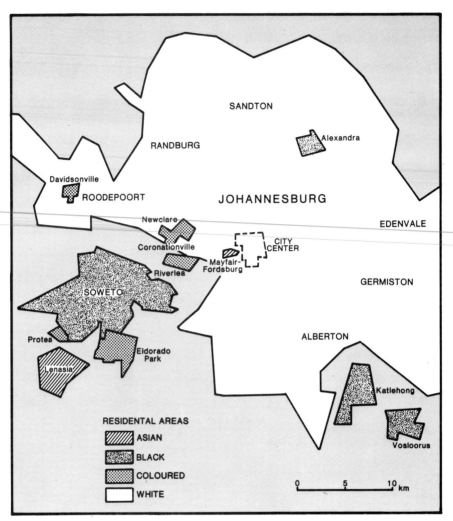

Racial-group residential areas in greater Johannesburg

of many mining companies, banks, and commercial houses. The South African Stock Exchange is located here. Downtown Johannesburg strongly resembles many American cities. Looking down Eloff Street, the main street of the city, one sees skyscrapers, busy traffic, hurrying pedestrians. There is a sense of urgency and bustle. Central Johannesburg cannot be called beautiful. In its hundred-year history it has been rebuilt more than once, but everyone was apparently so busy seeking fortunes that no one had time to pay attention to the planning of the city. There are very few parks in the extensive business center, but the affluent white suburbs to the north, which were planned in more recent times, are attractively laid out with stretches of water, parks, colorful gardens, and a wide variety of trees.

There are many fine buildings in Johannesburg. And there are two tall towers. One of them, named after a former Prime Minister, J. G. Strijdom, lies on top of a ridge in the cosmopolitan suburb of Hillbrow. It was built to serve the needs of the South African Post Office. The other is in the suburb of Brixton. It was built for the South African Broadcasting Corporation and transmits radio and television programs.

In parts of southern, western, and eastern Johannesburg strange man-made hillocks dominate the skyline. These are mine dumps and

Johannesburg skyline. Ingrid Hudson

were formed by dumping waste rock left over from the process of gold extraction. Today very little gold mining is carried out in the vicinity of Johannesburg, but the dumps remain. At one stage the yellow and gray mounds were something of an eyesore, and the fine sand that blew off them eddied down into the streets and filtered into shops and houses. Recently grass and trees have been planted on most of the dumps. Slowly the dumps are disappearing from the landscape as they are reworked by modern methods for extracting remaining gold traces; the residue is pumped underground into abandoned gold mines.

Thousands of people work in the gold mines of the Highveld. Most of the laborers are black and come from all over southern Africa—other parts of South Africa, Lesotho, Botswana, Swaziland, Zimbabwe, Mozambique. In the past the miners were forced to leave their families behind and were housed in large compounds near the mines where they worked. The compound system was a bad one, for it separated husbands from their wives for long periods, and fathers from their children. In the earlier part of the century appalling conditions existed in the compounds, but recently there have been considerable improvements. Wages, at first shocking, have also improved, but the newly established National Union of Mineworkers (NUM) is constantly negotiating for higher wages and improved conditions. While many miners still come to work without their families, some mining houses now provide married and family accommodation.

Johannesburg is a divided city and a city of great contrasts. Wealthy whites live in comfort in plush suburbs, many of them in the northern part of the city. Large houses, opulent cars, swimming pools, and tennis courts abound. Thousands of black servants are employed as maids and gardeners, and some as chauffeurs. But it would be wrong to say that *all* whites are wealthy and that *all* blacks are poor. Some whites struggle to make ends meet in this expensive city, and there are many "poorer" suburbs where whites live. Conversely, a relatively small but growing number of affluent blacks lives in parts of greater Johannesburg.

Like any other South African city or town, Johannesburg's residential areas are divided up according to the Group Areas Act, which ensures that South Africa remains a segregated society. There are areas for whites, areas for blacks, areas for Indians, areas for coloureds. It is illegal for members of one race to live in (except for domestic workers) or own property in areas other than their own. In the late 1980's this policy is being challenged to some extent, and all races have taken up residence in certain suburbs that were once white, contrary to government policy. These have been referred to as "gray areas." Will the government allow these areas to continue and new ones to develop? Will the government eventually abolish the Group Areas Act? At the moment no one knows.

Alexandra Township

There are many black townships in Greater Johannesburg, not only Soweto. One of these is called Alexandra Township. The poet Mongane Serote was born there. Here is a poem he wrote about his ambivalent feelings toward his place of birth. (A *donga* is a dry, eroded riverbed filled only in times of heavy rain.)

Alexandra

Were it possible to say,
Mother, I have seen more beautiful mothers,
A most loving mother,
And tell her there I will go,
Alexandra, I would have long gone from you.

But we have only one mother, none can replace,
Just as we have no choice to be born,
We can't choose mothers;
We fall out of them like we fall out of life to death.

And Alexandra,
My beginning was knotted to you,
Just like you knot my destiny.
You throb in my inside silences
You are silent in my heart-beat that's loud to me.
Alexandra often I've cried.
When I was thirsty my tongue tasted dust,
Dust burdening your nipples.
I cry Alexandra when I am thirsty.
Your breasts ooze the dirty waters of your dongas,
Waters diluted with the blood of my brothers, your children,
Who once chose dongas for death-beds.
Do you love me Alexandra, or what are you doing to me?

You frighten me, Mama,
You wear expressions like you would be nasty to me,
You frighten me, Mama,
When I lie on your breast to rest, something tells me,
You are bloody cruel.
Alexandra, hell
What have you done to me?
I have seen people but I feel like I'm not one,
Alexandra what are you doing to me?
I feel I have sunk to such meekness!
I lie flat while others walk on me to far places.

I have gone from you, many times,
I come back.
Alexandra, I love you;
I know
When all these worlds became funny to me,
I silently waded back to you
And amid the rubble I lay,
Simple and black.

Sophiatown

Again and again the tragic aspects of life in South Africa come to the surface. At one stage blacks were allowed to live much closer to the center of Johannesburg than they do now. Sophiatown was a suburb of well over 150,000 people in the west of Johannesburg. Like District Six in Cape Town, Sophiatown was both vibrant and colorful, grimy and squalid.

Don Mattera, the poet whose poems were quoted in Chapter I, spent much of his early life in Sophiatown. In his novel *Memory Is the Weapon* (1987) he gives this description of "Kofifi," the nickname of Sophiatown:

The yards were small and stinking wherever people lived in this crowded communal way. And you would find a man or woman lying drunk in the grime and slime and debris, breathing the foul air of a dispossessed and forsaken life. . . .

Sophiatown, the city of many faces: kind, cruel, pagan, Christian, Islamic, Buddhist and Hindu, and the face of what was called Law and what was made

Criminal. Each face told its own story; held its own secrets and added to the book that was Kofifi—the little Chicago of Johannesburg.

Another suburb for blacks called Western Native Township adjoined Sophiatown. After coming to power in 1948, the Nationalist government began to implement more and more apartheid legislation. Under the Group Areas Act thousands and thousands of people, nearly all "nonwhite," were uprooted from their homes and sent to other areas. By the late 1950's Sophiatown and Western Native Township were doomed. They were far too close to "white" Johannesburg. Sophiatown was declared a white area and Western Native Township a coloured area. All blacks were forcibly removed and sent to new "homes" in the rapidly growing South Western Township (Soweto), far, far away from "white" Johannesburg. In the case of Sophiatown the homes of the black residents were bulldozed to the ground, and a new suburb for whites only, insensitively called "Triomf" ("Triumph"), was built on the same site. Sophiatown had been a township where blacks could purchase land and build houses. The owners received some compensation for the loss of their houses, but once in Soweto they were no longer permitted to purchase the land on which their houses were built.

Soweto

Soweto is possibly the best-known name in South Africa today. This vast, sprawling ghetto stretches from Diepkloof in the east to Emdeni in the west, a distance of 8 miles (13 km.). Approximately two million people live here. Soweto's setting is bleak—not many trees grow here. In the cold winters thick smog from thousands of coal fires hangs in the air. Only in recent times has electric power been supplied to the residents of Soweto. Perhaps the smog will thin out in the years ahead as

A section of Soweto. Ingrid Hudson

more and more inhabitants obtain electricity, though for poorer citizens it may remain too expensive. Most of Johannesburg's black workers live here, though there is also a growing number of professional black people in this sprawling city, Johannesburg's restless twin. Here are houses, shops, churches, schools. Crowded commuter trains snake to and from stations in Johannesburg. Thousands of cars and commuter taxis pour out of Soweto in the early mornings and claw their way back in the smoky afternoons and evenings. After dark Soweto can be a frightening place. Robberies, rapes, and murders occur every night. More than a thousand murders occur annually. The nearby Baragwanath Hospital is crowded every weekend with people who have been attacked. Acts of criminal violence occur in many parts of South Africa, not only in Soweto. Indeed, acts of criminal violence occur in all large cities where there is overcrowding and unemployment. Crime in Soweto is no different from crime in overcrowded areas of London, Calcutta, Detroit, etc. In recent times in Soweto there have also been victims of political violence. Some of the victims have been injured or killed in clashes with the South African police, while others have been attacked by rival black organizations.

A Second Look at Johannesburg

In spite of the terrible residential segregation some blacks and whites *do* meet and attempt to get to know each other in certain areas of the city. One of these areas is the Market Theatre complex, where many exciting plays that challenge the status quo in South Africa are performed. Here blacks and whites together watch or perform in plays. Here many of the plays known to American audiences had their first performances—*Sizwe Bansi Is Dead* and *Master Harold and the Boys* by Athol Fugard, *Woza Albert*, and *Sarafina*. Unfortunately, however, many plays that whites do not see are performed in the black townships.

The University of the Witwatersrand, adjoining the suburbs of Braamfontein and Parktown, was attended by 17,000 students of all races in 1987. The university has played an important role in combating racism. While most students are white, thousands of black, coloured, and Indian students also attend the university. In 1987 and 1988 there were several clashes between students and police on the campus, and the government threatened to cut the subsidies of universities that failed to "discipline" their own students.

This area is commonly referred to as the P.W.V. (P = Pretoria, W = Witwatersrand and V = Vaal area, including Vereeniging, Vanderbijlpark and Sasolburg).

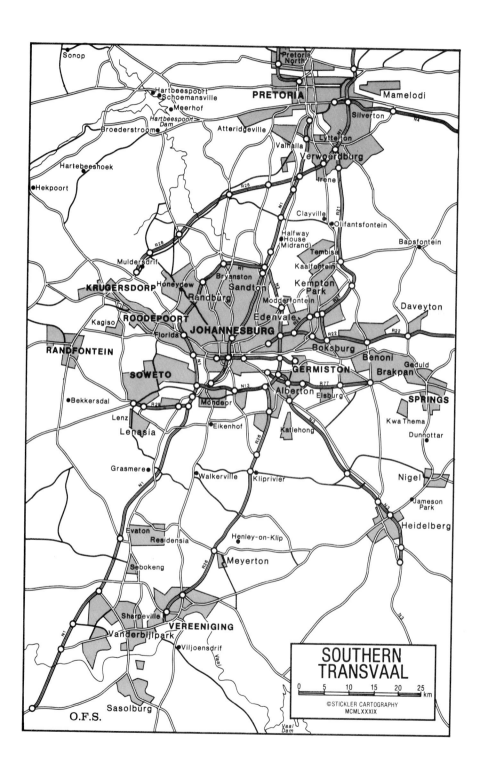

SOUTHERN
TRANSVAAL

0   5   10   15   20   25
└────┴────┴────┴────┴────┘ km

©STICKLER CARTOGRAPHY
MCMLXXXIX

Smaller Transvaal Cities

Apart from Soweto and the black townships, there are several smaller cities that spread out westward and eastward from Johannesburg along the gold reef. On the outskirts of many of these Witwatersrand cities (such as Springs, Germiston, and Krugersdorp), mine dumps bear witness to the countless ounces of gold that either have been or are still being brought to the surface.

Thirty miles (50 km.) south of Johannesburg lies the industrial town of Vereeniging where the peace treaty was signed at the end of the Anglo-Boer War in 1902. Near Vereeniging is the giant Vaal Dam, which supplies the water requirements of the Pretoria–Witwatersrand–Vereeniging industrial region.

Miners drilling holes in gold-bearing rock at Vaal Reef's gold mine in the Transvaal.
Jason Laure

Pretoria

About 37 miles (60 km.) north of Johannesburg, and at a slightly lower altitude, is the capital city of South Africa—Pretoria, the fourth-largest city in the country. In 1985 greater Pretoria had a population approaching 1 million.

Johannesburg is on the whole an English-speaking city, whereas Pretoria is predominantly Afrikaans-speaking. Pretoria was founded in 1855 and was named after the Voortrekker leader, Andries Pretorius. It was the capital city of the old Transvaal Republic. Today the city is the home of the Public Service (Civil Service) which is overwhelmingly staffed by Afrikaners.

Pretoria has the most striking city square in South Africa, Church Square. It is flanked by many fine buildings, one of which is the *Raadzaal*, the Council Hall, which was the home of the *Volksraad* (Legislative Assembly) of the old Transvaal Republic. Flying from it is the official South African flag. On this flag there are three miniature flags in the very center. In the middle is the Union Jack, the flag of Great Britain. On either side are the flags of the old republics, the Transvaal and the Orange Free State. This flag was a compromise and was intended to satisfy all white groups in South Africa, but black sentiment was totally ignored. At one stage "God Save the Queen" was the national anthem of South Africa, but since the Afrikaner Nationalists came to power the national anthem has been *"Die Stem van Suid-Afrika"* ("The Call of South Africa"), the Afrikaner anthem. But for most black people the national anthem is *"Nkosi Sikelel' iAfrika"* ("God Bless Africa"). This is often sung at political, church, and other gatherings where most of those present are black, and will probably one day be the national anthem of South Africa.

Nkosi Sikelel' iAfrika

The first stanza of the anthem sung by most black people in South Africa was composed and written in Zulu in 1897 by Enoch Sontonga, a schoolteacher from Kliptown, near Johannesburg, and was completed by a Xhosa poet named Samuel E. Mqhyai. The author of the Sotho section is unknown. Originally meant to be sung by school students and church choirs, it was later adopted by the African National Congress to close their meetings.

ZULU

Nkosi sikelel' iAfrika	God bless Africa
Maluphakamis'u phondo lwayo	Let the horn of her people rise high up
Yizwe imithandazo yethu	In your love hear our prayers
Nkosi sikelele	
Thina lusapho lwayo	God bless our people
(Woza moya) Woza woza	Come down, O holy spirit
(Woza moya) Woza woza	Come down, O holy spirit
Woza moya oyingcwele	
Nkosi sikelele	
Thina lusapho lwayo	God bless our people

SOTHO

Morena boloka	Lord preserve
Sechaba sahesu	Our nation
Ofedise dintoa lematsoenyeho	Remove wars and troubles
(Oseboloke) Oseboloke	You should preserve it
(Oseboloke morena) Oseboloke	(You should preserve it, O Lord) You should preserve
Sechaba sahesu	our nation
Sechaba sa Afrika	The nation of Africa

Makube njalo	May it be forever
Makube njalo	May it be forever
Kude kube nguna phakade	May it endure unto eternity
Kude kube nguna phakade	May it endure unto eternity

DIE STEM VAN SUID-AFRIKA

The Afrikaans title of South Africa's official national anthem is often translated as "The Call of South Africa." The words of the anthem were written by the Afrikaans poet C. J. Langenhoven in 1918. Here is the opening section of the anthem:

Uit de blou van onse hemel, uit die diepte van ons see,
Oor ons ewige gebergtes waar die kranse antwoord gee,
Deur ons ver verlate vlaktes met die kreun van ossewa—
Ruis die stem van ons geliefde van ons land Suid-Afrika.

Ons sal antwoord op jou roepstem, ons sal offer wat jy vra:
Ons sal lewe, ons sal sterwe, ons vir jou, Suid-Afrika.

Here is the English version of the above:

THE CALL OF SOUTH AFRICA

Ringing out from our blue heavens, from our deep seas breaking round;
Over everlasting mountains where the echoing crags resound;
From our plains where creaking wagons cut their trails into the earth—
Calls the spirit of our Country, of the land that gave us birth.

At thy call we shall not falter, firm and steadfast we shall stand,
At thy will to live or perish, O South Africa, dear land.

In Church Square is the statue of President Paul Kruger. He was President of the Transvaal Republic in 1886 when gold was discovered on the Witwatersrand. Kruger saw the independence of the Republic threatened by the inrush of gold-seeking strangers from around the world. He fiercely resisted the efforts of these new immigrants to obtain political power. Kruger typifies for Afrikaners courage and sturdiness in the face of opposition. He wore a frock coat and a top hat, and was bearded and patriarchal, a faithful reader of the Bible, and a lover of a pipe.

Many white residents of Pretoria are keen gardeners and take pride in the beauty of their city. Pretoria is well known for its magnificent jacaranda trees. In October and November these trees burst out in a blaze of striking mauve flowers. Even after these flowers drop to the ground, they do not fade, and wonderful mauve carpets lie stretched out in the city's streets and avenues.

There is indeed much beauty in the white suburbs of Pretoria. These suburbs contrast sharply with the many black townships on the out-skirts of Pretoria. These townships are smaller than, but in many ways similar to, Soweto. Here the houses are small and very few beautiful trees and flowers are to be seen. Thousands of people crowd into buses, trains, and taxis on their way to and from their jobs in the city.

The finest building (or collection of buildings) in Pretoria is surely the one known as Union Buildings, the administrative home of govern-ment. The Union Buildings are surrounded by spacious gardens, and from them there is a magnificent view of the city of Pretoria. Among the buildings to be seen are those of two universities, the University of South Africa (UNISA), and the University of Pretoria. The students of the former, who belong to all races, do not live at the university but study by correspondence from all over the country and from abroad. UNISA is the largest university in South Africa and in 1988 had over 90,000 students. The University of Pretoria, an Afrikaans-speaking

School groups still visit the Voortrekker Monument, in Pretoria.   *The Star*, Johannesburg

university, is the largest residential university in the country. In 1988 21,000 students were enrolled here.

On a ridge on the southern side of Pretoria is a prominent structure known as the Voortrekker Monument. It is a monument to the Voortrekkers who left the Colony of the Cape of Good Hope in the 1830's and crossed the Orange River, seeking a country of their own where they might live free from British rule. This Great Trek* (as it was called) was made by ox wagons, and both the ox and the wagon play a great part

---

*TREK: Word of Dutch origin meaning as a verb to pull a load or to travel by ox wagon or to migrate. As a noun, it means the journey itself.

in Afrikaner thought, poetry, and symbolism. This massive granite memorial is surrounded at its base by a wall of sculptured oxen and wagons, joined together in what is called in Afrikaans a *laager*. The *laager* of ox wagons was the defense of the Voortrekkers against the black inhabitants who contested their passage.

On December 16 each year many Afrikaners gather at the monument to commemorate the Battle of Blood River, in which a small group of Voortrekkers defeated thousands of Zulu tribesmen. On this day rays of sunlight fall through an opening in the dome of the monument and illuminate the words *"Ons vir jou, Suid-Afrika"* ("We for you, South Africa"), which are inscribed on the wall. But the monument and the commemoration have little meaning for the majority of English-speaking South Africans and arouse emotions of intense anger and pain in the hearts of millions of black South Africans.

The Orange Free State Highveld

Most of the province of the Orange Free State is a rolling prairie, situated 4,600 feet (1,400 meters) above sea level. The summers are warm to hot, and dramatic thunderstorms occur frequently. The winters are cold and crisp, and the grass of the veld changes from green to brown. On many winter mornings a white blanket of frost covers the ground but then evaporates as bright sunshine warms the earth. On the gently undulating fields of the northern and eastern Free State farmers grow wheat, corn, and vegetables. In the drier southern section the landscape is more like that of the Karoo. Thousands of sheep graze on stunted bushes. Windpumps lift water from under the earth's surface to fill their drinking troughs.

A large industrial town, Sasolburg, is situated in the northern Free State near the Vaal River. This town is built around the huge chemical plant established by the South African Coal, Oil and Gas Corporation (SASOL). In the vicinity of Sasolburg is a vast coalfield. The plant uses the coal to manufacture gasoline-related products and was, until recently, the only plant in the world to produce large quantities of gasoline from coal. SASOL has since built two other plants at Secunda, in the eastern Transvaal.

SASOL is one of South Africa's most important industries because the country has no domestic oil. The economy of South Africa would be seriously harmed if oil sanctions were applied by oil-producing countries in an effort to force the government to dismantle apartheid, but as long as SASOL exists, the economy could continue to function. Sasolburg was the target of a rocket attack in 1980.

Gold was discovered in the 1940's in the central Orange Free State, and many gold-mining towns with names like Welkom and Virginia grew rapidly on what was once farming territory. For example, Welkom (meaning "Welcome") was the name of a farm on which gold was discovered in 1948. Today Welkom is the second-largest town in the Free State.

Bloemfontein

Bloemfontein, the provincial capital of the Orange Free State and the judicial capital of the Republic of South Africa, is the largest city in the province, with a population in 1985 of well over 300,000 people. It was established in 1846 on a farm of the same name. Its name in English means "flower spring," and the farm may have been named after flowers that grew near a spring on the property. This spring can still be seen in the city.

Like Pretoria, Bloemfontein is a predominantly Afrikaans-speaking city.

Eastern Orange Free State

The eastern Free State borders on the mountainous country of Lesotho and is scenically very beautiful. In the Golden Gate Highlands National Park, there are many striking rock and mountain formations. The rock layer known as cave sandstone has been eroded by water over thousands of years. The result is a series of bizarre, flat-topped mountain shapes.

A river in the Orange Free State.   Department of Information, South Africa

Huge cliffs rise up dramatically from the hills beneath them and resemble strange castles and fortresses built on another planet. These cliffs are usually grassed on the top but most of them are impossible to climb. In the cliffs are many large caves in which the San people found shelter centuries ago. In the sunlight the cliffs glow with magnificent orange, red, and yellow colors. To the south lie the majestic mountains of Lesotho.

Middleveld, Escarpment, and Lowveld

The plateau on which the Highveld is situated ascends toward the east near the Drakensberg escarpment. On the eastern side of the escarpment there is a spectacular drop to the Lowveld, which lies hundreds of feet below the plateau. The eastern Highveld is well above 6,000 feet (1,800 meters) above sea level, with some of the peaks of the Transvaal Drakensberg range reaching far greater altitudes. The Lowveld, a few miles from the escarpment, is never more than 2,000 feet (600 meters) above sea level.

Middleveld

There is a third area of the Transvaal that is sometimes referred to as the Middleveld. Strictly speaking, Pretoria is just inside the boundary of the Middleveld, which stretches west, east, and north of the city. The western boundary is Botswana, the northern boundary is formed by the Soutpansberg range near the Zimbabwe border, and the eastern border is formed by the Transvaal Drakensberg range bordering the Lowveld. The Middleveld lies between 3,300 and 5,000 feet (1,000 and 1,500 meters) above sea level. The natural vegetation of much of this terrain is called bushveld. The country is flattish and is covered with thorn forest. To some it is not the most beautiful section of the country, but the bird life is more plentiful and more striking in color than in the higher and colder regions. The Middleveld has hotter summers and milder winters than the Highveld.

Over 90 percent of the population of the Middleveld is black. Most of the black inhabitants live in the homelands of Bophuthatswana, Kwa-Ndebele, Lebowa, and Venda. The largest towns (excluding Pretoria) are Rustenburg in the western Transvaal and Pietersburg in the northern Transvaal. A substantial section of the Middleveld excluding the homelands is occupied by white farmers. These farmers produce a wide variety of products ranging from citrus fruit and tobacco to corn and sunflowers. Large sections of the Middleveld are suitable for the herding of beef cattle. The white farmers of the Middleveld are among the most politically conservative people in the country. Most of them are Afrikaans-speaking and a substantial number of them favor a return to the old-style apartheid that existed in the 1950's and 1960's. Sometimes the northern Transvaal is referred to by political analysts as the "Deep North" in a humorous attempt to compare it with the "Deep South" of the United States.

The Eastern Transvaal Escarpment

The escarpment of the eastern Transvaal is one of the most scenic parts of South Africa. Many would say that it is *the* most beautiful part of

South Africa. The views of the Lowveld from the top of the escarpment are breathtaking. The escarpment stretches for about 200 miles (300 kilometers) from north to south, though the sudden transition from high to low ground is more dramatic in the south. Along the length of the escarpment there are splendid gorges, buttresses, waterfalls, streams, rivers, and mountain passes. The names are magical: God's Window, the Pinnacle, Lisbon Falls, Berlin Falls, Three Rondavels, World's End View. Particularly impressive is the Blyde River Canyon. *Blyde* is an old Dutch word meaning "joy" or "happiness." The canyon was given this name after an incident in which a group of Voortrekker women feared that their husbands had died. However, they were suddenly reunited with them at the river next to the canyon, which was then called "Happiness River." The Blyde River flows from the mountains and plunges into a spectacular gorge. There are several striking views of the valley below from the top of this gorge. The vegetation is lush—ferns, cycads, and proteas abound. But they may not be picked, for this is a nature reserve. In the *krantzes* (overhanging sheer cliff faces) and *kloofs* (deep ravines) baboons, buck, and an occasional leopard are to be found. Many birds live here as well.

The passes linking the escarpment with the Lowveld are as dramatic as those in the Cape, though scenically different. The Cape passes are rugged, and many of them are situated in arid country. The escarpment, on the other hand, is lush and the roads pass through many thickly forested areas. Perhaps the most awe-inspiring of the eastern Transvaal passes is Long Tom Pass, which is 35 miles (56 km.) long and at its summit is 7,052 feet (2,150 meters) above sea level. It links the old Boer town of Lydenburg with the Lowveld. An old wagon trail ran along a similar route in the nineteenth century, connecting the Boer republics with the Portuguese port of Lourenço Marques (now Maputo) in Mozambique. Long Tom Pass is named after a gun used by the Boers in 1900 in a battle with British forces. It was given this nickname by the British.

The majestic Drakensberg range, Natal. This section of the range is called the Amphi-theatre. South African Tourism Board

The battle raged in the pass for several days, and to this day craters made by the gun's shells can still be seen.

Long Tom Pass descends dramatically toward Sabie, an old gold-mining town but now the center of a vast timber industry. Huge forests of pine and eucalyptus trees cover the hills and valleys around Sabie. Next to the town flows the Sabie River, at peace at last after its tumbling descent from the escarpment. Along its journey are many splendid waterfalls with beautiful-sounding names like Bridal Veil, Horseshoe, and Lone Creek. Twenty-eight miles (45 km.) from Sabie is a romantic old town called Pilgrim's Rest. The town was a lively gold-mining center in the 1870's. Today virtually every building in Pilgrim's Rest is a museum in itself. It is not, however, a ghost town. People still live there.

The Transvaal Lowveld

The Transvaal Lowveld is a hot, humid region. In parts of the Lowveld, summer temperatures of over 104° F (40° C) are often recorded. There is reasonably heavy rainfall in summer and winters are warm and dry. Many indigenous trees grow on the Lowveld, including mopani, marula, the fever tree, and the baobab. The latter, also called the Cream of Tartar tree, is a huge tree with a gigantic trunk that stops suddenly and breaks into branches. To some it gives the impression that it has been planted upside down.

The largest town of the Lowveld is Nelspruit, which is a market center. Many rivers flow in the vicinity of Nelspruit on their journeys from the escarpment to the sea. The local farms are irrigated by these rivers, and a wide variety of agricultural products are grown. These include citrus fruits, bananas, pawpaws, and tobacco. In the Tzaneen area to the north are tea and coffee plantations.

Kruger National Park

To the east and north of Nelspruit lies the vast game reserve known as the Kruger National Park. This haven for wildlife was proclaimed a sanctuary by President Paul Kruger in 1898, when it formed part of the Boer Republic of the Transvaal. When the Transvaal became a British colony in 1902, the British agreed to abide by Kruger's proclamation, and the sanctuary was not threatened. Today it is one of the finest game reserves in the world. It comprises a tract of country about 200 miles (320 km.) long and 30 to 60 miles (50 to 100 km.) wide. It covers an area of about 7,700 square miles (20,000 square km.), about the same size as Massachusetts. Kruger Park has over 450 species of birds, 300 species of trees, and 106 mammal species.

There are birds everywhere. Most notable and frequently seen are the lilac-breasted roller, various hornbills, the gray loerie, the wood shrike and the long-tailed shrike, the various glossy starlings, and flocks of Arnot's chats. The bateleur, one of the most magnificently colored of all the birds of prey, sails majestically overhead, sometimes uttering a deep cry, sometimes clapping its wings. The vultures hover in the sky over a lion kill. Their heads are bald, and to some they appear repulsive, but their work is useful: They are the scavengers of the wilds, and will pick a carcass clean of any scrap of flesh. The biggest bird in the park is the ostrich. It stands 8 feet (2.5 meters) high, and is sometimes seen in small parties. Ostriches have a powerful kick and are fast runners, often reaching speeds of 30 miles (50 km.) an hour, but they do not fly.

Thousands of tourists flock to Kruger Park every year and stay at one or more of the many camps. These camps have wonderful names like Punda Maria, Shingwedzi, Letaba, Olifants, Satara, Skukuza, Pretorius-kop, Crocodile Bridge, and Malelane. At one stage apartheid or segregation existed in the camp facilities, but now *all* facilities are open to *all* races. In spite of these changes not many black tourists visit the Park. Perhaps they do not feel welcome; perhaps there are other reasons. One day the majority of visitors will be black.

Motorists are allowed out of the gates of the camp at sunrise and must return by sunset. Many visitors stay in the park for a week or more, often in a different camp each night.

While some tourists are absorbed by the beauty of the birds and the trees, others come to see the game. And game there is aplenty. The most common mammals are the impala, which move about in large herds. They are small antelopes that are graceful beyond description whether moving or at rest. Other buck include waterbuck and kudu. The kudu bull carries two great horns that are deadly weapons. Even the lion will think twice before attacking him. Common sights are fleeing warthogs,

Zebra run in Kruger Park.   Photo Researchers

with their tails in the air, and baboons searching for scorpions under stones and defleaing their young. Often the visitor comes across large herds of zebras and wildebeests. They can be seen separately, but for some reason they are usually found together. The long-necked giraffe fascinates many a tourist. This fabulous creature peers out from the tops of tall trees, stops eating, and stands motionless as cameras click. Soon many other heads appear at varying heights, and the bodies come into view. If disturbed, the giraffe will break off into a strange, ungainly canter.

Some animals are rarely seen. One of these is an antelope called the klipspringer or rock jumper. He stands still on a rock, high above the road, beautiful and motionless, silhouetted against the sky. But any minor disturbance will cause him to vanish in less than a second. Another rare and beautiful sight is that of the cheetah. For a second a party of cheetah may be seen crossing the road, but then the animals disappear in the depths and shadows of the sunset bush.

Most visitors are determined that they will see an elephant or a lion. And sometimes, suddenly, a whole herd of elephants will appear. Bulls, cows, and calves move along in slow procession. With their trunks they pluck leaves and branches from the many trees and leave wide swathes of destruction—and piles of dung—behind them.

But it is the lion, the King of Beasts, that most visitors hope to see. A pride is often found lying next to the road. It may consist of one or two males and several lionesses and cubs. They pay little attention to the motorists who may not, under any circumstances, get out of their cars. Very few tourists are lucky enough to see lions pursuing their prey, and even fewer manage to see a kill.

Lions in the Kruger Park.   Anglo-American Corporation

The King

Here is a humorous poem about tourists and an old lion. It was written by one of South Africa's finest poets, Douglas Livingstone.

Old Tawny's mane is moth-
eaten now, a balding monk's tonsure,
and his fluid thigh muscles flop
slack as an exhausted boxer's;

Creaks a little and is
just a fraction under fast (he's lame)
in those last short lethal rushes
at the slim white-eyed winging game;

Can catch them still of course,
the horny old claws combing crimson
from the velvet flanks in long scores,
here in the game-park's environs;

Each year, panting heavily,
manages with aged urbanity
to smile full-faced and yellowly
at a thousand box cameras.

Here is a description of the park from a book called *A South African Eden.* This book was written by the Irish-born Colonel James Stevenson-Hamilton, who became known as the "father" of Kruger National Park. He became chief game warden of the park in 1902 and lived there until his retirement in 1946. He died in 1957 at the age of ninety. This is what he wrote:

From a place of concealment, you are looking over an African river scene. Tree-clad banks and green reeds fringe the water, which reflects the pure blue of the sky. Hippos splash and grunt, crocodiles float lazily about among unheeding fishes; otters protrude their heads, turn over in the water like seals, or lie lazily on stones by its edge; a pair of Egyptian geese are preening themselves on a sandbank; kingfishers poise and dive; bush pheasants strut about, and call raucously to one another; a bateleur sails overhead; two fish-eagles perch side by side on a dead bough; a long line of impala makes its slow way towards the water, stealthily watched by a leopard extended along the horizontal limb of a great fig tree.

It is hard to realize that so peaceful a scene is all a part of the great process of eating and being eaten. And then, the moment you show yourself, what a change! The hippos and the crocodiles dive; the others disappear in water or burrow; the birds fly away; the impala snort and rush off; the leopard has simply vanished. In a few seconds not a sign of animal life is left visible to the human eye. Unvarying reaction to the recognition of wild nature's arch-enemy.

Natal

Natal is often called "The Garden Province." It is the smallest of South Africa's four provinces in area, but it has a considerably larger population than that of the Orange Free State. Its climate and scenery are remarkably varied. The huge Drakensberg range separates Natal from Lesotho, the Orange Free State, and the Transvaal to the west and north. Here too there is an escarpment, but the drop to lower-lying ground is not as sudden as it is in the eastern Transvaal. In Natal the escarpment of the great interior plateau drops in a series of wider steps toward the sea.

From towns like Ladysmith, Bergville, and Estcourt the wall of the Drakensberg presents an impressive sight, though in summer the massive range is often covered in cloud. The mountains rise to heights of over 10,000 feet (3,000 meters) above sea level and are 5,000 feet (1,500 meters) above the surrounding country. They are wild and magnificent, the greatest mountain mass in southern Africa. In winter the mountains are often covered in snow, a rare sight in most parts of South Africa.

Northern Natal and Natal Midlands

It was in northern Natal that much of the fighting in the Anglo-Boer War of 1899–1902 took place. This was a crucial conflict between the Dutch-speaking white settlers (the Boers) and the British, who wanted to retain control of the area. Ladysmith was the scene of an important siege in 1899. The Boer forces penned up the British, and delayed their advance into the Transvaal. In Ladysmith there is a beautiful Anglican church, with many stained-glass memorial windows and marble tablets bearing the names of 3,200 soldiers who fell during the siege.

Northern Natal is an important coal-mining district with coal mining centers at Newcastle, Dundee, and Vryheid. As one moves farther southward and eastward, the region falls away in a series of steps toward the coast. The area adjoining northern Natal is known as the Natal Midlands. This is a most attractive part of the country. There is a local beauty of hill and valley, tree and field, which is seldom seen in the higher sections of the interior. The farms are smaller, and signs of human habitation more frequent.

Several large forests have been planted in the Natal Midlands, an area that is lush and enjoys a good rainfall. The forests include large numbers of pines, bluegums, and wattles. Centers of the forestry industry are Pietermaritzburg, Greytown, Richmond, and Ixopo.

Ixopo is a small town 53 miles (85 kilometers) southwest of Pietermaritzburg. This town, founded in 1878, was the setting for Alan

Paton's novel *Cry, the Beloved Country.* The author worked in Ixopo as a schoolteacher in the 1920's, and it was here that he met and married his first wife. The opening of the novel describes in lyrical prose the beauty of the hills surrounding the town:

There is a lovely road that runs from Ixopo into the hills. These hills are grass-covered and rolling, and they are lovely beyond any singing of it. The road climbs seven miles into them, to Carisbrooke; and from there, if there is no mist, you look down on one of the fairest valleys of Africa. About you there is grass and bracken and you may hear the forlorn crying of the titihoya, one of the birds of the veld. Below you is the valley of the Umzimkulu, on its journey from the Drakensberg to the sea; and beyond and behind the river, great hill after great hill; and beyond and behind them, the mountains of Ingeli and East Griqualand.

The main highway from Johannesburg to Durban—a distance of 370 miles (600 km.)—runs through the Natal Midlands, passes close to the spectacular Howick Falls, and continues to Hilton. A vast stretch of country lies to the south of Hilton. Immediately below is the city of Pietermaritzburg, and in the distance lie many flat-topped mountains. The largest of these is another Table Mountain, which keeps guard over the Valley of a Thousand Hills.

Pietermaritzburg

Pietermaritzburg is the administrative capital of Natal province. It is the second-largest city in Natal, though much smaller than its coastal sister, Durban. The 1988 population of Greater Pietermaritzburg was unofficially estimated at about 400,000 people. The city was founded in 1838 and was named after two Voortrekker leaders, Pieter Retief and Gert Maritz. Today it is largely an English-speaking city, though in the 1987 all-white elections the white voters of the city voted overwhelmingly in favor of National Party candidates, who support racial separation. The

Zulu residents of Pietermaritzburg call their city *"um Gungundhlovu,"* which means "The Place of the Elephant."

Alan Paton describes the city of his birth as "the lovely city" and goes on to say "my hometown was a paradise." It is tragic that in 1987 and 1988 there was terrible violence in the black areas surrounding Pietermaritzburg. Bitter feuding occurred between supporters of the United Democratic Front (U.D.F.) and members of the Inkatha movement, a militant pro-Zulu group. Hundreds of people died in these clashes.

The Valley of a Thousand Hills

Pietermaritzburg and Durban are 50 miles (80 km.) apart. Midway between the two cities on the old main highway lies the Valley of a Thousand Hills, a most appropriate name for this scenic valley. There are rivers and streams everywhere, and many tropical birds can be seen and heard. The central river is the Umgeni, which flows into the Indian Ocean at Durban. The valley is inhabited by Zulu-speaking people. Some of them wear western clothing, but others, mostly women, still wear traditional clothes. They also wear colored cloth, even colored towels, which contrast vividly with one another. Sometimes the hair of a married woman is piled high up on her head and dressed with reddish clay. Multicolored beads play a great part in traditional Zulu dress, in the shape of necklaces, head circlets, and bangles around arms and legs, even around the waist.

Durban

Greater Durban was officially South Africa's third-largest city in 1985, with a population of about one and a half million people. Unofficial estimates, however, which take into account the large black "shack-dwelling" population (which, it is claimed, is rapidly approaching two million people) put greater Durban's population in 1988 at over 3 million. If this figure is correct, Durban has a considerably larger population than Cape Town and is South Africa's second-largest city. It has been said that Durban is one of the fastest-growing cities in the world. Durban has a far larger Indian population than any other South African city.

Durban has a fine natural harbor, and is one of the busiest cargo ports in Africa. The city is South Africa's principal port and also the country's leading holiday resort with a series of magnificent beaches.

Durban's most prominent feature is the Bluff, a long, high hill that protects the bay from the Indian Ocean. The first recorded sighting of the Bluff by a European was made by the Portuguese sailor Vasco da Gama on Christmas Day in 1497. Da Gama called the region "Terra do Natal," the land of the birth of Christ. British traders arrived in Port

The yacht basin in Durban Bay.   South African Tourism Board

Natal in the 1820's and set up their huts in the tropical bush. In 1835 the name was changed to Durban in honor of one of the governors of the Cape Colony, Sir Benjamin D'Urban. When the settlers first arrived, elephants roamed freely, and hippos, crocodiles, and pelicans lived in the swamps. But soon all these animals were exterminated. One has to travel for hours from Durban today to spot these creatures in their natural habitat.

In the historical chapters the clashes in Durban between the British and the Voortrekkers will be discussed, as well as the ride of Dick King, hero of the British settlers. His statue is found on the Esplanade of Durban Bay. Another reminder of this history is the Old Fort, where the British were besieged by the Voortrekkers. After the departure of the Voortrekkers southern Natal's white population became largely English speaking. Today English is spoken by most of Durban's white citizens as well as by the majority of Indian and coloured citizens.

The region consisting of Durban and the Natal coastal belt has a hot, wet subtropical climate. Summers are warm and humid, with temperatures often around 80 degrees F (27° C) in central Durban. When this is combined with a high humidity, as it often is in the months of January and February, the days and nights are sticky and uncomfortable. Durban enjoys a good summer rainfall, and some rain also falls in winter. The winters are mild to warm, and even in winter months the beaches are crowded.

Many tropical trees and bushes grow in Durban and along the coastal belt. Tropical fruits are found in abundance. Fields of bananas are a common sight, and one also sees hundreds of pawpaw, mango, litchi, and avocado trees. The gardens of the wealthier citizens of Durban are full of the vivid and barbaric colors of poinsettia and bougainvillea. Orange sheets of the flower called "golden shower" hang from roofs and pergolas. Another magnificent tree, the erythrina, puts forth blood-red blooms in the late winter and early spring. Two other colorful trees to be found in Durban's suburbs are the jacaranda and the flamboyant. Both jacaranda and flamboyant come from outside Africa; both jacaranda and flamboyant are prodigal with blossom; both jacaranda and flamboyant carpet the roadways with their flowers. The flamboyant flowers are scarlet, the jacaranda ones mauve. Still another striking flowering tree is the spathodea, the African flame, with masses of great orange-red bell-shaped blooms. All these trees and shrubs are to be seen in profusion in Durban. They line the streets and fill the gardens, making this city for many one of the most fascinating and beautiful in the world.

Yet even more fascinating are the people of Durban, a richly diverse community. Durban is without doubt the most cosmopolitan city in South Africa, a meeting place of Asia, Africa, and the West. From the sea the skyline of Durban looks like the skyline of any like-sized American city. Here is a city with plush hotels and office blocks, commercial banks, and scurrying traffic. Away from West Street, the main street of Durban, is the Indian city. Here are streets crowded with Indian and black shoppers, many of the Indian women wearing their brightly colored saris. Here are large wholesale houses and hundreds of smaller shops owned by Indian merchants. Here is the Indian Market, one of the most colorful and lively places in Durban. Here are schools and mosques. And here too, in the streets, in the shops, and at the crowded bus and railway stations are thousands of Zulu people who have come to seek work in this bustling city.

To what extent is Durban "a meeting place"? In a way it is, and in a way it isn't. There *are* friendships between members of different racial groups, but Durban is also a city of division and of racial and ethnic tension. It has witnessed violence between Indians and blacks, and some of its white citizens have expressed strong prejudices against other racial groups. The Group Areas Act applies in Durban as in all other

South African cities. Blacks live in black areas, whites live in white areas, Indians live in Indian areas, and coloureds live in coloured areas. In the past, as a result of the Group Areas Act, many Indians and blacks were forced to quit their homes and to live in areas set aside for their own racial groups. In Cape Town District Six was destroyed. In Johannesburg blacks were forced out of Sophiatown. In Durban there were similar mass removals of blacks from an area called Cato Manor. Most of Durban's black people live in the townships of Umlazi and Kwa-Mashu. As in Soweto there has been a great deal of violence in these black areas in recent years, and while many have died in clashes with the police, much of it has been black-on-black violence. The reader may be puzzled to discover that black-on-black violence has occurred in recent times in South Africa. The reasons for this are complex and may become clearer once the historical sections have been read. The causes of this violence have to do with denial of political rights, with poverty, with unemployment, and with strongly held, clashing beliefs.

The municipality of Durban is making an attempt to desegregate the city's beaches. At one stage there were separate beaches for whites, Indians, blacks, and coloureds. But segregation has been breaking down rapidly, and it is to be hoped that in the 1990's apartheid will have disappeared forever from Durban's beaches.

The waters of the Indian Ocean are warm, even in winter. Sharks are a danger to swimmers, but all Durban's beaches are protected by shark nets. There are also dangerous currents, and consequently bathers must bathe in appointed places, where there are lifeguards on duty. Other beach attractions in Durban are the Snake Park and the Durban Centenary Aquarium. In the former many dangerous snakes, most of them indigenous to Natal, can be seen. The deadliest is the black mamba, one of the most venomous snakes in the world. It reaches a length of 13 feet (4 meters) or more, and terrible stories are told of its speed and ferocity. At one time it was common in all the coastal regions of Natal, but luckily it retreats from built-up areas. Other snakes to be seen include green mambas, cobras, and puff-adders, snakes that are found in many parts of South Africa. In the aquarium there are considerable numbers of species of fish, including several types of shark.

Greater Durban, which includes the areas of Pinetown and New Germany, is a large industrial center. Hundreds of factories are found in this area. Raw materials for these industries are obtained from the oil refinery in Durban, from inland forests, and from the vast sugar plantations on the coastal belt.

Natal Coastal Belt

Sugar is the main product of the Natal coastal region. Most of Natal's sugarcane is grown on the coast north of Durban known as the North Coast. The main road from Durban along the coast to the Tugela River passes through endless fields of cane. In this hot and humid climate the sugarcane flourishes, and many farmers (mostly white) have become very wealthy through sales of the crop. The cane is cut by hand, then transported to a sugar mill without delay. Some sugarcane is also grown on the Natal South Coast, south of Durban.

Seaside resorts along the Natal coastline rejoice in Zulu names like Umdloti, Umhlanga, Isipingo, Amanzimtoti, Ifafa, Umtwalumi, Umtentweni. The sun is bright, the sands golden, the sea blue, the water warm. This was and still is the playground of white South Africa, but changes are taking place. As South Africa fumbles toward the dismantling of apartheid, more and more beaches are being opened to all South Africans.

Zulu workers on a sugar farm, Natal North Coast. Tony Savino, Impact Visuals

Floods

On September 26, 1987, Natal recorded its highest monthly rainfall for September in living memory. More than 60 inches (150 centimeters) of rain had fallen. The previous average was 25 inches (64 centimeters). This was only the beginning of the worst floods that have ever been recorded in South Africa. Rain continued to fall unabated, and many Natal rivers flooded their banks. Some places recorded 2 feet (600 millimeters) in only four days. A few days later there were more than three hundred dead and more than half a million people left homeless. The overwhelming majority of dead and homeless were black people. Many Indians too suffered tremendous losses. In early 1988 there was also heavy flooding along the Orange and Vaal rivers in the Orange Free State and northern Cape. Again tremendous damage was caused to property, but fortunately there was very little loss of life. It is ironic that floods should have been so widespread in a country that for so many years had suffered severe drought.

Zululand

One part of Natal that has not yet been mentioned is Zululand, a region of the province that lies to the north of the Tugela River. Coastal Zululand is hotter and more humid than the coastal stretch to the south. Vast quantities of sugarcane are grown along the Zululand coast, and the rapidly growing port of Richards Bay is now the chief South African port used for the export of coal from the Transvaal coalfields. There are several fine nature reserves in Zululand, some along coastal stretches and others inland. The two most popular of these reserves are Umfolozi and Hluhluwe. Here lives a wide variety of game, including the rare white rhinoceros and the even rarer black rhinoceros.

Though white farms occupy a substantial section of Zululand, most of the territory belongs to the homeland of KwaZulu. The sections of Zululand that belong to KwaZulu do not constitute the *whole* of KwaZulu. The KwaZulu homeland consists of nine separate pieces which stretch from the Mozambique border in the north to the Transkei border in the south. The largest concentration of KwaZulu blacks lives in the Umlazi district near Durban. Of South Africa's almost 6 million Zulu-speaking people, about half live in KwaZulu. The Chief Minister of KwaZulu, Chief Mangosuthu Buthelezi, has refused to ask for "independence" for his homeland. He would like to see—as would many Natal whites—the merging of KwaZulu and Natal into a nonracial region of South Africa, but at the time of writing the government has refused to give this venture its blessing. Chief Buthelezi is a controversial figure for other reasons as well, and has both strong supporters and fierce enemies among blacks and whites.

The Homelands

Soon after the National Party came to power in 1948, the policy of "separate development" was enforced with new, more restrictive, laws. Certain areas, which had traditionally been the home of rural blacks, were set aside by the government to be occupied and governed exclusively by blacks. These are called "homelands" or "black homelands," and the "independent" ones are referred to as "national states." The homelands occupy about 13 percent of the total land area of South Africa. They were divided along ethnic lines, and the government laid the foundation for each homeland to become "independent" if it so wished. Of South Africa's ten homelands four have thus far chosen "independence." They are Transkei (independent October 1976), whose citizens are mainly Xhosa speaking; Bophuthatswana (indepen-

The legend reads:

- NON-INDEPENDENT HOMELANDS
- INDEPENDENT HOMELANDS

ZIMBABWE

M O Z A M B I Q U E

Limpopo

Venda

Gazankulu

KRUGER

Lebowa

NATIONAL

Lebowa

PARK

T r a n s v a a l

Kwa Ndebele

NELSPRUIT

Rustenburg

PRETORIA

B o p h u t h a t s w a n a

Mafikeng

MIDDELBURG

JOHANNESBURG

WITBANK

Kangwane

MAPUTO

Molopo

ERMELO

SWAZILAND

POTCHEFSTROOM

Vaal

Vaal

Wilge

Kroonstad

N a t a l

WELKOM

Dundee

BETHLEHEM

HARRISMITH

Ladysmith

Kwa Zulu

KIMBERLEY

Orange Free State

Fouriesburg

Qwa Qwa

Tugela

Ficksburg

Estcourt

Greytown

Bop.

BLOEMFONTEIN

Ladybrand

LESOTHO

PIETERMARITZBURG

DURBAN

Tixei

C a p e

Tixei

Port Edward

P r o v i n c e

Transkei

INDIAN OCEAN

Ciskei

King Williams Town

GRAHAMSTOWN

EAST LONDON

Bathurst

Knysna

PORT ELIZABETH

0   100   200
km

The "homelands" of South Africa

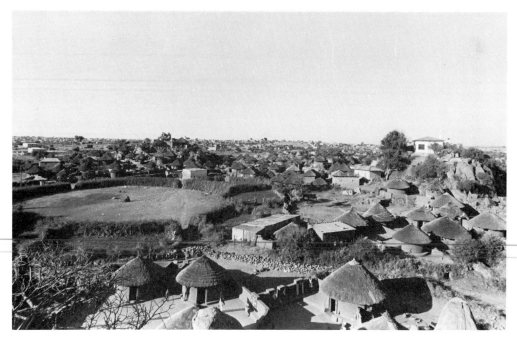

Village in Lebowa.   *The Star,* Johannesburg

dent December 1977), citizens mainly Tswana speaking; Venda (independent September 1979), citizens mainly Venda speaking; Ciskei (independent December 1981), citizens mainly Xhosa speaking. The remaining six homelands are Lebowa (mainly North Sotho), Gazankulu (mainly Shangaan), KwaNdebele (mainly Ndebele), KaNgwane (mainly Swazi), Qwaqwa (mainly South Sotho), and KwaZulu (mainly Zulu). Of these some may yet seek independence, but others like Gazankulu and KwaZulu are opposed to independence, regarding themselves as integral parts of South Africa.

The inclusion of a chapter on the homelands does not imply that the author approves of government policy, or recognizes the areas as independent states. Every nation outside of South Africa officially views their "independence" as a sham. But it cannot be denied that the homelands exist as geographical units.

Transkei

The largest of the independent homelands is the Transkei, sometimes also called Transkei. The word *Transkei* means "across the Kei River." The population of the Transkei is about 3 million. This homeland consists of three separate pieces, the largest of which borders on the Cape Province to the south and Natal to the north. The capital of the Transkei is Umtata.

The vast majority of Transkei inhabitants live in the country. Many of them are subsistence farmers, planting corn or sorghum and owning small numbers of cattle, sheep, and goats, which wander about in search

These two Transkei women still lead a traditional way of life and rely on herding and subsistence farming to make a living. South African Tourism Board

of grazing. Cattle in particular play an important part in traditional life. *Lobolo*, or the bride price, is paid in cattle to the father of the bride.

Many early missionaries made the mistake of supposing that wives were *purchased* in this manner, but the bride price is something more significant than that. It signifies a contract every bit as important as Western marriages, a contract not between two persons but between two kinship groups.

Cattle and goats are essential providers of milk and meat. But they bring problems, for in parts of the Transkei the land has been over-grazed and terrible soil erosion has resulted. The peasant farmers struggle to survive and seek work in the cities. The children do not get enough food and suffer from malnutrition. It is a similar story in many rural parts of South Africa as this excerpt from *Cry, the Beloved Country* shows:

The great red hills stand desolate, and the earth has torn away like flesh. The lightning flashes over them, the clouds pour down upon them, the dead streams come to life, full of the red blood of the earth. Down in the valleys women scratch the soil that is left, and the maize hardly reaches the height of a man. They are valleys of old men and old women, of mothers and children. The men are away, the young men and the girls are away. The soil cannot keep them any more.

Yet there is also great beauty in the Transkei. Pondoland in the northeast of the territory is particularly attractive. Here, as in Natal, the high land falls to the sea in a confusion of hills, valleys, kloofs, rivers, and waterfalls with stretches of evergreen forest, in which grows the Cape chestnut. In summer this tree puts forth a profusion of pink blooms that entirely cover its crown.

Until the middle of the last century many wild animals were to be found in this area—the lion, the elephant, the hippopotamus. The latter animal is remembered in the name of the Umzimvubu River (umzimvubu is a Xhosa word meaning "home of the hippopotamus"), which flows out to the sea at Port Saint Johns through a magnificent gateway. Along much of the Transkei coast the escarpment has contained itself in patience and has taken its last leap into the Indian Ocean itself. One cliff after another stretches out along the coastline, but every now and then there is a break giving way to superbly flat and isolated beaches.

Ciskei

Not far from the Transkei's western boundary is another independent homeland, the Republic of Ciskei, often shortened to Ciskei. The word *Ciskei* means "this side of the Kei river." More than 700,000 people live in this homeland. Both Transkeians and Ciskeians are Xhosa speaking. The capital of Ciskei is Bisho.

Ciskei is a very poor area. Many of its male inhabitants are migrant workers who earn money in the large industrial cities. Agriculture has been developed in the Ciskei, and some areas produce a great deal of citrus fruit. Yet in other parts it is also a case of "the young men and the girls are away. The soil cannot keep them any more."

In the town of Alice is the University of Fort Hare. This university was once held in high esteem, for many of Africa's and South Africa's black leaders, including Nelson Mandela, studied here. But in 1959 the Nationalist government passed legislation that tried to prevent South Africa's liberal universities from continuing as multiracial institutions. Fort Hare suffered along with many other universities. Those staff, both black and white, known to be opposed to government policies were dismissed. Today the university is controlled by the so-called independent country of Ciskei, but it has been through many unhappy years. Hundreds of students and many staff members have been dismissed because of their opposition to the totalitarian policies of the Ciskei government.

Bophuthatswana

The wealthiest homeland is Bophuthatswana, which became "independent" in December 1977. It has a population of about 1.5 million
people, most of whom speak Tswana. Bophuthatswana is a very strange
country because it consists of seven separate land units. One of these
is completely surrounded by the Cape Province, one shares borders with
the Cape and Transvaal provinces, a third shares borders with the Cape,
Transvaal, and Botswana, three are completely surrounded by the
Transvaal, and a seventh piece is completely surrounded by the Orange
Free State. The capital is Mmabatho, which was built shortly before
"independence" and is today a bustling and growing town that has
never experienced apartheid.

Bophuthatswana is rich in minerals. Some of the world's richest
platinum mines are in the homeland near the western Transvaal town
of Rustenburg. Chrome, asbestos, manganese, and coal are also mined.
Bophuthatswana is a semiarid homeland and does not produce many
crops. Many thousands of goats and sheep are raised in drier areas, and
beef cattle graze on the Highveld grasslands.

One of Bophuthatswana's chief tourist attractions is the luxurious
hotel complex called Sun City. The hotel was built in semiarid country
about 30 miles (50 kilometers) north of Rustenburg. Attractions at Sun
City include a casino (illegal in South Africa), a huge area for glittering
shows and performances, and a golf course where some of the world's
richest golf tournaments are held. Cinemas show many semiporno-
graphic films, which are banned in South Africa. Small wonder that Sun
City is sometimes called "Sin City." Stars such as Frank Sinatra and
Dolly Parton have performed at Sun City, and some of the world's major
boxers have taken part in world title fights. But as the opposition to
apartheid has mounted, more and more performers and sportsmen have

argued that in fact Sun City is an integral part of apartheid in South Africa and should be boycotted.

Venda

The homeland of Venda achieved "independence" in September 1979. Venda is considerably smaller in area than the Transkei or Bophutha-tswana and is situated in the far northern Transvaal. It lies east of the Transvaal town of Louis Trichardt and consists of two separate pieces: The southern section is smaller and is *almost* linked to the northern section. The northern boundary is close to the Zimbabwe border, but a narrow strip of the Transvaal separates the two "countries." Its capital is Thohoyandou, a Venda word meaning "head of the elephant." The capital boasts a small and very new university. Venda is the most fertile of the "independent" homelands. Local inhabitants grow considerable quantities of fruit and vegetables, but nevertheless there is also a great deal of poverty in parts of this "country."

The Future of the Homelands

By and large the four "independent" homelands have suffered a history of instability and restlessness. Several leaders have been charged with corruption. Opposition has been ruthlessly stamped out. Most nonindependent homelands have experienced similar problems.

If the African National Congress were to come to power, all the homelands would be declared part of the Republic of South Africa. They would almost certainly retain their respective languages and cultures, but the excessive powers of the chiefs would be abolished.

The Early Inhabitants of South Africa

Until the 1960's South African schoolchildren were taught that when the first Dutch settlers arrived in 1652, large parts of South Africa were empty and unexplored. Teachers admitted that at that time parts of the Western Cape were inhabited by Khoikhoi and San. But they claimed that the forefathers of the Bantu-speaking peoples arrived in the northern parts of present-day South Africa at much the same time as the Dutch colonists arrived in the southwest. Apparently, large parts of South Africa had been there for the taking. According to this view, one that is still taught today by some teachers, the white settlers were courageous men and women who fought off hordes of fierce, heathen black warriors to open up the country, a tale similar to the old myths about cowboys and Indians in the United States. But a newer view is that these settlers unfairly took much of the land for themselves and set aside only certain smaller regions for black settlement. Most of the country's natural resources were monopolized by the white minority, and the blacks were left with very little.

As a result of the old way of teaching, all South African schoolchildren were misled. Black pupils failed to learn about their heritage, and white students were presented with myths rather than facts. Now scholars, community activists, and even students themselves are rediscovering history. They are reclaiming a different past, at odds with the teachings of the white government. Indeed, they are trying to shape a more inclusive nation that puts to rest the old teachings that made blacks out to be inferior to whites.

Southern Apes and Modern Humans

When was southern Africa first inhabited? There is strong evidence to suggest that earliest humans lived in the southern and eastern parts of the African continent about 2.5 million years ago.

Technological and Social Attributes of the Stone and Iron Ages

STONE AGE	IRON AGE
• Hunting (bow and arrow)	• Hunting (spears) and herding cattle
• Gathering plants to eat	• Growing plants for food
• Small mobile groups	• Large sedentary groups in organized villages
• Stone knapping (making stone tools)	• Metal technology
• Egalitarian	• Ranked society

Outline of
South African History

c. 2.5 million years ago: Southern Africa is first inhabited by australopithecenes

c. 100,000 years ago: Modern humans arise in Africa. These first species develop into a variety of physical types, one of which becomes the ancestor of the modern San.

c. 2,000 years ago: Khoikhoi first appear in southern Africa

c. A.D. 500: First Bantu-speaking people already settled in parts of southern Africa.

500–1000: Further waves of Bantu speakers arrive from the north

1488: Bartholomew Diaz rounds the Cape

1497: Vasco da Gama passes the Cape and names Natal

1503: Antonio de Saldanha enters Table Bay

1602: Dutch East India Company formed

1652: Jan van Riebeeck arrives in Table Bay

1657: Some colonists allowed to farm for the first time
First slaves imported from other parts of Africa and southeast Asia

1688: First Huguenots arrive at the Cape

1737: Moravian Missionary Society establishes mission station to work among the Khoikhoi

1778: After several clashes between Boers and Xhosas the Dutch East India Company intervenes and declares the Fish River to be the boundary between the warring factions

c. 1785: Birth of Mosheshwe

c. 1787: Birth of Shaka

1795: First British occupation of the Cape

1798: Dutch East India Company becomes insolvent

1799: London Missionary Society begins working in the Cape

Archaeologists have called these earliest inhabitants "australopithe-cines," also known as "southern apes." The australopithecines were not toolmakers. Toolmaking began between 2 and 1.5 million years ago with the advent of the first species of true humans. The advent of this species marked the beginning of the Stone Age. There is evidence that about a hundred thousand years ago the modern human arose in Africa. Africa was thus the birthplace of both "southern apes" and modern humans. Humankind was born in Africa.

This first species of humans further developed into a variety of physical types. One of these became the ancestors of the modern San.

The San

There are not many San left in southern Africa today. Most of them live in the Kalahari Desert in Botswana, one of South Africa's neighboring countries. The San have been given a variety of names by various inhabitants. They were called "Twa" by the Xhosa and "Bushmen" by the early Dutch settlers. Many people still refer to them as Bushmen,

A San hunter in the Kalahari Desert. South African Tourism Board

San art. This scene of hunters and animals is typical of San rock paintings.   South Africa Tourism Board

but the name that is increasingly being used is San, which is what the Khoikhoi used to call them. According to some experts *san* means "men" in the Khoisan languages. (Khoisan languages are those spoken by the Khoikhoi and San peoples.) Other experts argue that "San" denotes people of low status, and prefer to use the word "Bushmen."

The San have always been hunter-gatherers and are famous for their hunting ability. They are a short yellow- or reddish-skinned people who speak a variety of click languages, which very few non-San speakers understand. Some groups of San are unable to understand the language spoken by other San groups. At one stage the San were scattered over wide areas of South Africa, as we can see from the many rock paintings drawn by the San in caves throughout the country. In past centuries many San have been killed by their "enemies," both black and white. And some San have intermarried with other groups.

The Khoikhoi

About two thousand years ago sheep and goat herders related to the San first appeared in South Africa. They have become known as the Khoikhoi, and like that of the San, their language was full of click sounds.

Click Languages

A click is a sound formed by trapping a pocket of air against the palate (or roof of the mouth) between the back of the tongue and the front of the tongue or lips. Through subtle adjustments of the tongue either "popping" or "sucking" clicks will result.

Most of us are familiar with the sucking click written as "tsk" and used to express annoyance. A different click is the sharp popping sound used to imitate a cork being drawn from a bottle.

The San languages make extensive use of four or five clicks as well as a variety of more usual consonants. Over 70 percent of words in a San language begin with a click, and because most words are very short, consisting of only one or two syllables, the effect created by the spoken language is a most dramatic stream of clicking sounds.

Although all humans can produce clicks, the San use of clicks as parts of words is found nowhere else in the world. This observation has often led to farfetched claims that clicks are a leftover of earlier stages of human evolution or that they enable the San hunter to blend with the natural sounds of his environment. However, these ideas are very difficult to prove and remain pure speculation. So far as we know, clicks do not offer their users any special advantages.

Some believe that as a result of their improved diet they were taller than the San. The Khoikhoi were called "Hottentots" by the early Dutch settlers, and this name continues to be used. But "Khoikhoi" is being used more and more by experts. The Khoikhoi no longer exist as a separate group in South Africa, although there are pockets of old people who can still remember aspects of their customs and language.

Early Iron Age People

At the time of the birth of Jesus there were many Khoisan people scattered throughout present-day South Africa. It was once believed that no other groups lived in South Africa for the next thousand years. But archaeologists have found evidence that Iron Age people were settled in parts of present-day Natal and the Transvaal before A.D. 500. These people were neither Khoikhoi nor San. They were negroid and may well have been the first Bantu-speaking people to settle in South Africa.

"Iron Age" is used to define a way of life, but in terms of South African history it is a term used by archaeologists to refer to a period when people lived in villages, grew crops, kept cattle, made pottery, and smelted iron. Controversy still rages about the language or languages spoken by these Early Iron Age settlers and about their origins. Many experts agree, however, that the Bantu languages of South Africa originated in central Africa and that the Early Iron Age people came to settle in South Africa after migrating from the north. Did all the Bantu speakers arrive at the same time? Apparently not; there was not one period of migration but several.

Late Iron Age People

Archaeologists also speak of the Late Iron Age. In southern Africa, the Late Iron Age began about A.D. 1000 when new groups arrived in the region. Iron tools allowed these people to grow more food. Soon the population greatly increased and many villages grew rapidly. By about A.D. 1500 some of these people began to live on the open grasslands. These open grasslands (today called the Highveld) were virtually tree-less. There was no wood for fuel or for building. As a result stone was used for building and dung for fuel.

An important feature of Late Iron Age life was an increase in the number of cattle kept by the inhabitants. Cattle need grass to graze on. And in South Africa grass grows on valuable land. The struggle for land was to become one of the most crucial areas of conflict in the centuries that lay ahead. It is still divides the peoples of South Africa today.

The conflicts were initially between the San, the Khoikhoi, and the Bantu-speaking groups. Some of the early victims of the struggle were the San hunter-gatherers. They found that they had less and less land on which to hunt. The rock paintings of the San in the eastern parts of the country tell of fighting between them and Nguni herders. Thousands of San were killed in these conflicts, as well as in conflicts with other groups, both black and white. The San who survived were those who lived in the Kalahari Desert.

The Coming of the Dutch

It is likely that sailors from the Mediterranean saw the mountain masses of the Cape 2,500 years ago, but the first certain record is that of the Portuguese sailor Bartholomew Diaz, who rounded the Cape in 1488. Diaz called it the Cape of Storms, but later either he or King John of Portugal renamed it the Cape of Good Hope.

In 1497 another great Portuguese navigator, Vasco da Gama, passed beyond the Cape to an area that he named Natal. He also found a sea route to India.

In 1503 Antonio de Saldanha entered Table Bay, and his ship was perhaps the first ever to lie under the great mountain. He was almost certainly the first white man to climb it, and it was he who gave it the name of Table Mountain. As the sixteenth century went on, more and more ships, particularly from Holland and England, anchored in Table Bay, and the crews bartered with the Khoikhoi who had been living in the area for centuries. The sailors especially prized the red meat that the cattle herders could provide.

The Arrival of Jan van Riebeeck

In 1602 the Dutch East India Company was formed to trade between Holland and the Dutch East Indies (modern-day Indonesia). So many ships were now passing on this route that in 1652 the Company sent

Extracts from Jan van Riebeeck's Journal in the first years of the settlement

June, 1652: Out of 116, only sixty, from sickness, fit for labour; dysentery and severe fevers. Only one cow and calf obtained from the natives. . . .

July, 1652: All the vegetables, and also wheat, grow delightfully close to the fort, but all drowned and destroyed by heavy rain; weather such as hardly to admit of a dog being driven out, and the mountains in several places covered with snow, increasing the sickness.

January, 1653: It appeared as if the lions would in the night take the fort by storm, that they might get at the sheep; they made a fearful noise as if they would destroy all within, but in vain, for they could not climb the walls.

out Jan van Riebeeck to found a refreshment station at the Cape, where green vegetables could be grown to provide the vitamin C needed to prevent the dread disease of scurvy, where outgoing sailors could leave letters to be taken back to the Netherlands by some other ship, and where the sick could be left for attention.

The Khoikhoi

The establishment of the station was not easy. The Khoikhoi were ready enough to barter cattle with passing ships. However, this was to be a more or less permanent settlement, and the Khoikhoi soon realized that the more cattle the Company acquired, the more land it would need for grazing. Quite naturally the Khoikhoi did not wish to lose their land, and so for a while they refused to barter at all. Instead they continued to graze their fine herds within sight of van Riebeeck's fort. Van Riebeeck would have liked to capture as many Khoikhoi as he could, make slaves of them, and seize all their cattle. Fortunately the Company would not give him permission to do so. It was certainly contrary to Dutch law for native people to be enslaved.

But the Khoikhoi's desire for tobacco, food, and alcohol made them dependent upon the Dutch, while the devastation caused by new diseases, as well as the power of the Dutchman's gun, put the Africans at an even greater disadvantage. Many of the Khoikhoi moved away from the Cape into the hinterland. Here their way of life survived a little longer. But those who remained became the Dutchman's servants. By the middle of the nineteenth century the Khoikhoi were lost in the turbulent melting pot of black and white. Their culture was no more. Even their language was no more.

The Introduction of Slaves

The Dutch East India Company did not at first intend the settlement at the Cape to become a colony. Nevertheless in 1657 it allowed nine *burghers* (citizens) to farm on their own, but placed many restrictions on them. Soon the *burghers* grew impatient with the rule of the Company. In turn the Company found both the *burghers* and the local Khoikhoi to be unsatisfactory sources of labor, so they imported slaves from West Africa. Increasingly the whites began to rely on slave labor, and a further group of slaves were imported from Malaya in southeast Asia. It has been said that the treatment of the slaves at the Cape was not as harsh as that of slaves on the plantations of the West Indies and on the plantations in the Deep South of the United States. But no doubt the treatment of the Cape slaves was inhuman enough.

There are many rough parallels between the history of South Africa and that of the United States. Settlers from Europe went to both countries, settlers and indigenous peoples clashed in both countries, slavery was introduced in both countries. Both countries were later to free their slaves, but the United States has chosen a slow path of integration and South Africa has maintained a path of racial separation.

Before 1700 there existed in the Cape a community of Khoikhois, white settlers, slaves, and ex-slaves. There was naturally a great degree of sexual contact and even intermarrying. White prejudice against marriage across racial lines developed slowly. Only centuries later would there be legislation against it. The result of this mixing of peoples was a group who came to be called "Cape coloureds." A section of this group was called the "Cape Malays," a term still used today to refer to coloureds of Asian descent who are practicing Muslims.

Marriages between white and black were sometimes referred to as "mixed marriages." One such marriage took place between a young

Cape coloured performers in the annual Coon Carnival in Cape Town. The title of the festival, as well as the costumes and gestures of the performers, were originally drawn from visiting American minstrels.   Jason Laure, Impact Visuals

Khoikhoi convert to Christianity named Eva and a Danish surgeon, Pieter van Meerhoff. Eva had been brought up in van Riebeeck's household and become a translator. But as more and more Khoikhois learned Dutch, Eva's services were no longer indispensable. She was deserted by the van Riebeeck family when they sailed for Batavia (modern-day Djakarta), and spent her time in the company of sailors. She bore two illegitimate children. But her life flourished once more after her marriage to Pieter van Meerhoff. She and her husband had three children before she was widowed.

Settlers from Europe

The white people of the Cape grew slowly in numbers, and consisted of German, Dutch, and French immigrants. The largest number were Germans, not Dutch, and many of them were peasant farmers. It was the French Huguenots who were the most cultivated. They were Protestant victims of religious persecution in France, and they were largely responsible for the development of South Africa's wine industry. But whatever their different origins, these people all adopted Dutch, since it was the official language at the Cape and the only language taught in the schools. The polyglot mixture of Khoikhoi, slaves, and ex-slaves from other parts of Africa and Malaya also naturally adopted Dutch as their medium of communication. But they simplified its forms, softened some of its sounds, and enriched it with words of their own. In fact, what began to evolve was a new language, more in harmony with Africa, and which in the course of time their "white masters" adopted too (some might say appropriated). The language came to be called *die taal* or "the language," but today it is called Afrikaans. The people who speak it are called Afrikaners, or people of Africa. It is also the language of the majority of coloured people who live in South Africa today.

What was becoming clear, even as early as 1700, was the interdependence of one group with another in that part of the African continent that was to become South Africa. By 1700 mixed marriages had already taken place (though these were to be frowned upon by the white establishment later on), translators had to be found to aid communication between the various groups, Dutch was learned and spoken by non-Dutch speakers, and several groups contributed to the formation of the Afrikaans language. Even today no one group in South Africa could survive without the support of other groups.

Many of the settlers were townspeople, and stayed in Cape Town, or Kaapstad, as the city built at the foot of Table Mountain was called. The more adventurous (and sometimes the more lawless) were attracted by the land farthest from the cities. In South Africa, the attraction was initially for the great mountains and fertile valleys of the Cape Peninsula. These settlers became herders of flocks rather than farmers and trekked with their flocks and herds farther and farther away from the Company's control into the wastes of the Karoo. They lived in increasing isolation from the "civilizing" influences of Europe.

The Trekboer

The expansion over the Karoo was rapid. A similar expansion westward took place in the United States. In the United States the white pioneers displaced, massacred, or swindled most of the Native Americans on their trek into new territory. The Dutch trekkers annihilated the Khoikhoi and the San or turned them into what they called "apprentices." In fact they enslaved them. There was little to stop the advance of the trekker, or "trekboer." The word *trekboer* means a farmer who treks about, looking for grazing. The Company tried to control this migration, but was not successful, and this hard but free life made the trekkers independent and impatient of control.

In their isolation and wildness the Boers turned to their own version of Dutch Reformed Protestantism, which exercised a powerful influence on them. The official church, like the Company, found it difficult to keep in touch with the trekkers. However the trekkers formed their own religious groups and every night the father of the family would read aloud from the Bible.

In particular the Boers were attracted by the stories of the Old Testament, which seemed most relevant to their hard and lonely lives. They identified with some of the Old Testament leaders as they moved in the wilderness with their flocks and herds, with their "menservants" and their "maidservants," among wild men and wild beasts, with no

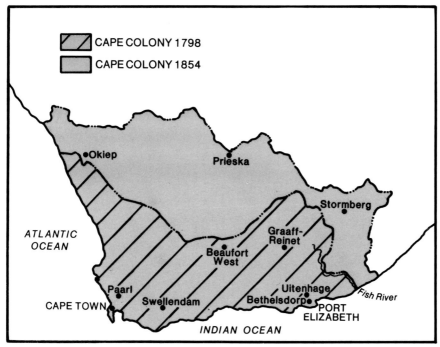

The expansion of the Cape Colony between 1798 and 1854

protection but their guns and their God. Small wonder that in their isolation they tended to delude themselves into believing that they were a "Chosen Race" with special rights and privileges over the "inferior" heathen tribes around them.

These trekboers were the forefathers of today's Afrikaans-speaking population. While many Afrikaners have acknowledged their reliance upon others, right-wing extreme Afrikaners still believe in a policy of isolation. Like the trekboers of old they wish to separate themselves from other peoples and to rely on their guns and their God for protection. At the heart of this desire for isolation is the *fear* that their language and their culture will be destroyed if black people come to power in South Africa.

The Xhosas

It was just about this time that those trekkers who moved east rather than northeast and who remained nearer the coast encountered certain Bantu tribes moving in the opposite direction, largely in the coastal country below the southern and eastern escarpments. This was one of the supreme events in the history of South Africa. These opponents were more numerous and more formidable than the San and the Khoikhoi. They were called the Xhosas. They were noble warriors of *assegai* (spear) and shield, they were masters of song and dance, and they had a highly developed system of law and custom. They were cattle breeders, and their interests conflicted sharply with those of the trekboers. Both groups had need of grazing for their beasts, which suffered in times of drought. Both were extending their frontiers. Again and again in South African history competition for land lies at the heart of racial clashes and conflicts.

The Xhosas were not a single united nation but a conglomeration of Nguni racial groups who spoke the same language and shared the same culture. Each group was ruled by a chief, who owed a loose allegiance to a central overlord.

Though the Xhosa were moving westward when they first encountered the Boers, their movement was a gradual one. For long periods of time they would live in one area before they moved on with their cattle in search of new grazing. J. B. Peires describes the Xhosa homesteads in his book *The House of Phalo*:

The Xhosa chose to live on the ridges intersecting the valleys of the hilly country where wood and water were most often found. Their homesteads were built facing the rising sun and near the tops of the ridges, where they could be sheltered from the wind and drained by the downward slope. Most homesteads consisted of eight to fifteen beehive-shaped dwellings, a framework of branches plastered with clay and dung and thatched with long grass. The only opening was a low door, and the smoke from the hearth in the centre escaped through the roof. These dwellings were arranged in a semi-circle around a cattle-enclosure made of Mimosa thorn-bushes.

Many frontier wars were to be fought between the Boers and the Xhosas. In these wars, as Peires has pointed out, "neither Xhosa nor Colonists were wholly innocent or wholly culpable."

Frontier Wars

After several skirmishes between Boers and Xhosas the Company entered into a treaty with some Xhosa chiefs in 1778, and declared the Fish River to be the boundary between the Boers and the Xhosas. This

Somerset's plan for a neutral zone in the eastern Cape. The plan failed as both colonists and Xhosas invaded and occupied the territory

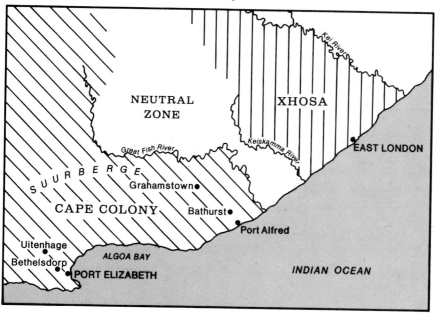

act was useless. Individuals crossed the river, on both sides, primarily in search of grazing land but also to steal cattle or to retrieve them. There was incessant trouble, raiding, thefts, reprisals, breaking out into war.

In this situation the Company was of little use. It had made the Fish River the boundary, but could do little to defend it. One company official openly sided with the Xhosas. But the trekboers were becoming increasingly rebellious, and the Company ceased to have any control over them. Soon the whole border was in a state of chaos.

In the early 1800's the British annexed the Cape and inherited its turbulent frontier troubles. The British actually occupied the Cape twice, first from 1795 to 1803 and again in 1806. The Dutch East India Company had become insolvent in 1798, and the days of the Netherlands as a great power were over.

Britain was eager to acquire a new colony at the Cape for two reasons: First, the Cape was of considerable strategic importance, providing Britain with trade links with India and other countries in the east; second, expanding British industry desperately needed a new market for its goods.

At the time of the final British annexation of the Cape there were about 25,000 white people in the colony and about 30,000 black slaves.

So began the turbulent nineteenth century.

The Coming of the British and the Great Trek

With the arrival of the British officials at the Cape, there came also a number of vigorous missionaries. The white farmers were used to officials, but the missionaries were something new. As might be expected, the attitude of the missionaries toward the Khoikhois and the Xhosas was not the same as that of the farmers; to the farmer the Africans were laborers whose educational and social advance was of little interest. The missionaries objected to the farmers' ill treatment of Khoikhois, Xhosas, and slaves. Officials, missionaries, and farmers lived in an uneasy triangular relationship. The officials had to consider the difficulties of the farmers, but they had also to consider the powerful support in England for the missionaries. These missionaries sent back reports to England, many of them hostile to the colonists.

But the colonists were also hostile to the missionaries. Many Khoikhois flocked to the mission stations, where they found conditions better than on the farms. The farmers were angry at losing their labor, and were totally unsympathetic to the plight of the Khoikhoi who had been forced to give up their traditional ways and to adopt an economic system that was designed to exploit them.

The missionaries played a dual role in the history of South Africa. On the one hand they began the "liberal" tradition, one to be followed by small groups, mainly white, in the nineteenth and twentieth centuries. These liberals fiercely defended the underdog and fought courageously for justice and for peace. On the other hand the missionaries undermined the order that existed in traditional society.

The Moravian and London Missionary Societies

The Moravian Missionary Society, which had worked among the Khoikhoi from 1737 to 1744, returned to the Cape in 1792 to resume its work. The London Missionary Society (L.M.S.) followed in 1799. The farmers were angered when the L.M.S. representative, Dr. J. T. van der Kemp, married a Khoikhoi woman much younger than himself. Things had changed since Eva married surgeon van Meerhof with a degree of approval from the local white community. Van der Kemp's marriage affronted local white opinion. Antagonism among white farmers toward missionaries was growing. They could not accept Khoikhois being treated as equals.

Slagter's Nek

In 1815, under a new law, a Khoikhoi servant complained of the treatment he had received from his master, Frederick Bezuidenhout.

Outline of
South African History

1806: Second British occupation of the Cape

c.1815: Mosheshwe becomes ruler of the Basotho

c.1818: Mfecane wars raging among Nguni factions. Dingiswayo is killed. Zulu kingdom is born under the rule of Shaka.

1820: First British settlers arrive in eastern Cape

1823: Mzilikazi flees from Shaka

1824: Shaka cedes parts of Natal to British

1828: Death of Shaka. Dingane becomes king in his place.

1833: Emancipation of slaves in all British colonies, including the Cape

1834: Fighting between Xhosas and Boers continues on eastern Cape boundary. White settlers lose land when British government removes boundary from Kei River to Fish River. Boers furious.

1836: Start of Great Trek

1838: Murder of Pieter Retief and his followers by Dingane. Dingane defeated by Boers at Battle of Blood River. Republic of Natal established by Boers.

1840: Dingane killed. Mpande becomes new Zulu king.

1842: Britain annexes Natal

1848: Britain annexes territory between Orange and Vaal rivers, which becomes known as the Orange River Sovereignty

1852: Boers north of Vaal River unite to form South African Republic (later to merge with other Boer republics and to be known as Transvaal)

1854: After Bloemfontein Convention Orange River Sovereignty becomes a Boer republic known as Orange Free State

1857: Nongquase's vision, which leads to the mass killing of Xhosa cattle. This eventually results in Xhosa defeat by British.

1860: First Indian immigrants arrive in Natal

1866: Boers attack Mosheshwe and capture a great deal of Sotho territory

Bezuidenhout treated the court summons with contempt, and at last a British officer with Khoikhoi soldiers was sent to arrest him. Sending Khoikhois to arrest a white man had never been done before. Bezuidenhout fought the party from a cave, but was killed. At his funeral his brother swore to avenge the outrage, and he and his friends rebelled. The rebellion was soon put down, and five of the men were hanged at Slagter's Nek; but many of the farmers regarded them as martyrs who had died for the cause of the white man against the government, the missionaries, and the cursed doctrine of equality.

The 1820 Settlers

In 1820 came the first large group of English-speaking colonists, about five thousand in number. Most of the settlers came to the disturbed frontier area, and they founded the towns of Port Elizabeth and Grahamstown. One result of their coming was that the British government attempted to make the Dutch (who would be called Afrikaners by the early twentieth century) as English as possible. English took the place of Dutch as the official language. The Dutch *landdrosts* were replaced by magistrates, the Dutch *rix-dollars* by pounds, shillings, and pence,

Arrival of the 1820 settlers in Algoa Bay. They went ashore at Fort Frederick, which in 1820 was renamed Port Elizabeth by Sir Rufane Donkin, Acting Governor of the Cape, after his deceased wife, Elizabeth Frances.

and only English and Latin were taught in the state-aided schools. This attempt at anglicization angered the Dutch. Much of their anger was directed at the Governor, Lord Charles Somerset, who had introduced the changes.

The Emancipation of the Slaves

In 1833 the slaves in all the British colonies were emancipated, some thirty years before the freeing of slaves in America. For slaves worth £3 million, compensation of £1.25 million was to be paid. Many whites now found themselves without slaves or compensation.

Severe drought struck the eastern Cape in 1833 and 1834. During this time the Boers sought pasture for their cattle in Xhosa country. In December 1834 the Xhosas retaliated and attacked Boer farms as far west as the Fish River Valley. But they were driven back by British and Boer forces. The Governor of the Cape, Sir Benjamin D'Urban, fixed a new frontier on the Kei River, giving the settlers more territory.

However, the British government reversed D'Urban's policy and brought the border back to the Fish River. The British government declared that " 'the Kaffirs' had an ample justification" for the war.

The Great Trek

This was the last straw for the Boers. Of British government, British missionaries, British public opinion, they had had enough. So five thousand of them set out north on what came to be called the Great Trek, leaving the eastern coasts, climbing the mountains up onto the great interior plain, in the direction of Kimberley and Bloemfontein and Johannesburg, all yet unborn. Among the trekkers was a lad of ten, whose name was Paul Kruger. The year of the Great Trek is usually set down at 1836. "We quit this Colony," wrote Pieter Retief, one of the foremost Voortrekkers, "under the full assurance that the English Government has nothing more to require of us, and will allow us to govern ourselves without its interference in future."

A Voortrekker woman, Anna Steenkamp, wrote of "the shameful and unjust proceedings with reference to the freeing of our slaves." She continued: "Yet it is not so much their freeing which drove us to such lengths, as their being placed on an equal footing with Christians, contrary to the laws of God, and the natural distinctions of race and color, so that it was intolerable for any decent Christian to bow down beneath such a yoke; wherefore we rather withdrew in order to preserve our doctrines in purity." There seems to be no doubt that one of the deepest causes of the Great Trek was the implication in British law and administration that white and black were in some way equal. In addition, the Voortrekkers resented the imposition of English language and culture on their own way of life, and also felt threatened by Xhosa attempts to expand westward.

The Courage of the Voortrekkers

Though the heroic role of the Voortrekkers has been greatly exaggerated by twentieth-century Afrikaner nationalist historians, there is no doubt that the trekkers had great courage and determination. They set off into the unknown interior with their families and their black servants (even in the Great Trek, whites relied on the assistance of black servants), their cattle, their sheep, and their goats. Their possessions were loaded into ox wagons in which the women and children traveled. The servants walked with the animals, and the Voortrekker men traveled on horseback, their guns at their sides.

Some of the treks were large and involved a hundred wagons or more. Others were considerably smaller. Half a dozen families would decide to travel together. The treks were slow-moving affairs. The Voortrekkers did not travel on Sunday because this was a day of rest and family prayers. Along the way the Voortrekker women attended to the cooking, looked after their children, and made soap and candles. The men repaired their gear and their wagons and attended to the herds. They would also go hunting, and depended a great deal on buck and other wild animals for their food.

The methods of travel of the Voortrekkers and of their defense against indigenous tribes were very similar to those employed by the American pioneers in the west. The Americans fought with the Native Americans; the Voortrekkers with native Africans. When the Boers had warning of an attack, they would form their ox wagons into what they called a *laager*. Wagons were lashed together to form a circle. The openings were filled with thorn bush. In the center of the *laager* additional wagons were placed as a shelter for women and children. Horses were also brought into the center, but sheep and cattle were left outside. The Boer men would then attempt to stave off the attack with their guns.

Afrikaner women in Voortrekker dress celebrating the centenary of the Great Trek in 1938.

An illustration of one such attack was the Battle of Vegkop in the present-day Orange Free State. A Boer *laager* was attacked by Ndebele warriors riding on horses and hurling *assegais*. In this instance the Boers were victorious but lost great numbers of cattle and sheep, which were taken by the Ndebele. In other battles the Boers were defeated. Their wagons were destroyed and many of them were killed.

The Voortrekkers traveled vast distances. And, as in the United States, some areas were flat like the prairies and others mountainous like the Rocky Mountains. Their treks across the Drakensberg range into present-day Natal were particularly terrifying. They often had to take their wagons apart in order to get them down the steep precipices.

The commencement of the reenactment of the Great Trek. Mrs. Marthia du Plooy waves farewell as the replica ox wagon sets out from Cape Town on its marathon journey to Pretoria on the 150th anniversary of the Trek (1988). Adil Bradlow, Afrapix, Impact Visuals

Sometimes their supplies ran out and they starved to death. Sometimes they were stricken by diseases such as malaria, and sometimes their sheep and cattle would die after being bitten by the dreaded tsetse fly. Often Voortrekker women would die in childbirth. And the infant mortality rate was high.

Another Look at the "Great Trek"

Many South African schoolchildren are still taught that the Great Trek was one of the most important events in South African history. There is no doubt that it was a significant event. Yet to what extent was it really a "Great" Trek? Many Afrikaners still look upon the Voortrekkers as heroes. Fanatical right-wing Afrikaners almost worship them. But increasingly their "heroic" role in South African history is being questioned. It was not the Trek itself that shifted the balance in South Africa's history to one of white domination, but subsequent developments such as the intervention of the British and the discovery of diamonds and gold.

Though the Voortrekkers defeated many indigenous groups, they suffered several setbacks themselves. While the trekkers were involved in bitter political squabbles, many of their African neighbors prospered. The survival of some of the Boer communities was thanks to the cooperation and goodwill of their African neighbors.

It is sad that some of the descendants of the Voortrekkers still believe that they can prosper only by going it alone, instead of learning the lesson that survival is possible only through sharing and mutuality.

The "Mfecane" and the "Difaqane"

The period of South African history discussed here is complex and confusing. Historians are still battling to make sense of the events that occurred in various areas occupied by Bantu groups in the eighteenth and early nineteenth centuries. Conflicting accounts of this period have been given by missionaries and travelers who moved about in remote areas. Further skimpy evidence has been obtained from oral history that has been handed down over the decades. One thing is certain: Tragedy on a vast scale struck the Bantu-speaking communities in the early part of the nineteenth century. The catastrophe has been well summed up by Professor Rodney Davenport:

The first great tragedy of South African history was that in the early years of the nineteenth century the Bantu-speaking communities began to tear each other apart in what is generally assumed to have been one of the bloodiest conflicts ever to have affected Africa in historical times.

These tragic events have been referred to by the Nguni word *Mfecane*, meaning "the crushing." The *Mfecane* refers on the whole to the conflicts in the northern Nguni chiefdoms. A Sotho word, *Difaqane*, meaning "the scattering of tribes," refers to related disturbances among Sotho and Tswana tribes on the Highveld.

"Mfecane," "Difaqane," "Xhosa"

It is hard for nonnative speakers to pronounce *Mfecane*. The "c" is pronounced with the click that is the "tsk" sound. The word *Mfecane* is pronounced more or less as M-feh-*tsk* ah-neh.

One or two clicks spread into the Sotho languages. One of these is the "q" click as found in the word *Difaqane*. This click is the sharp popping sound used in imitation of a cork being drawn from a bottle. The pronunciation of Difaqane might be given as Dee-fah-*pop* ah-neh.

Yet another click is to be found in the *Xh* of the name "Xhosa." This imitates the sound used to urge a horse on. The suggested pronunciation is *Cluck* aw-sah.

The Nguni People

By the end of the eighteenth century the Nguni speakers had emerged as a distinct and separate group from the Sotho speakers. The Nguni speakers may be further subdivided into two major groups.

The southern Nguni were the Xhosas, described in the previous chapter. They moved gradually southward and westward in search of grazing land and eventually came into conflict with Boer and English settlers on the eastern edge of the Cape Colony. These early clashes took place before the events of the Mfecane.

The northern Nguni occupied much of present-day Natal and lived there long before the arrival of the first white settlers. A major subgroup of the northern Nguni was to become known as the Zulus.

Both northern and southern Nguni lived in small settlements that were usually family units and were controlled by a chief. Contact between ancestors and ancestor worship were very important to the Nguni, and their chief was the link between themselves and their ancestors. Not surprisingly, the chief was almost considered divine by the clan. He had

This drawing of a typical kraal points out how the arrangement of homes provided for defense from attack, control of cattle, and indicated the relative importance of each family. History for Today Standard 6, Juta & Company Ltd.

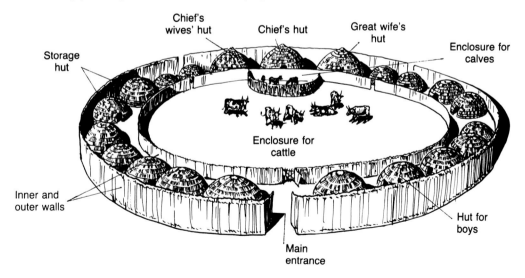

a great wife and a right-hand wife. On his death he was succeeded by the oldest son of his great wife or, if she had no sons, by the oldest son of his right-hand wife. These family units lived in settlements called kraals. Cattle were the most important resource to the Nguni and were allowed by herders to range widely in search of grazing.

Several of the family units merged with other units, thus forming larger and more powerful ethnic groups. Three of the larger groups were the Ndwandwe, the Ngwane, and the Mthetwa. At the end of the nineteenth century there was a quarrel among the royal family of the Mthetwa, and one of the sons, Dingiswayo, broke away. After the death of his father he defeated his brothers and became King of the Mthetwa in 1806. This was the same year in which Britain finally took over the Cape Colony. Dingiswayo reorganized the Mthetwa and became very powerful. Under his leadership many other groups were defeated in battle. The Mfecane had begun.

Causes of the Mfecane

Many worse conflicts were to follow. What were the causes of these conflicts? One of them was the rising population among the northern Nguni. Corn had been introduced from the Americas. The good rains at the end of the eighteenth century meant good crops, which certainly accelerated the growth of the population. As the population grew, there was more competition for grazing land, and for land on which to cultivate crops. There was also competition for the control of elephant hunting and the ivory trade. Dingiswayo in particular acquired considerable control over the latter and had many of his competitors put to death.

Between 1800 and 1810 there was a marked change in the weather pattern. The heavy summer rainfalls of previous years came to an end.

A terrible drought set in and the parched land struggled to survive. Food ran short, and many people resorted to eating grass and the flesh of dogs. Cattle were starving and the people who owned them desperately sought new grazing lands.

Opposition to Dingiswayo and his Mthetwa kingdom mounted. One of his main rivals was Zwide, leader of the Ndwandwe group. A bloody battle took place in 1818 between the Mthetwa and Ndwandwe. Dingiswayo tried to flee, but he was captured and killed. Thousands died in bloody fighting. The Ndwandwe were victorious but were not to remain so for long.

One of Dingiswayo's chiefs was named Shaka, and he headed a clan of the Mthetwa called the Zulu. Shaka took over the leadership of the Mthetwa after the death of Dingiswayo, and soon his Zulus dominated the group. One could say that the Zulu kingdom had been born.

Devastation caused by the Mfecane

The areas where most of the bloody conflicts involving Zulus and other ethnic groups occurred were later to be called Natal and Zululand. Here

---

The Warrior:
Shaka, King of the Zulus

Shaka was born in approximately 1787. His father was King Senzangakhona of the Zulus, then a small clan living in the heart of the much larger territory that later came to be called Zululand. When Shaka was still a boy, his father cast him out with his mother, Nandi, who was aggressive and unpopular. Wherever they found asylum, he was ridiculed and rejected by the other boys; but as he grew up into a powerful, handsome, and brave young man, wise beyond his years, he was hailed as a leader, and the fame of his exploits soon spread.

He attracted the attention of King Dingiswayo, a remarkable ruler who had formed a confederation of Nguni groups, including the Zulus. Shaka became a general in the King's army, and when his father, Senzangakhona, died, Dingiswayo assisted in making him King of the Zulus.

Farther north another powerful king, Zwide, was the head of a rival confederation. In 1818 he killed Dingiswayo, but within two years Shaka had taken over his old benefactor's power structure. Then he lured Zwide's army into a trap, smashed it, and sent the survivors scattering northward into Mozambique.

Shaka was in the process of forging a powerful, centralized Zulu state. The basis of his strength was military. His growing army was drilled until it became a ruthlessly efficient machine, comprising 50,000 men divided into 20 regiments. His warriors were made to put aside their light throwing spears and to depend on a short, long-bladed stabbing spear, which was as effective in close fighting as the short sword of the ancient Roman legions. The regiments were based on age groups, not clan origins. They were distinguished from one another by the color of their large ox-hide shields.

Speed and surprise were all-important. In those days a European army could march fifteen miles a day on good roads. A Zulu *impi* (army) could cross fifty miles of trackless country in the same time. In battle they attacked on the run, maintaining perfect formation. The younger regiments were placed on the wings (called "horns"). Their object was to outflank and encircle the enemy army, while the main body, or "chest," attacked. A short way behind, the "loins," or reserves, waited.

Every year Shaka sent his regiments either north, south, or west, to conquer, destroy, and bring back plundered cattle; and every year they had to go farther and farther through the wastelands they themselves had made. While one might admire Shaka's power and organizational genius, one should not forget the victims of that yearly devastation, estimated at over a million people. The destitute survivors fled or hid in the mountains, where they starved.

Shaka held his growing nation together by a combination of charisma and terror. Anyone who displeased him was in danger of being put to death instantly. On one occasion more than a hundred of his concubines and their suspected lovers were summarily executed. On another occasion a regiment accused of cowardice submitted to being driven into the sea and drowned. In 1827, when Shaka's mother, Nandi, died, the day of national mourning in the capital became an orgy of hysterical killing in which over five thousand people were slaughtered. (Shaka was not the first despot who sought to relieve his grief by steeping it in blood!)

Power had gone to Shaka's head, upsetting his judgment and blinding him to the resentment his excesses were causing. In 1828, when his *impis* returned from their annual expedition (this time to the south, deep into what is today the Transkei), he promptly sent them on a second expedition to the north. When they returned again, defeated more by exhaustion and lack of provisions than by their enemies, they dreaded Shaka's wrath. But he was dead, assassinated by two of his brothers. One of them, Dingane, became king in his place. He was far less dynamic than Shaka in almost every respect, but the change came as a relief to the nation Shaka had built.

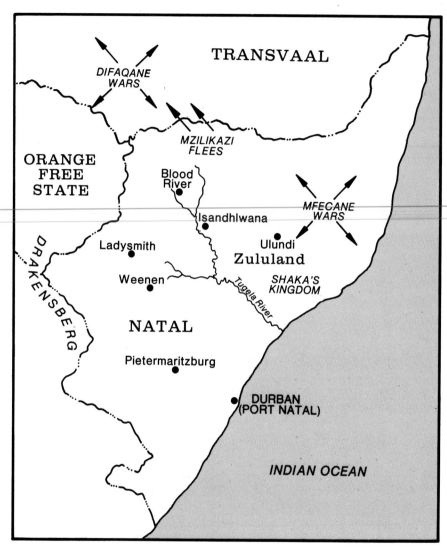

Natal and Zululand in the nineteenth century

is a description of the slaughter in a section of this territory given by an American missionary named L. Grout in 1836, several years after many of these battles had taken place. Grout wrote:

From Natal to Tugela, there is not a single inhabitant. Yet 15 years ago this country was densely populated; its inhabitants have been completely destroyed by Shaka. We see the ruins of several kraals; the people who accompanied us told us that if it were not for the long grass, we would see the ground strewn with human bones. . . .

Some historians have claimed that such accounts are exaggerated. There is no doubt, however, that devastation took place on a vast scale. Shaka now controlled a very large area, but opposition to him from the ranks of his own Zulus was mounting. He now feared assassination, and many suspects were executed. But in 1828 Shaka was killed by his two brothers, Dingane and Mhlangane. Dingane eventually emerged as the new Zulu king. The clash between Dingane and the Voortrekkers will be described in the next chapter.

The Difaqane

The ripple effect of the Mfecane extended not only to the Drakensberg range but beyond it onto the high plateau, the present-day Highveld. Those fleeing over the mountains from the south and east clashed with other inhabitants of the plateau. The Difaqane, as it came to be called, was an extension of the Mfecane in other parts of the country.

One of the leading figures of the Difaqane was Chief Mzilikazi, who had fled from Shaka in 1823, moving with his followers northward over the Drakensberg and onto the Highveld. Mzilikazi and his warriors defeated many peoples. By 1836 Mzilikazi had established a large kingdom in the western Transvaal.

The Difaqane was a scattering and relocation of ethnic groups. Many Sotho and Tswana groups were displaced by Mzilikazi, and some, like the Baralong, were almost totally destroyed. Meanwhile, in the country that would be called Lesotho, a new leader was emerging. He was

The Statesman:
Mosheshwe, King of the Sotho
(c. 1786–1870)

As a powerful young warrior Mosheshwe became the leader of a
small tribe in a place called Butha-Buthe in what is now northwest
Lesotho. At the time of the Difaqane his people were threatened
with total destruction, so he trekked with them over the rocky
mountains to a chosen place 60 miles (100 km.) south. This was an
impregnable mountain with a perfectly flat top, a bit over a mile in
length and nearly half a mile wide. He named it *Thaba Bosiu*
("Mountain of Night"). It became his citadel, and here his real
power began, for he gathered around him many refugees of the
Difaqane and in a remarkably short time welded them into the
Sotho nation.

He saw the advantage of horses and guns and urged his people to
acquire these things. He persuaded the men to work in the fields
with the women, contrary to general African tradition. In 1833 he
welcomed the missionaries for the religious and other benefits they

headman of a Sotho village and his name was Mosheshwe. He offered
refuge at his home village of Butha-Buthe to all those fleeing from the
invading Nguni tribes. Quietly he built up a following, and by 1840 had
40,000 supporters. Mosheshwe was now established at Thaba Bosiu, a
mountain fortress to which he had moved for safety. By the end of the
Difaqane Mosheshwe was by far the most powerful leader in the area.

By 1836 the Highveld was beginning to settle again after the devas-

could bring his people (though he himself was never baptized and never learned how to read and write).

His power and influence continued to expand, but when the Boer trekkers crossed the Orange River, a long struggle began for his people's land in what is now the eastern Orange Free State. Mosheshwe asked the British for protection and even annexation, seeing in this the best way to hold off the encroaching Boers. But when Britain became embroiled in the dispute over the land, it was on the Boer side.

Mosheshwe's greatness lies in the fact that unlike leaders such as Shaka and Mzilikazi, he was essentially a man of conciliation and peace. But he fought when he had to. And when he fought, he did not throw away his men in futile assaults, as at Blood River; he employed a defensive strategy and in this way defeated the British twice, and twice fought the Boers to a standstill.

But in the end the Boer pressures were too great. A short time before he died, Mosheshwe was relieved to learn that Britain had agreed to turn what remained of his diminishing country into a protectorate. Lesotho, as it is called today, owes its independence very largely to its founder, Mosheshwe.

tating Difaqane wars. But new conflicts were to develop as the first parties of Voortrekkers entered the scene.

Effects of the Wars

The Mfecane and Difaqane wars certainly caused large-scale suffering and destruction. In several areas the population was drastically thinned out, making it easier for white settlers to move in and claim the territory as theirs. Even today many conservative Afrikaners believe that whites were entitled to claim vast, seemingly empty areas of land for themselves. But as Professor Davenport has pointed out, these areas were not "empty." The clashes between black and white that were to occur in the nineteenth century were due to "outright competition for land."

Some conservative whites in South Africa like to claim that the Mfecane wars prove that blacks had and still have a warlike mentality and that even today ethnic conflict is rife. This is a very dangerous and racist view and fails to take into account the numerous and bloody conflicts that have taken place throughout human history. Europe, for example, has had a dismal record of "intertribal" conflicts during its centuries of history.

And not all the effects of the Mfecane were negative. New states were born as a result. Two of these were to be called Lesotho and Swaziland. Many of the new states were established along the lines of the Zulu kingdom. And still another positive result was that new and powerful leaders emerged after the wars.

Yet, sadly, new clashes were beginning. Mention has already been made of the wars that took place between the settlers on the frontiers of the eastern Cape and the Xhosas. From 1836 on the conflicts expanded and included Voortrekkers, English settlers, and many other black groups.

CHAPTER XIII

Conflict—Blacks, Boers, and Britons

The growing conflicts in South Africa now became three-sided. First, there were increasing numbers of clashes between Voortrekkers and various black groups both on the Highveld and in Natal. These clashes were nearly always about claims to land. Then later the Voortrekkers fought the British in Natal after the British had annexed territory that the Boers laid claim to. Then even later the British were involved in many battles with the Zulus, again over land claims. All these conflicts produced outstanding leaders. There were Boer heroes, British heroes, and black heroes. But not all these leaders are regarded as heroes by all South Africans today, so strong are the divisions within the country. Those who are heroes to one group are sometimes regarded as villains by others—like Crazy Horse and General Custer in the United States.

With the British-controlled Cape Colony behind them the Voortrekkers trekked into the rugged interior of the country that would one day be called South Africa. In battles for land between the Voortrekkers and various Bantu-speaking peoples sometimes the blacks were victorious and at other times the Voortrekkers gained the upper hand. Initially these battles took place on the Highveld but then the conflicts spread to present-day Natal after a group of Voortrekkers crossed over the Drakensberg escarpment in their wagons.

Voortrekkers versus Zulus

The leader of the Natal party was Pieter Retief. At the beginning of 1838 he went with sixty of his followers to see the Zulu King Dingane. He wanted to make a treaty in order to acquire more land, but he and his whole party were murdered. The King then sent ten thousand warriors to the Voortrekker camp, where a few men had stayed behind to guard the women and children. All the Voortrekkers were killed. Thereafter the place was called Weenen, a Dutch word meaning "weeping."

Much has been written about Dingane's treachery. But not nearly enough has been said about the Voortrekkers' insatiable greed for land. Retief's followers had occupied land in Zulu territory without Dingane's permission. There is no doubt the Voortrekkers would have demanded more and more land or would have tried to seize it by force. Treacherous as Dingane's actions were, he was defending his people against a serious threat.

The remaining Natal Voortrekkers decided to form a new state and established a township some distance inland from the port of Durban. This they called Pietermaritzburg after their leaders, Pieter Retief and

Gerrit Maritz. Maritz died in September 1838. A new leader, Andries Pretorius (after whom Pretoria was named), was sent to Natal to help the Voortrekkers and to avenge the murder of Retief and his followers. Pretorius prayed to God to give him victory and vowed that the Voortrekkers would keep the day of victory holy.

Heroes and Villains

On December 16, 1838, a Zulu army attacked the camp of Pretorius and his followers on the banks of the Ncome River. Hundreds of Zulus were trapped in a ditch and fired upon by the Voortrekkers. Two to three thousand Zulus were killed, and it is said that the Ncome River flowed red with their blood. This came to be called the Battle of Blood River. Once again, an event was transformed into a myth.

December 16 was called Dingaan's (an old spelling of Dingane) Day for more than a century. Then it was changed to the Day of the Covenant, and only recently its name was changed to the Day of the Vow. It is religiously observed by many conservative Afrikaners (descendants of the Voortrekkers), but not by English-speaking South Africans, who, until prevented by a growing uneasiness, and finally by law, used the day to hold races and cricket matches. It is fair to say that the Day of the Vow means little or nothing to English-speaking South Africans, while to blacks it gives great offense. And indeed this is not surprising, for December 16 is often used by Afrikaner speakers to dwell on the bitter enmities of the past, and the necessity for continuing them into the future. Nothing could show more clearly than the Day of the Vow the terrible divisions within South Africa.

The Republic of Natal, established by the Boers in 1838, was short-lived. British traders and missionaries had been active at Durban Bay and along the Natal Coast since 1824, and had actually obtained a grant of land from Shaka. However, the British government paid little attention to this British settlement until the Boer Republic, in 1841, sent a punitive expedition to the south against the Bacas, who had allegedly stolen some cattle. The neighboring Pondos (Bacas and Pondos were Nguni speakers) were alarmed and appealed to the Cape government, whereupon the British annexed Natal in 1842. The Boers besieged the British in Durban, and Dick King, a British settler, undertook a daring ride of 595 miles (960 kilometers) to Grahamstown in ten days, through a wild and unknown country, to call for reinforcements. Most of the Boers then gave up the siege, and Natal, as a result of immigration from Britain, became largely English speaking, if we consider only its white inhabitants. Dick King became a hero and even today is looked on with pride by many English-speaking South Africans.

In the meantime what had happened to Dingane? He did not die in the Battle of Blood River, but he suffered great humiliation and was forced to hand over much of his land to the Boers. Only Zululand, the area lying to the north of the Tugela River, remained under his control. In October 1839 Mpande, Dingane's half-brother, met with a committee of Boers. He promised his friendship to them as long as they protected him from Dingane. Boer commandos helped Mpande to seize some of Dingane's cattle. Dingane fled to the north and was killed near the Swaziland border. Mpande became the new Zulu king.

The Zulu kingdom enjoyed a long period of peace under Mpande's rule. Mpande showed friendship to both Boers and British and also established good relations with the Pedi and Sotho kingdoms to the north and west, over the Drakensberg range. Mpande was a model diplomat, unlike his predecessors. He has been criticized for being too conciliatory toward the Boers, but there is no doubt that he had the interests of his people at heart. By 1873 Mpande was old and frail, and his son Cetshwayo became the new Zulu ruler.

Boer Republics on the Highveld

The Boers who had trekked to the Highveld desperately tried to obtain as much land as they could. Sometimes they entered into a series of treaties with local black chiefs, sometimes they took land through conquest, sometimes they "purchased" land by giving cattle to local chiefs in exchange. Various Boer leaders also vied with each other for power, and there was bitter competition.

Meanwhile, the British in the Cape carefully monitored the various activities of the Boers in the interior of the country. The British were anxious to keep the peace with various black sovereignties to the northeast and east of the Cape and were determined that the Boers were not going to upset this peace. Thus when the Winburg Boers, greedy for land, attacked the neighboring Griquas, the British intervened and drove the Boers northward. But disputes between Boers and blacks continued, and eventually the Governor of the Cape Colony, Sir Harry Smith, annexed the territory that was to become the Orange Free State. From 1848 to 1854 the territory was under British rule and was known as the Orange River Sovereignty. One of the Boers' fiercest opponents was the Sotho leader Mosheshwe. The British now also clashed with Mosheshwe but were defeated in a battle in 1851. In 1852 the new Governor of the Cape, Sir George Cathcart, led another attack on Mosheshwe. The battle was indecisive, and a temporary truce followed. Finally, in a total reversal of their previous policies, the British decided to withdraw. Then they signed an agreement with the Boers and abandoned all treaties with black rulers except for one part with the Griqua Chief, Adam Kok. The pattern of British intervention followed by withdrawal was to be repeated again and again in South African history. In 1854 the new Boer republic of the Orange Free State was formed.

Tension between the Sotho and the Boers continued. Both were in

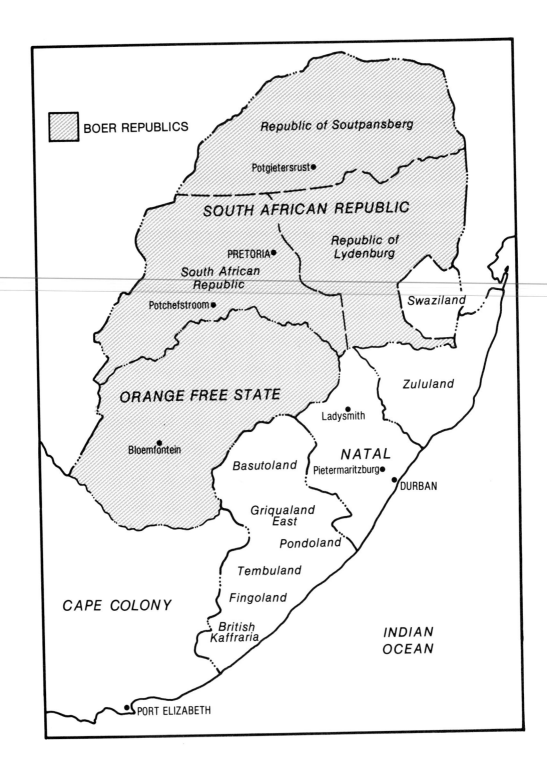

BOER REPUBLICS

Republic of Soutpansberg

Potgietersrust•

SOUTH AFRICAN REPUBLIC

Republic of
Lydenburg

PRETORIA•

South African
Republic

Swaziland

Potchefstroom•

Zululand

ORANGE FREE STATE

Ladysmith•

NATAL

Basutoland

Pietermaritzburg•

Bloemfontein•

•DURBAN

Griqualand
East

Pondoland

Tembuland

Fingoland

CAPE COLONY

British
Kaffraria

INDIAN
OCEAN

•PORT ELIZABETH

fierce competition for fertile land in the Caledon valley. In 1858 the Boers launched an attack on Mosheshwe's mountain fortress at Thaba Bosiu, but were soundly defeated. In 1866 the Boers attacked again and destroyed Sotho cattle and crops. Mosheshwe was forced to give up a great deal of territory and desperately appealed to Britain to help him save what was left. The British agreed, and Basutoland became a British protectorate in 1868. Today it is the independent country of Lesotho, totally surrounded by the Republic of South Africa.

Zulus versus British in Natal

Relationships between the Zulus and the British began to sour soon after Cetshwayo became King of the Zulus. Cetshwayo was angry that Boers were moving into Zulu territory and occupying land in the region of Blood River, but the British paid little attention. They put down a rebellion in 1873 and kept a wary eye on Cetshwayo's attempts to revive a Zulu army. In 1877 the British sent Theophilus Shepstone from Natal to annex the South African Republic (the Transvaal). He attempted to persuade the Boers that the annexation was in their interest and that the Zulus were a threat. The Transvaal Boers had also lost a costly war against the Pedi and needed help.

The British had decided to establish a white confederation in the region. The annexation of the Transvaal was the first step in their plan. The next step was to disarm all the black kingdoms in the country. The Zulu kingdom was seen as the most powerful. And so in January 1879 the British invaded Zululand from Natal under Lord Chelmsford. The Zulus were prepared for them. Cetshwayo assembled his warriors and addressed them as follows:

The eastern half of South Africa in the latter part of the nineteenth century. Toward the end of the century the South African Republic became known as the Transvaal.

I am sending you out against the White men who have invaded Zululand and driven away our cattle. You are to go against the column and drive it back into Natal. You will attack by daylight as there are enough of you to eat it up and you will march slowly so as not to tire yourselves.

British troops numbering over one thousand infantry and a "Native Contingent" (i.e. black soldiers) of about two thousand camped on the slopes of a mountain named Isandhlwana, but made minimal preparations for defense. Chelmsford and some of the other British troops did not camp there but searched for the Zulu army elsewhere. On the morning of January 22, 1879, the British at Isandhlwana were taken by surprise by thousands of Zulus who advanced on them from different sides. The British fired at them with artillery and rifles, but the Zulus advanced in a seemingly endless succession of warriors, attacking the British with their *assegais.*

Here is a description of the last stages of the battle from C. T. Binns's book *The Last Zulu King* (Cavaye, Mostyn, and Younghusband were all British officers):

The Zulus surged forward, till the Native Contingent broke and fled. Through the gap in that vital angle the enemy poured in a solid mass. Then frightful slaughter began, for at in-fighting no army in the world could excel the Zulus. Before Cavaye and Mostyn had time to reform or even to fix bayonets, the warriors were among them and slew them to a man. Younghusband and his men succeeded momentarily in retreating to a terrace on the southern slopes of the mountain, but they too soon fell to the deadly assegais.

So ended the bloody Battle of Isandhlwana. Nearly every British soldier was killed. And thousands of Cetshwayo's Zulu warriors also died, drastically weakening his army. Chelmsford was devastated when the news of the British defeat was disclosed to him.

The British sent for reinforcements and again invaded Zululand in July 1879. The Zulu capital, Ulundi, was captured and Cetshwayo was defeated. He was exiled to Cape Town but later went to England to see

Queen Victoria. He returned to Zululand and continued to rule, but with diminished powers. He died in 1884.

Meanwhile the British divided Zululand into thirteen chiefdoms. Dinizulu, Cetshwayo's son, refused to accept British rule and rebelled against it. He was arrested, convicted of treason, and exiled.

The Xhosa Cattle Killing

The tragedy that befell the Zulu people was repeated over and over again. The Pedi, the Griqua, and the Xhosa were all eventually defeated by the British. Particularly tragic for the Xhosa was a catastrophe that occurred in 1857. A young Xhosa girl named Nongquase had a vision in which her ancestors told her that if the Xhosa slaughtered all their cattle, a wind would sweep the whites up into the sea. The Xhosa were so desperate to rid themselves of the whites that they were willing to try anything. Nongquase's prophecy was believed, and about 200,000 cattle were killed. Twenty thousand people died of starvation in the Ciskei and 30,000 migrated to work on white farms. This event is sometimes referred to as "the national suicide of the Xhosa people." The Ciskei became part of the Cape Colony. And in 1885 the British annexed the Transkei, having put down a Xhosa rebellion there.

Loss of Black Territory

By the end of the nineteenth century the black people of South Africa had been disarmed and had lost most of their land. A small percentage of the total land area was set aside for the black population. These black areas are today referred to as homelands. In addition the British established three "protectorates." These were Basutoland (today independent Lesotho), Bechuanaland (today independent Botswana), and Swaziland (today independent under the same name).

The Discovery of Diamonds and Gold, and Further Conflict

The Mfecane and Difaqane, the Great Trek, and the clashes between Boers, British, and various black peoples had brought about considerable changes in the country that would later be called South Africa.

But even bigger changes were to follow after the discovery of diamonds and gold. The discovery of these minerals attracted hundreds of fortune seekers to the interior of the country. And this discovery was to lead to a new major clash between the British and the Boers.

Outline of South African History

1867: First diamond discovered in Griqualand West

1868: Basutoland becomes a British protectorate

1870: Death of Mosheshwe

1873: Cetshwayo becomes new Zulu ruler

1876: Boers defeated by the Pedi in the Transvaal

1877: South African Republic (Transvaal) annexed by Britain

1879: British defeated by Zulus at the Battle of Isandhlwana
British win Battle of Ulundi; Cetshwayo captured

1880: Transvaal Boers rise up against the British; beginning of
First Anglo-Boer War

1881: Pretoria Convention grants self-government to Transvaal
Boers, but Britain retains control of foreign affairs

1883: Dinizulu becomes new Zulu ruler
Kruger elected President of the Transvaal

1884: Death of Cetshwayo

1886: Discovery of gold on the Witwatersrand and foundation of
Johannesburg

1890: Rhodes becomes Prime Minister of the Cape

1895: Jameson Raid fails; Rhodes resigns as Cape Prime Minister

1897: Milner sent out as British High Commissioner for South
Africa and Governor of the Cape

1899–1902: Anglo-Boer War

1902: Treaty of Vereeniging. Both the Transvaal and the Orange
Free State become British colonies, the Orange Free State now
being called the Orange River Colony
Death of Rhodes

1904: Kruger dies in exile in Switzerland

1906: Gandhi leads a passive resistance campaign against pass laws for Indians

Transvaal granted self-government

1907: Orange River Colony granted self-government

1908–1909: Meeting of all-white National Convention

1909: Meeting of black South African Native Convention

Delegation of black leaders and white liberals fails to persuade the British government to extend the franchise to blacks

1910: Formation of the Union of South Africa

The Discovery of Diamonds

In 1867 the first diamond was discovered at Hopetown in an area claimed by both Boer republics, the Transvaal and the Orange Free State, and by the Griqua Chief, Nicholas Waterboer. Then more diamonds were discovered. The British, eager for new markets following an economic depression in Britain, decided to end the dispute by grabbing the diamond fields for themselves. They annexed the land claimed by Waterboer and declared the area a new British colony called Griqualand West. Four diamond pipes, or veins, were discovered on a farm in the new colony. The biggest of these was named Kimberley in honor of the British minister responsible for the colony at the time. The pipes were divided into 3,600 small-claim holdings, each one owned by a "digger." Soon the diggings began, and the "Big Hole" was born. In the meantime Britain paid the Orange Free State £90,000 in compensation. This was considered insufficient, and the Boers were angry.

Thousands of diggers flocked to Kimberley seeking their fortunes. White claim holders came from other parts of South Africa, from Europe, America, and Australia. There was also a minority of nonwhite claim holders including Griquas, Malays, and Indians. The whites accused the blacks of illicit diamond buying, and soon the British authorities canceled all claims for "non-Europeans"—excluding white

A view of the Kimberley mine in 1875 showing the many small claims being dug into the neck of an extinct volcano. De Beers Consolidated Mines

Americans and Australians! Another group of blacks who flocked to the mines were laborers, mostly Sotho and Xhosa speakers who had lost land to the whites. Many black laborers chose to spend long periods on the mines in spite of the relatively low wages they received. Their families remained behind. Migrant labor had begun.

But there was in addition a smaller group of shrewd businessmen who also descended on Kimberley. One of these businessmen was Cecil Rhodes, a clever young man from England. Hundreds of small-claim holders soon went bankrupt, and Rhodes took over their claims.

The First Anglo-Boer War

Meanwhile dramatic events were taking place in the Transvaal. As has been mentioned, the British annexed this Boer republic in 1877. The Transvaal Boers, facing bankruptcy after disastrous wars against the Pedi, were in no position to offer resistance.

However, this step further antagonized not only Boer opinion in both republics, but also many Boers who had remained in the Cape Colony. Inadvertently the British government was uniting the Boers throughout South Africa; it was about this time that the unifying name of Afrikaner, as distinct from Transvaaler, Free Stater, and Cape Colonial, began to come more and more into use, though the word "Boer" was also frequently used. In 1880 the Transvaal *burghers* (citizens) rose in rebellion; the British suffered a severe defeat at Majuba, on the Natal–Transvaal border. In 1881 the war (sometimes called the First Anglo-Boer War) ended without victory; self-government was restored to the Transvaal, but in foreign affairs it was to be subject to the control of the Queen of England. But the Transvaal Afrikaners wanted complete independence, and they were led by Paul Kruger, whom, in 1883, they made their President.

The Discovery of Gold

In 1886 gold was discovered on the Witwatersrand, though there had been discoveries elsewhere prior to this date. Cecil Rhodes, now in control of the Kimberley diamond fields, had great dreams of an all-British route across the length of Africa from Cape to Cairo, and of the unification of South Africa under the British flag. But Kruger stood in his way. Rhodes had to find a way to prevent the expansion of the Transvaal Republic. He became Prime Minister of the Cape Colony in 1890, brought about the annexation of what was then called Bechuanaland (present-day Botswana), and the establishment of the new country of Rhodesia (named after Rhodes; now Zimbabwe). So with Portuguese Mozambique to the east, and Natal to the south, Kruger was contained.

The area in the Transvaal where gold was discovered was named the Witwatersrand, a word of Dutch origin meaning "ridge of white waters" and referring to the gold reef that stretched for miles underground. It was to the Witwatersrand that Rhodes now turned his attention, for this was an area in which he had great financial interests.

The discovery of gold attracted thousands upon thousands of prospectors to the Witwatersrand, far more than those who went to Kimberley. On the bare Highveld soil a new city called Johannesburg sprang up. It was soon nicknamed "the city of gold." By 1895 the Witwatersrand was producing a quarter of the world's gold supply. The whites who came from other parts of South Africa and from many parts of the world were called *uitlanders* ("foreigners") by the Boers. Kruger altered the voting qualifications in the Transvaal to prevent the *uitlanders* from securing control. Tensions began to mount. But also, as in the case of Kimberley, thousands of blacks flocked to the Witwatersrand. Blacks had lost much of their land and struggled to survive on what they had left. They now had to pay taxes to colonial governments and also had

Market Square, Johannesburg, about 1902.   Barnett Collection

to buy implements like plows to farm their land. Many came as laborers. But some sought other work in the growing city of Johannesburg. For many of those who came to Johannesburg, and to other areas of the Witwatersrand, their old way of life disappeared forever. Now they had to work for wages, buy food and clothing, and live in "compounds" (mineworkers' living quarters) or in hastily constructed shacks.

Apart from Rhodes, other mining capitalists also moved from Kimberley to the Witwatersrand gold mines. Within ten years of the discovery of gold, Johannesburg boasted several gold-mining millionaires.

Kruger's dislike of Rhodes and the other *uitlanders* grew. The Boer leader did not trust Rhodes, and with good reason. For Rhodes began to hatch a secret plan to stage an *uitlander* rebellion that would oust Kruger and lead to a British takeover of the Transvaal. Rhodes's friend Dr. Leander Jameson was to cross into the Transvaal from Bechuana-

President Paul Kruger, September 1899.

land with five hundred followers. When he reached the Witwatersrand, other *uitlanders* would join the rebellion. But Dr. Jameson arrived too early, and the Jameson Raid (as it came to be called) of 1895 was a dismal failure.

That was the end of the influence of Cecil Rhodes in South Africa. He resigned as Prime Minister of the Cape Colony. Multimillionaire Rhodes was to be remembered for many years to come both through the money that he left in his will for promising students to study at Oxford University in England (Rhodes scholarships) and through the incorporation of his name in the country that until 1980 was called Rhodesia. But in many other ways his name is not remembered with pride. He was unscrupulous and believed that the ends justified the means. He claimed to believe in "equal rights for every civilized man south of the Zambezi." But as Prime Minister of the Cape Colony he kept on altering the law to allow the vote to only the wealthiest of blacks. Rhodes died in Cape Town in 1902, shortly before the end of the Anglo-Boer War.

Kruger, encouraged by the failure of the Jameson Raid, now took a stronger line with the *uitlanders*. But in 1897 the British government sent out a new High Commissioner for South Africa and Governor of the Cape, an opponent harder and colder than Rhodes, Lord Alfred Milner. Milner inflamed Boer emotions by snubbing Kruger's proposed voting rules. The Boers had had enough of British law and British rule. War was imminent.

The Anglo-Boer War

On October 11, 1899, the Boer republics suddenly declared war on Britain. This was to be called the Boer War or the Anglo-Boer War or the South African War or the *Vryheidsoorlog*, meaning "War of Freedom." Initially there were 40,000 Boers versus 20,000 British in the conflict.

At first the Boers fared well. British troops were besieged in three towns: Ladysmith (Natal), Mafeking, and Kimberley. Thirty-two thousand Boers were involved in these sieges, leaving their fellow Boers with insufficient troops to stage an invasion of the Cape Colony. Britain sent for reinforcements, and 85,000 additional troops arrived. The sieges were broken in all three towns, and the British began to win battle after battle. Pretoria was taken by the British in June 1900. The Boers appeared to be on the retreat.

The British were convinced that the war was almost over. But they were mistaken. The Boers now resorted to guerrilla warfare and controlled much of the countryside for another two years. For food and shelter they relied on their farms and farmhouses. The British countered by adopting a scorched-earth policy: Boer crops and houses were burned, and Boer women and children were put into protected villages called "concentration camps."

A White Man's War?

Disease was rife in the concentration camps and food was in short supply. Twenty thousand Boer women and children died in the camps. As a result thousands of Boers continued to hate the British for many years after these events. Even today hatred lingers on in the hearts of many conservative Afrikaners. Yet little is said about the thousands of blacks who died in separate concentration camps. Black farmers were placed there by the British when their farms were destroyed. And black miners were sent to the camps after the temporary closure of the mines. It is estimated that there were more black than Boer deaths in the camps. Thousands of blacks also died in the fighting. Some had fought for the Boers, but a larger number had supported the British. The Anglo-Boer War was by no means exclusively a "white man's war."

The war was finally won by Britain, and on May 31, 1902, the Treaty of Vereeniging was signed. The two republics of the Orange Free State and the Transvaal became British colonies; the Orange Free State was now called the Orange River Colony. The unification of South Africa was thus brought nearer, but its two white groups, the English speakers and the Afrikaners, had never been farther apart. And the black people, who constituted the majority of the population, were left with no voice in their own future.

The Twentieth Century: 1902—1948

The first thirty years of the twentieth century witnessed the passing of discriminatory legislation against blacks, Indians, and coloureds as well as the growth of new political movements. It also witnessed a number of dramatic events. There was the establishment of the Union of South Africa with an all-white Parliament. The second decade of the century saw the outbreak of the First World War, which led to sharp divisions of opinion in South Africa. It was also in this decade that a militant Afrikaner group gained support, in opposition to more liberal Afrikaners who attempted to heal the breach between English- and Afrikaans-speaking South Africans. Among blacks there was growing unhappiness about their exclusion from government. Black workers began to react strongly against their exploitation by white industrialists, and a number of trade unions were founded. White miners, strongly influenced by socialist ideas, went on strike against their bosses. But many of the white miners were also racists and showed little sympathy for their black fellow workers.

Plans for Union and Black Resistance

After the Anglo-Boer War there was a period of energetic reconstruction in which the Governor of the two new colonies, Lord Milner, played a leading part. But he was an autocrat and insensitively attempted to force the Boer population to accept English culture. Milner's plans were fiercely opposed in South Africa and by liberals in Britain. In 1905 the Liberal Party came to power in Britain, and in 1906 it restored self-government to the Transvaal, and in 1907 to the Orange River Colony. The first Prime Minister of the Transvaal was General Louis Botha, one of the Boer generals. His Secretary of State was another Boer leader, General Jan Smuts. The first Prime Minister of the Orange River Colony was Abraham Fischer, with General J.B.M. Hertzog as his Attorney General. English was to be the official language, but Dutch (as opposed to what began to be called Afrikaans) could be freely used in governmental debates. The vote was limited to white adult males in these two colonies. In all four colonies—Cape, Natal, Transvaal, and Orange River—whites discussed the possibility of forming a Union of South Africa. Blacks were not invited to join these discussions.

While the British Liberal Party government and Boer leaders such as generals Louis Botha and Jan Smuts strove for Boer-British reconciliation, little attention was given to the rights of the majority of the population—Africans, Indians, and coloureds. Dissatisfaction was growing among all these groups, and new political movements were springing up. One of these was the Natal Indian Congress, founded by the young lawyer Mohandas Gandhi soon after his arrival in Natal in 1893. Gandhi and the Congress fought for the rights of disenfranchised Indians in Natal.

Mahatma Gandhi in South Africa

Mohandas Karamchand Gandhi (called the *Mahatma*, or "great soul") was born in India in 1869. As a young man he studied law in England, and in 1893 went to South Africa to practice law. He was to spend twenty-one years in that country. Indians were severely discriminated against, and Gandhi himself was thrown off a train for occupying a "white" seat. He later described that incident as a turning point in his life, which made him decide to stay in South Africa and assist the Indian community in its struggle against discrimination and prejudice.

Overcoming his habitual shyness, Gandhi gave public speeches and discovered his gift of leadership. He returned temporarily to India to fetch his wife and son, and while there spoke in public about the treatment of Indians in South Africa. This was widely reported in the press, and when Gandhi returned to Durban, South Africa, he was met by a hostile mob of whites who threatened his life. But he was saved by a white woman and the superintendent of police, who disguised him as a policeman and smuggled him past the crowd.

Gandhi began to campaign actively on behalf of the Indians in South Africa, establishing an influential newspaper to express Indian opinion. He also established communities at Phoenix

In 1902 coloured and African leaders formed the African Political Organisation in Cape Town. Their original concern was with the rights of coloured people in the Cape, but they soon joined other organizations

Settlement near Durban and Tolstoy Farm near Johannesburg, where his ideas of self-help and *satyagraha* (passive resistance) were developed. He challenged unjust laws—for example, the requirement that Indians had to carry registration certificates from the age of eight. He also led a march into the Transvaal to defy the ban on the entry of Indians into that province. He encouraged the protestors to submit peacefully to the attacks of the police, and himself spent several periods in jail. The Reverend Dr. Martin Luther King, Jr., used similar techniques in the struggle to gain civil rights for all in the United States.

The passive resistance campaign achieved some improvement in the position of the Indians when the Indian Relief Bill was passed by the South African Parliament in 1914. Feeling that his task in South Africa had been completed, Gandhi returned to India, where he was to play a major role in the political process that finally led to that country's independence from Britain in 1947. The following year Gandhi was assassinated by a Hindu extremist.

Before leaving South Africa, Gandhi sent General Jan Smuts, the white political leader, a pair of sandals he had made in jail. Smuts wore them for nearly twenty-five years and then returned them to Gandhi with the message that "I have worn these sandals for many a summer, even though I may feel that I am not worthy to stand in the shoes of so great a man."

in calling for an end to racial discrimination before the Union of South Africa was established.

In 1908 and 1909 white representatives of the four colonies met at a national convention in Durban and Cape Town to plan a united South Africa. The four colonies were to merge into a Union. The coloured and black male voters of the Cape (those who were qualified) were allowed to retain the vote, but black voters were not given that option in the other provinces (as the colonies would now be called) of the Union. The franchise (or right to vote) for the so-called nonwhite males of the Cape was entrenched in the constitution and could be removed only by a two-thirds majority of both Houses of Parliament—the Senate and the House of Assembly—sitting together. All four colonies agreed that no black, Indian, or coloured might be elected to either House of Parliament.

There was strong reaction to these plans from black leaders. In March 1909 a new group called the South African Native Convention met in Bloemfontein. This Convention was called by three Africans: Dr. Walter Rubusana, who had studied at McKinley University in the United States; John Tengo Jabavu; and Dr. John L. Dube, an educator who had been strongly influenced by the American black leader Booker T. Washington. They demanded that *all* adult males be allowed to vote in the new South Africa. They joined members of the African Political Organisation on a delegation to Britain led by a white liberal named W. P. Schreiner to attempt to persuade the British government to extend the franchise before the Union of South Africa was formed. But they received scant attention, and the proposals of the all-white national convention went ahead.

Even though they fought two wars against the Afrikaners, the British were unwilling to intervene to protect the rights of the black people. Once again they had interfered in the affairs of others and been responsible for the spilling of a great deal of blood, both black and white. Much bitterness had been created. Now they withdrew, leaving the local inhabitants of South Africa to sort out their affairs.

The Formation of the Union, and Discriminatory Legislation

The Union of South Africa came into being on May 31, 1910. The first Prime Minister of the new country and leader of the newly formed South African Party was Louis Botha. His deputy was Jan Smuts. Both English speakers and Afrikaners (the term which will be used from now on instead of Boers) supported the new party, though some very conservative Afrikaners joined reluctantly.

In January 1912 delegates at the Native Convention formed themselves into the South African Native National Congress (SANNC). The Congress's first President was Dr. John Dube, and the Vice-President was Dr. Walter Rubusana. Pixley Seme was elected Treasurer, and Solomon T. Plaatje, a writer and journalist, was the Secretary. The new Congress protested vigorously against the proposed Natives Land Act but to no avail. This new organization was to become very powerful. Later titled the African National Congress (ANC), it was outlawed in 1960 but is still influential today.

In 1913 the government passed the Natives Land Act, by which approximately 10 percent of the whole of the Union of South Africa was set aside for black "tribal" ownership. The rest of the country was for white development. Blacks would be encouraged to be workers on white-owned farms and mines, but would never be allowed to own land in "white areas." Wages paid to blacks were miserable, and the conditions under which many mineworkers and farm laborers had to live were appalling.

The Indian community also received shabby treatment. In 1913 the government became alarmed at the number of Indians now living in South Africa, and so passed the Immigration Bill that prevented any further Indian immigration to the country. Indians were not allowed to enter the Orange Free State and were prevented from purchasing land in the Transvaal. Protests against the treatment of Indians grew. These were led by Mohandas Gandhi. Gandhi gained minor concessions in his negotiations with General Smuts. But by the time Gandhi returned to India in 1914, Indian rights in South Africa were still very limited.

The First World War

Meanwhile, what was happening in "white" politics? Many Afrikaner Nationalists were becoming increasingly dissatisfied with the South African Party's attempts to reconcile English and Afrikaner South Africans. These embittered Afrikaner Nationalists argued that if they had their own party, they could strive for a new Republic of South Africa, independent of Britain. White rule and Afrikaner traditions would triumph. In 1912 General Hertzog broke away from General Botha and soon thereafter formed the small National Party. In 1914 the First World War started, and General Botha took South Africa into it on the side of Great Britain. However, many Afrikaans-speaking South Africans would have nothing to do with a "British" war. They staged a short-lived revolt soon after the outbreak of war. The rebel Afrikaners supported the Germans in German South-West Africa. Eventually the Germans were defeated by South African forces, and soon after World War I ended, South-West Africa (now Namibia) was placed under South African administration with the understanding that it would eventually become independent. Thousands of blacks joined the South African forces during the war, and worked mainly as laborers. Seventeen thousand blacks accompanied white South African troops to East Africa. And 21,000 blacks served in the armed forces as the South African Native Labour Contingent in France during 1917 and 1918.

Both Botha and Smuts attended the Versailles Peace Conference after the war. Both were present at the signing of the treaty in the Hall of Mirrors on June 28, 1919. Botha died shortly after his return to South Africa, and Smuts became Prime Minister.

Smuts returned to a restless South Africa. The cost of living in South African cities was soaring. Thousands of blacks poured in to the Witwatersrand to seek work in the mines. They were not able to bring their families with them and left them behind in the "native reserves." By 1921 white miners were being paid wages ten to fifteen times greater than those paid to blacks.

The Pass Laws

Pass laws have a long history in South Africa. In 1760 pass laws were applied to the slaves in the Cape. By 1827 all Africans who visited the Cape from elsewhere had to carry passes. "Hottentots" (Khoikhoi) also had to carry them if they moved from one place to another. After the discovery of diamonds in Kimberley, all Africans in the Transvaal had to carry passes. This was partly to prevent farm laborers from leaving white farms and seeking work on the mines.

The Pass
What was a "pass"? A way to control and monitor where people went. At the beginning of the twentieth century any white or policeman could stop an African and ask to see his pass. The following information was contained in it:
· the name and address of the bearer, as well as his father's name and his chiefdom, so that the bearer could easily be traced;

• the name of the district where the pass owner was allowed to look for work;
• the date on which the pass was issued—the pass bearer had only six days to find a job, or he had to try for another district;
• the names and addresses of all the employers of the pass bearer, past and present; how long he had worked for each of them; what kind of work he had done and what the employer thought of him.

In addition, the pass bearer's wages for each job were recorded. The job seeker was therefore at the mercy of all his employers. What they said about him decided whether he would get a job in the future. The wage he had been paid in the past decided the wage he would be paid in the future.

The pass laws underwent minor modifications as time went on, but basically the system was used to control the movement of blacks to the cities. This system became known as influx control. It was a cruel system. Often women and children were unable to join their husbands and fathers in the cities. Every decade was marked by strong protests against the pass system. Black opposition to the pass laws reached a climax in the Defiance Campaign of 1952. In the same year the Nationalist government passed the Natives Abolition of Passes and Coordination of Documents Act, an absurd title for an act that did not abolish passes at all, but simply renamed them "reference books." In 1956 African women were also compelled to carry passes. Huge protests followed this decision. Twenty thousand women of all races marched on the Union Buildings in Pretoria to voice their protest, but the Prime Minister, J. G. Strijdom, refused to see them.

The number of pass arrests dropped after the Sharpeville Massacre in 1960, but by the early 1970's more than 600,000

A policeman inspects an old man's pass in the 1950's.   IDAF Publications Ltd.

Africans were being arrested per year for pass offenses (usually for not carrying their passes with them when stopped by a policeman). Those found guilty were fined, sent to prison, or deported to the rural area from which they had supposedly come.

In 1985, as part of his "reform" measures, P. W. Botha, the Prime Minister, declared that Africans would no longer be forced to carry reference books. However, Africans from the "independent" homelands would still have to be in possession of "passports." In this way the movement of Africans from the homelands to South African cities is still controlled. Only citizens of the non-"independent" homelands benefitted from this legislation.

Some of the information on passes was adapted from Gold and Workers 1886–1924 *by Luli Callinicos.*

Strikes and Changes in Government

Many black trade unions were being formed and strikes for higher wages were taking place. In 1920 nineteen black demonstrators were killed by police in Port Elizabeth following a strike by black workers. More and more workers, both black and white, were becoming socialists. The South African Labour Party, open to whites only, had socialist sympathies but at the same time was being drawn toward Afrikaner nationalism. In Cape Town a group of white socialists broke away from the Labour Party and organized an African trade union in 1918. The Union was called the Industrial and Commercial Union (ICU), and it was led by Clements Kadale, a black immigrant worker from Nyasaland (present-day Malawi). The ICU's aim was to obtain better wages and abolish restrictions based on race. By 1928 the membership of the ICU was 200,000 and there were branches throughout southern Africa. But sadly, it declined after much internal squabbling and was finally suppressed by the Nationalist government in 1929.

By the early 1920's the price of gold was falling on the world market. In a desperate attempt to meet rising costs the mining companies reduced white wages and planned to employ blacks in jobs previously reserved for whites. This led to a strange reaction from the white miners. They took up the cause of socialism and protested against capitalist exploitation. But they showed no sympathy whatsoever for the plight of the *black* mineworkers. The white miners went out on strike. A small group of white socialist workers called the Newlands Red Commando led the strike at one stage. Their slogan was: "Workers of the world, fight and unite for a White South Africa," an odd reversal of the usual slogan "Workers of the world, unite!" On March 19, 1922, Smuts sent in the army to break the strike. The strikers were defeated after five days of violence. More than one hundred died, and four rebel miners were hanged.

Soldiers versus strikers in Braamfontein, Johannesburg, 1922.

Many white mineworkers lost jobs after the strike or had their wages reduced. They hated the Smuts government, which they felt was on the side of capitalist mine owners. But unlike their black fellow workers, they still had the vote. And so they voted for a new government in 1924. Two parties constituted this government—the Afrikaner National Party and the largely English-speaking Labour Party. These two parties formed a pact to successfully oust Smuts and became known as the "Pact Government." General Hertzog was the new Prime Minister.

Though the Pact Government was hostile to wealthy industrialists, it also vowed to control "communists and agitators." The new government looked after the interests of white workers at the expense of blacks. From now onward the "colour bar" was to be applied in factories throughout South Africa. "Job Reservation," as it was called, separated white from black workers and prevented black workers from doing

Black Trade Unions

Trade unions for black workers are not new in South Africa. They first emerged after World War I to lead the protest against the miserable wages paid to black workers in all industries. In the 1920's a huge Industrial and Commercial Workers Union grew rapidly and dramatically. But the government refused to recognize it, and eventually it collapsed.

Black workers suffered from many forms of exploitation. The movements of black workers were controlled by the pass system, so they were not free to offer their labor to the highest bidder. Their wages were deliberately kept low. By law they could not leave a job if they were contract workers (as most workers were). They were also prevented from training for skilled jobs. Black workers were not allowed to strike. Nor could they negotiate for minimum wages in their own right. South African blacks had no vote.

Unions for black workers reemerged after a wave of mass strikes in Durban in 1973. These unions concentrated on work issues and on establishing democratic trade unions. They avoided national political issues, fearing they would be crushed as other unions had been during the 1960's. In spite of hostility from management and the state, these unions were to survive. In 1979 the state was forced to recognize the legality of black trade unions for the first time in South African history.

Trade unions grew rapidly in the 1980's, giving a voice to black

skilled work. Mine owners restricted the wages that black workers could receive.

In 1925 the Pact Government established Afrikaans as an equal

workers. One of their most significant gains was that management can no longer fire workers without a hearing. In 1985 the Congress of South African Trade Unions (COSATU) was launched, a giant federation of over a million workers organized into industrial unions in all the major sectors of the economy. Undoubtedly the most significant union within the federation is the National Union of Mineworkers (NUM), which grew spectacularly among the migrant mineworkers housed in the vast compounds of the South African gold-mining industry.

COSATU soon found itself in a head-on confrontation with the state when it expanded its focus from work issues to the national liberation movement. At the same time it fiercely asserted its independent role within the liberation struggle.

While COSATU remains the most powerful of the black union federations, it still faces considerable difficulties in organizing workers and dealing with management. As many as 30 to 40 percent of the work force are unemployed, constituting a pool of cheap labor throughout the region. The labor movement also remains divided between the dominant nonracial tradition of COSATU and the blacks-only tradition of NACTU (the National Council of Trade Unions). In spite of these obstacles the black trade-union movement has a greater capacity to mobilize power than any other legal organization in South Africa. Where the majority of the working population does not have the vote, the trade union has become its political voice.

language with English. And South Africa now had its own flag, the Union flag. No longer would the British Union Jack be South Africa's official flag.

Striking members of the National Union of Mineworkers (NUM) being bussed home to the Transkei after being fired from their jobs. Eric Miller, Impact Visuals

Hertzog was reelected again in 1929. In 1930 he granted the vote to white women, but there was no question of any extension of the vote to blacks. Now *all* adult whites had the vote, but the erosion of black rights continued unabated.

Economic Depression and Further Divisions in the 1930's

The decade of the 1930's was dominated by the economic depression that struck the world economy. White political opponents were reluctantly forced to unite, but extremist Afrikaners still remained aloof. In black politics there was also division. Some leaders were pro-Communist, others anti-Communist. But one pattern remained constant—whatever the white government in power, discriminatory legislation against blacks continued to be passed.

In the early days of the Depression, as the economy worsened, Hertzog was forced to form an alliance with Smuts. The new party, called the United Party, came to power after the elections of 1934. English-speaking South Africans on the whole supported Smuts. They saw him as a liberal Afrikaner, which in some ways he was, at least as far as English–Afrikaner relations were concerned. Smuts had studied at Cambridge University in England and was a great admirer of the British Royal Family. However, he was more conservative in the matter of black-white relations. He was responsible in his lifetime for passing discriminatory legislation against various black groups. Yet conservative Afrikaner nationalists hated Smuts and refused to associate themselves with the new United Party. They formed another new party called the Purified National Party. The Reverend D. F. Malan, a Dutch Reformed Church minister, was their leader.

It was not only Afrikaner nationalists who were deeply divided in the 1930's. African nationalism also went through a period of dissension. Tougher segregation laws and harsh police action had to some extent suppressed the militant actions of black workers. In 1930 the African National Congress (ANC)—as the South African Native National Congress had renamed itself in 1923—expelled its president, James Gumede, because he had pro-Communist sympathies. The new leader was Pixley Seme, who adopted a much more cautious approach.

Like Dr. Walter Rubusana and Dr. John L. Dube, Pixley Seme also had American connections. Seme graduated from Columbia University in 1906. At his graduation he delivered a prize-winning address entitled "The Regeneration of Africa," in which he said, "The giant is awakening! From the four corners of the earth Africa's sons are marching to the future's golden door bearing the record of deeds of valor done."

A somewhat more powerful black voice was the All-African Convention, which met in Bloemfontein in 1935 under the chairmanship of Dr. A. B. Xuma. Dr. A. B. Xuma, also educated in America, was strongly influenced by his college roommate, Floyd McKissik. McKissik was an important black civil rights leader actively involved in the Congress of Racial Equality in the United States. The Convention met to discuss Hertzog's proposed "Native Bills." The first of these, called the Natives Representation Act, removed the 16,000 African voters in the Cape from the common roll, as the list of eligible voters was called, and placed them on a separate list. These voters would be represented in Parliament by three white members. All other Africans in South Africa would be represented in Parliament by four white senators and by a new body outside Parliament called the Natives Representative Council. Another bill was the Natives Trust and Land Act. A body called the South African Native Trust would buy large areas of land to add to the "native reserves." The reserves would thereby comprise about thirteen percent of South Africa's total land area.

Hertzog persuaded the All-African Convention that the Natives Representative Council would truly serve black interests. Accordingly some of the leaders of the Convention agreed to be elected to this body. The bills were passed in 1936 and represented a further erosion of black rights in South Africa. Both the ANC and the Convention seemed to be out of touch with the masses of black workers who had been pouring into the cities of South Africa seeking employment. But African nationalism was to become a powerful voice in the decades that followed.

The Second World War

On September 3, 1939, Britain declared war on Nazi Germany. Hertzog was against joining in, while Smuts was strongly in favor of supporting the Allies. Finally Smuts, with a majority of thirteen votes in Parliament, became Prime Minister once again and led South Africa into war on the side of Great Britain. Many South Africans of all races decided to join the armed forces in the fight against Nazism. By the end of 1940 the South African Defence Force had enlisted 137,000 men. By 1945 335,000 South Africans had served in the Defence Force.

As in the First World War black South Africans were not allowed to carry firearms and, as before, served as laborers and servants. The body to which the black servicemen belonged was known as the South African Native Military Corps. Most coloured recruits also served in non-combatant roles such as stretcher bearers and batmen (officers' servants), but there were also coloured gunners and sailors.

Afrikaner opinion on participation in the Second World War was deeply divided. General Smuts, an Afrikaner, played a leading role in the war and was a regular visitor to the front in Africa and Europe. He was often accompanied by his wife, and the couple—known as *Oubaas* (Old Boss) and *Ouma* (Grandmother)—were very popular with the troops. Smuts and British Prime Minister Winston Churchill were in regular consultation. Smuts's former colleague, Hertzog, disliked Britain. He was reunited with Malan but died a disillusioned man in 1942.

Extreme factions of Afrikaners were not only opposed to Smuts and the Allies but positively favored the Nazi ideology of Adolf Hitler. The leader of one of these factions was Oswald Pirow, a former Minister of Defence in Hertzog's cabinet. Pirow had visited Germany in 1938 and was most impressed by Nazi discipline and racist attitudes. In 1940 he founded a pro-Nazi group called the New Order. Incredible as it may seem, a rival organization to the New Order was also formed. This was the Ossewa Brandwag (Ox Wagon Watch) whose members dressed in Nazi-type uniforms and were staunchly pro-Hitler. This organization, often called the O.B., was founded in 1938 after the Voortrekker celebrations marking the centenary of the Great Trek. Militants in the O.B. carried out several acts of sabotage in an attempt to undermine the Smuts government, and some of them were imprisoned. Other O.B. members were arrested without charge by the government and detained in camps. One of these was B. J. Vorster, who was to become Prime Minister of South Africa in 1968.

More Liberal or More Conservative?

Smuts returned triumphantly to South Africa in 1945. His South African forces had fought with great courage and had played a major role in forcing the Germans to retreat in both North Africa and Italy. Smuts was fortunate in having a brilliant and highly efficient deputy, Jan Hofmeyr, who ran affairs at home while Smuts was away. Hofmeyr was a child genius who had become Principal of the University of the Witwatersrand in his early twenties and who was appointed Minister of Finance and Education in Smuts's 1939 Cabinet.

Hofmeyr was more liberal than Smuts and accordingly wanted the United Party to grant more rights to black people. But in spite of Smuts's heroic fight for freedom abroad, and Hofmeyr's efforts at home, Smuts's United Party clung to a conservative path. During the war the Smuts government separated coloureds from other groups by establishing a separate Coloured Affairs Department. In addition the government also attempted to introduce legislation to prevent Indians from purchasing houses previously owned by whites. Hofmeyr was unhappy about this proposal and in 1946 announced in Parliament: "I take my stand for the ultimate removal of the Colour Bar from our constitution." Dr. Malan's Nationalists did not forget that remark. They could not tolerate the thought that South Africa might move in a more liberal direction.

Industrialization increased rapidly after the Second World War. Thousands of blacks had been allowed to move into the cities as new jobs were created. In the early 1950's Johannesburg's population had reached a million, half of whom were black. Soon blacks began to make demands for full political rights. Many whites grew insecure. Afrikaner nationalists spoke of the *swart gevaar* (black peril) and enlisted white support. Dr. Malan warned the electorate that the United Party espoused Hofmeyr's liberal ideas, which would be disastrous for whites.

Nevertheless Smuts was confident of victory in the elections of 1948, elections which were almost exclusively for whites only. (A few coloureds were still able to vote.) But he and his United Party were in for a dramatic shock. Dr. Malan's National Party came to power, in spite of having recorded a minority of votes. This was due to a system that favored rural voters. White fear, short-sightedness, and prejudice carried the day.

Apartheid

The National Party had promised the electorate that it would introduce apartheid (pronounced apart-hate and meaning separateness or segregation) if it came to power. Of course a great deal of apartheid and a great deal of racial discrimination already existed in South Africa. The concept was not a new one, but the word was. But from now on apartheid was practiced with a vengeance.

Repression: 1948—1976

Today South Africa is in a state of crisis—its economy is ailing, economic sanctions (or restrictions) have been applied against it on a considerable scale, and its armed forces have been involved in bloody clashes across its borders. It has been labeled "the skunk of the world." Yet at the start of 1948 South Africa was a popular country. It had played an important role in combating Fascism during the Second World War, and its Prime Minister, General Jan Smuts, was held in great esteem by many Western leaders. What has happened within South Africa in the past forty years to change its image so drastically? Just as racism was being challenged around the world, it grew stronger in South Africa.

The defeat of General Smuts and his United Party in May 1948 came as a shock to most white South Africans and to the entire Western world. The Afrikaner Nationalists under Dr. D. F. Malan took control of South Africa's destiny. Many of Malan's supporters had been pro-Nazi. The Western world found it difficult to understand why white South African voters voted out the government who had fought on the side of the Allies. The blacks and coloureds who had fought for freedom on South Africa's side now realized that the fight had to continue within its borders.

Implementation of Apartheid

The new repression that began in 1948 was for black people the stepping up of a process that had begun before the establishment of union. As has been mentioned, industrialization increased rapidly after the Second World War, and large numbers of black people moved from the country to the cities. Perhaps some had hoped that the Smuts government would move in a more liberal direction and that postwar policies would be those of integration rather than segregation. But the coming to power of Dr. Malan's Nationalists ended any such hopes. From 1948 onward apartheid was systematically implemented and began to reach into every aspect of the lives of individuals.

Apartheid was enforced in all public places. Notices reading *Europeans* and *Non-Europeans* (later changed to *Whites* and *Non-Whites*) were placed at entrances to post offices, railway stations, airports, and other public buildings. And there were separate movie houses, theaters, and restaurants for the various race groups.

Sexual contact across the color line was made illegal after the Nationalists came to power. In 1949 the Prohibition of Mixed Marriages Act was passed, declaring marriages between whites and other groups illegal. And the amendment to the Immorality Act in 1950 prohibited sexual intercourse between whites and other racial groups. The South African police kept a close check on friendships across the color line, prying into the private lives of individuals, hiding in bedrooms and behind cars, and surprising individuals in the act of lovemaking. Arrests were made, undignified medical tests were carried out, and charges were pressed. Prison sentences of several months' duration were imposed on those found guilty. In some cases black women were given stiffer sentences than their white lovers for the same "offense." Some of these cases led to tragic consequences. Several white men, in some instances Afrikaner policemen or clergymen, committed suicide rather than have to face total ostracism from the community.

The Group Areas Act

In 1950 the Nationalist government passed the Population Registration Act, by which every South African citizen had to be in possession of an identity card (or pass) on which the race of the holder was clearly stated. Many individuals were put through humiliating tests to determine whether they were "white" or "coloured." In some cases members of the same family were classified in different racial groups. In the same year the government passed the vicious Group Areas Act, which had the effect of implementing strict residential segregation—whites were to live in white areas, blacks in black areas, coloureds in coloured areas, Indians in Indian areas. Very few blacks were affected by this legislation, as they already lived in areas controlled under the Urban Areas Act, but thousands of Indian and coloured people were moved out of white areas to areas farther from the city center. Many Indian merchants were ruined by these moves. The Group Areas Act is still in force today in spite of government claims that apartheid is being dismantled.

Surprisingly, the South African Communist Party (open to all races) was still in existence in 1950. In that year the government passed a new law called the Suppression of Communism Act. Once this law was passed, the Communist Party became an illegal organization and was

Black tenants evicted from their homes surrounded by their possessions.   Anna Zieminski,
Afrapix, Impact Visuals

automatically banned. The Act also gave vast powers to the Minister of
Justice. He was now empowered to exclude any individual from public
life if, in his opinion, that individual was "furthering the aims of
Communism." Many people were labeled "Communists" who were in
fact not Communists at all. In the three decades following the passing
of this Act hundreds upon hundreds of South Africans of all races and
persuasions were banned. Most such "banned" individuals were restricted to certain areas, prevented from entering any educational institution, from preparing any material for publication, and from attending
any social gatherings. No banned person was allowed to be quoted in
the media or at public gatherings, and the courts were powerless to
intervene. Individuals were banned for periods of five, ten, or even, in
a few cases, fifteen years.

Dr. Hendrik Verwoerd, Prime Minister of South Africa from 1958 to 1966, lays a foundation stone in 1961. Dr. Verwoerd was assassinated in the Houses of Parliament in Cape Town in 1966. (The writing on the left-hand side of this photograph is in Afrikaans.) The Star, Johannesburg

It was in the early 1950's that a new and sinister leader was emerging from among the ranks of the Nationalists. His name was Dr. Hendrik Verwoerd. In 1950 he was appointed Minister of Native Affairs. Verwoerd was once described as the "supreme architect" of the ideology of apartheid. He was the driving force behind the legislation to remove the few remaining coloured voters from the list of eligible voters. In 1952 Dr. Verwoerd introduced the Bantu Urban Authorities Act, making it more difficult for blacks to live in "white" urban areas.

Further Resistance

The Afrikaner Nationalists remained in power following the elections of 1953 and, due to the system of voting that favored rural voters, they won thirty more seats than their opponents with a lesser number of votes. It was, of course, another nearly all-white election. But opposition to the Nationalists and their apartheid ideology was mounting. Veterans of the Second World War had joined together into a movement called the Torch Commando. More than 200,000 people joined the movement. The Commando was led by Group Captain "Sailor" Malan, a distinguished war pilot. The Commando opposed the growing totalitarianism in the Nationalist government. But the Torch Commando eventually failed because it made little attempt to woo coloured and black members.

Another resistance movement that developed in 1952 was called the Defiance Campaign. This was planned by the African National Congress and the South African Indian Congress. It was led by Walter Sisulu, full-time secretary of the ANC; the young Nelson Mandela; Patrick Duncan, son of a former Governor-General of South Africa; and Manilal Gandhi, one of Mohandas Gandhi's sons. They mounted a passive-resistance campaign against the government and deliberately broke some of the apartheid laws of the country. Thousands were arrested. The government passed a law called the Criminal Law Amendment Act of 1953. Protesters could be sent to jail, fined, or given ten lashes. The Defiance Campaign was crushed. But the African National Congress was not. By 1954 its membership had risen to 100,000. Its President-General in the early 1950's was Chief Albert Luthuli, later to be awarded the Nobel Peace Prize. Luthuli was banned in 1952, and the ban was renewed in 1954 and again in 1959. But the ANC continued to grow throughout these years.

Chief Albert Luthuli, ANC leader and Nobel Peace Prize Winner. Born: c.1898 Died: 1967.   The Star, Johannesburg

In May 1953 the Liberal Party of South Africa was formed. Margaret Ballinger, a member of Parliament, was the first President, and Leo Marquard and Alan Paton were Vice-Presidents. Later Alan Paton and Peter Brown were to become leaders of this party. It was a small party consisting of members of all racial groups and dedicated to the establishment of a nonracial democracy in South Africa. The ruling National Party and the opposition United Party (Smuts's former party) were open to whites only.

The Laws of Separation

In the meantime apartheid legislation continued unabated, including the Natives Abolition of Passes and Coordination of Documents Act. Under another law, rights of Africans to stay in urban areas were restricted. Many years later, in the 1980's, these laws were to be scrapped, after the government yielded somewhat to international pressure demanding the dismantling of apartheid.

In 1953 the government passed the Bantu Education Act. This Act placed all African schools under the control of the Department of Native Affairs. Church schools had financial pressures placed on them, and many were forced to submit to government control. Instruction was to be given in the home language in junior schools, and at a more senior level English and Afrikaans were to become compulsory subjects. The architect of Bantu Education was Hendrik Verwoerd, Minister of Native Affairs. At this time Dr. Verwoerd made a speech in Parliament in which he said that there was no place for Africans in the white community "above the level of certain forms of labour."

Dr. Malan resigned as Prime Minister in November 1954 at the age of eighty. His successor was J. G. Strijdom, a white supremacist and fanatical anti-Communist. Repressive legislation continued under his prime ministership, but much worse was to follow when he was succeeded after his death in 1958 by Hendrik Verwoerd. The supreme architect of apartheid was now in command of South Africa's destiny.

Afrikaner Nationalism Reexamined

Why was the Nationalist government passing all this repressive legislation? Why were so many new apartheid laws being enforced? Perhaps the reader would like to pause here and reexamine the history of the Afrikaner people. Many of the forefathers of the Afrikaners had trekked

away from British rule over a hundred years before Afrikaner nationalism came to power in 1948. Many wars had been fought against black
people, who had lost most of their land. Then Afrikaners had been
involved in a war with the British, who had attempted to grab the wealth
that had been discovered in territory regarded by the Boers as their own.
The Boers had lost the war and had suffered a great deal, though some
of their supporters had sought reconciliation with the British. But in
1948 the hard-core Nationalists had come to power at last.

From 1948 Afrikaner nationalism grew in strength. In later elections
the Nationalists captured a higher percentage of the vote. Even some
English-speaking South Africans were beginning to vote for apartheid.
For Afrikaner Nationalists apartheid meant security. It meant that their
language, their culture, their identity would be preserved. They felt
threatened by the large black population. They disliked the white liberals and radicals whose policy was integration, not apartheid.

Dr. Verwoerd in particular believed that a time would come when all
South Africans would live in separate states. The largest and wealthiest
part of South Africa would remain white, but there would be separate
homelands for each of the black "nations." Dr. Verwoerd's philosophy
was one of "divide and rule."

Mounting Opposition to Apartheid

The vast majority of South Africa's population was totally opposed to
the apartheid legislation, and resistance to it was growing steadily. This
opposition came from organizations like the African National Congress,
the South African Indian Congress, militant coloured organizations,
trade unions, and the small multiracial Liberal Party. Many individuals
were banned without recourse to a court of law or were charged with
various "subversive" activities. A large group of people were arrested
and charged with treason but were later acquitted. This trial, which

lasted five years, became known as the Treason Trial.

In June 1955 a most important gathering took place at Kliptown, just outside Johannesburg. There three thousand individuals of all races discussed and adopted a document that was to be called the Freedom Charter. They pledged themselves to a nonracial and democratic form of government and demanded nationalization of banks, mines, and heavy industry. The African National Congress, the South African Indian Congress, and the South African Coloured People's Organisation were heavily represented at the gathering, as was the all-white Congress of Democrats. The South African Liberal Party did not attend the meeting.

Father Trevor Huddleston, courageous fighter for human rights. He came to Sophiatown from the Community of the Resurrection in England in 1943, and ran the Church of Christ the King in Sophiatown and started a jazz band in the township. He fiercely but unsuccessfully resisted government attempts to destroy Sophiatown. He was recalled to England by his church in 1956 (some people say because church authorities feared for his safety) and remains to this day a strong opponent of apartheid. The Star, *Johannesburg*

The Freedom Charter

This is the preamble to the charter:

We, the people of South Africa, declare for all our country and the world to know:
That South Africa belongs to all who live in it, black and white, and that no government can justly claim authority unless it is based on the will of the people;
That our people have been robbed of their birthright to land, liberty and peace by a form of government founded on injustice and inequality;
That our country will never be prosperous or free until all our people live in brotherhood, enjoying equal rights and opportunities;
That only a democratic state, based on the will of the people, can secure to all their birthright without distinction of colour, race, sex or belief;
And therefore, we the people of South Africa, black and white, together equals, countrymen and brothers adopt this FREEDOM CHARTER. And we pledge ourselves to strive together, sparing nothing of our strength and courage, until the democratic changes here set out have been won.

Repressive laws and acts continued unabated. After years of manipulating the Senate, the government succeeded finally in 1956 in making coloureds ineligible to vote in white elections. An organization called the Women's Defence of the Constitution League protested vigorously. Its members wore black sashes to mourn the violation of the constitution and held banners stating that the tampering with the constitution was

ON'T JAIL
JECTORS
NSCRIPTS
NEED
ERNATIVES

FREE
THE PRESS
TO TELL
THE
TRUTH

SOWETO '76
THE
STRUGGLE
CONTINUES

HANDS
OFF
LANGA
HIGH
SCHOOL

Members of the Black Sash stage a silent vigil in Cape Town in June 1988. They were marking the government's renewal of the state of emergency.   Eric Miller, Impact Visuals

"Legal today: Immoral forever." These brave women proceeded to "haunt" cabinet ministers and to hold silent stands of protest throughout the country. The protests have never stopped. The League is more commonly known as the Black Sash and has been active in assisting victims of repressive legislation.

In 1958 the National Party again increased its majority at the polls and in the following year passed two further far-reaching laws. One of these was called the University Education Extension Act. This was an attempt to prevent black students from attending so-called "white" universities. New universities for blacks in various areas were planned. There were huge protests from universities, particularly those of Wit-

Women in the
Anti-Apartheid Struggle

"When you strike a woman you strike a rock" is a theme that has
often been heard in conversations about women in South Africa. It
stems from the 1950's, when women were the main source of
resistance against the government's pass system requiring blacks to
carry documents permitting them to be in white areas and the areas
surrounding them. The resisters were mainly black women who
came from both rural and urban areas, but they were also supported
by groups of white women.

When the National Party took control of the country and began
implementing its policy of apartheid, traditional family life in the
country was increasingly fragmented and destroyed. The
migrant-labor system that separated husbands from their wives and

watersrand and Cape Town. Nevertheless the legislation went ahead.
Also in 1959 the government passed the Promotion of Bantu Self-
Government Bill, which came into force the following year. The representation of Africans by a small number of whites in Parliament was
abolished and eight new Bantu national units were set up. These were
called, both seriously and mockingly, "Bantustans." In 1959 Dr. Verwoerd gave vague hints that these new territorial authorities might
become "independent."

The Progressive Party

A new party, the Progressive Party, was formed in 1959. Eleven members of the opposition United Party broke away to form it. In many ways

families put new pressures on traditional roles. South Africa was (and is) an essentially patriarchal society, with men heading the household. But increasingly women have taken on new responsibilities as men have gone off to work in the mines and other industries in the cities. Sociologists believe that apartheid has actually strengthened the role of women, particularly in black society.

In the 1980's many courageous women, black and white, have played leading roles in the anti-apartheid struggle. These include Albertina Sisulu, the wife of an imprisoned ANC leader; Sheena Duncan of the Black Sash; Nadine Gordimer, a leading South African writer; Professor Fatima Meer, a Durban sociologist; and Helen Suzman, veteran member of Parliament. And there are also many unsung women heroes who have suffered under detention without trial or who have struggled to support families with husbands in prison or in exile.

it was similar to the Liberal Party, yet somewhat more conservative. Where the Liberal Party stood for the universal right to vote, the Progressive Party supported a qualified franchise. Where the Liberal Party had a 50-percent black membership, the Progressive Party was mostly white with a trickle of black members. In the elections of 1961 the urban voters rejected ten of the eleven Progressive candidates. For many years Helen Suzman, the only successful candidate, remained the sole Progressive Party member of Parliament. She represented the constituency of Houghton in Johannesburg and fought with courage and vigor for the abolition of apartheid.

By 1959 South Africa was in a state of considerable unrest. The ANC strongly opposed the pass laws, which had now been extended to include African women. The ANC also resisted the attempt to establish "Bantus-

Helen Suzman, liberal campaigner for civil rights and veteran Member of Parliament.
Paul Weinberg, Afrapix

tans" and "tribal colleges" away from the "white" universities and denounced the whole idea of Bantu education. There was also quarreling within the ranks of the ANC. Witwatersrand University Professor Robert Sobukwe adopted a black-militant approach and opposed the more moderate policies of the ANC. In March 1959 Sobukwe and others formed the Pan-Africanist Congress (PAC) in opposition to the ANC.

The Sharpeville Massacre

March 21, 1960, was a day of shame for South Africa. For on that day a massacre occurred at Sharpeville, a black township near Vereeniging in the Transvaal. Both the PAC and the ANC had called for massive demonstrations against the pass laws. The ANC demonstrations were to take place on March 31, but Robert Sobukwe, leader of the PAC, called on his followers to protest on March 21.

Scene at the Sharpeville Massacre, March 21, 1960. The Star, Johannesburg

And so, on that day, several thousand unarmed blacks gathered outside the Sharpeville police station. There they met up with a group of armed white South African policemen. The protesters announced to the police that they had left their passbooks at home and demanded to be arrested.

The young policemen were jittery. In January that year nine policemen had been murdered in Cato Manor, near Durban, after conducting a liquor raid. As the crowd pressed against the high fence surrounding the police station, some of the policemen opened fire on the crowd. The protesters began fleeing in panic, but the police kept on firing. Sixty-nine people were killed and 180 injured. Most of the dead and injured were shot in the back as they were running away. The next day the name "Sharpeville" burst into world headlines. Condemnation of the police action poured into South Africa from many countries. The Sharpeville massacre began a new era in South Africa. Many black leaders began to argue that if people were killed for protesting peacefully, then perhaps it was time for violent resistance to bring about change.

The poet Don Mattera wrote a poem about Sharpeville. Here it is:

> *Day of Thunder*
> *day of Blood*
> *in the dusty streets of Sharpeville*
> *thunder roared from saracen skies*
> *blood flowed from Black men's eyes*
> *when they met the Hail of Dum-Dum.*
> *The calling*
> *the crying*
> *the falling*
> *the dying*
> *of men, women and children*

and the cold stern faces of them
who held the Thunder
and spat the Hail
while my people sang:
Return Africa,
O Africa return
Bitter was that day.

The government declared a State of Emergency and introduced what was practically martial law. Thousands of people were arrested at dawn on April 1. The detainees included African, Indian, white, and coloured people, drawn from the African National Congress, the Pan-Africanist Congress, other Congress movements, and from the Liberal Party. None of them was tried in a court of law, and most of them were kept in jail for periods up to five months. Robert Sobukwe was sent to prison for three years for his part in defying the pass laws, but a special Act of Parliament kept him in prison for a further six years. On his release he was restricted to the district of Kimberley. He died in 1978.

Beyers Naude

It would be very wrong to regard all white South Africans as racists and supporters of apartheid. There have been—and still are—many white South Africans who have vigorously opposed the racial policies of their government, and who have committed themselves to the struggle for a just and democratic society, often at a high cost to themselves.

One notable example of this group is Beyers Naude (pronounced

Bay-ers Nor-dee). What is particularly striking about him is that he is an Afrikaner, born on May 10, 1915, to conservative Afrikaner parents. His father was a clergyman in the Dutch Reformed Church who had served as an unofficial chaplain to the Boer forces in their war against Britain.

Beyers himself trained as a *dominee*, or clergyman, became a member of the secret Afrikaner organization the *Broederbond*, which was committed to Afrikaner political domination, and rose rapidly to a leadership position in the Dutch Reformed Church. Many viewed him as a possible Prime Minister under an Afrikaner Nationalist government.

But the shooting by the police of peaceful black demonstrators at Sharpeville in 1960 was a turning point in Naude's life. He began to question the morality of apartheid and to criticize both his church and his government. In 1964 he established the Christian Institute as a nonracial ecumenical body. Over the next ten years he was subjected to the strong hostility of many of his own people. The government confiscated his passport, he was prosecuted in the courts, and finally he and the Christian Institute were banned. This meant, among other things, that he could not attend meetings or speak in public, write anything for publication, enter a black area, or leave his hometown without permission. He could not be quoted in the press.

Despite these restrictions, Naude enjoyed an international reputation as a symbol of resistance to apartheid and received many

Dramatic events followed the Sharpeville massacre: The government banned the forty-eight-year-old African National Congress and the newly formed Pan-Africanist Congress; a white South African, David

Beyers Naude, Afrikaner theologian and fearless critic of apartheid. Paul Weinberg, Afrapix

international honors. When his ban was lifted in 1984, he served for a period as General Secretary of the South African Council of Churches, following another famous South African, Bishop (later Archbishop) Desmond Tutu.

At present, Beyers Naude lives in Johannesburg and is still very actively involved in ecumenical and other church affairs.

Pratt, attempted to assassinate Prime Minister Verwoerd, but succeeded in merely wounding him (the would-be assassin was later sent to a mental institution, where he finally committed suicide); several small countries refused to trade with South Africa, and companies began to leave the country. Britain, Russia, and the United States criticized the government in vigorous terms, and one prominent Nationalist promised a "new deal" in race relations—a promise later repudiated by Dr. Verwoerd.

The world outrage that broke out after the Sharpeville massacre was to grow in the years ahead following other disastrous events. But it was never to be sustained for very long, as other trouble spots on the globe attracted world attention. This pattern of involvement in South African conflicts followed by disengagement was by now familiar. In the latter part of the nineteenth century Britain had constantly jumped in and out of Boer affairs, sometimes to protect local blacks, sometimes out of self-interest. In more recent times the United States has demonstrated a similar pattern of outrage followed by disinterest.

In 1961, following a visit to London, Dr. Verwoerd withdrew South Africa from the British Commonwealth. After a referendum among the whites it was agreed that South Africa would become a republic. A decimal system of coinage was introduced in the same year. The rand, equivalent to the old ten shillings, became the new unit of currency. There were one hundred cents to the rand.

Sabotage and Torture

The wave of repression continued. Strikes were ruthlessly suppressed, and a law was introduced making the minimum penalty for sabotage five years' imprisonment and the maximum death. The law also laid down severe penalties for strikers and slogan painters. Hundreds of individuals were banned, and there were further infringements of the freedom of the press. Harsh detention laws were introduced. Individuals could be detained for 90 days without recourse to a court of law. This was later extended to 180 days and today is virtually indefinite. In 1962 the ANC top structure went into exile and vowed to continue the struggle against apartheid from abroad. At home Nelson Mandela, in hiding, formed a resistance movement called Umkhonto we Sizwe (the Spear of the Nation). Its aim was to sabotage installations such as electricity pylons and mailboxes. Initially it was opposed to the taking of human life. A similar movement, the African Resistance Movement (ARM), was started by some disenchanted liberals and others. Blasts occurred near mailboxes and at electricity substations throughout the country. Many electricity pylons were toppled, and power failures resulted. South Africa's tough Security Police took control. Hundreds of individuals were detained, interrogated, and in some cases tortured. Over sixty detainees have died in detention since 1963, but not one policemen has been found guilty of assault or murder in these cases. By 1964 many Umkhonto we Sizwe and ARM activists had been arrested and charged with acts of sabotage. One of the ARM members was an ex-Liberal named John Harris. He was found guilty of placing a bomb in the concourse of Johannesburg station in July 1964, injuring many people. An elderly woman died of her injuries. John Harris was hanged in Pretoria in April 1965.

Imprisonment, Assassination, and Death

But a big blow to Umkhonto we Sizwe was the arrest of Nelson Mandela in August 1962. A further seventeen Umkhonto leaders were arrested after a raid on a house in Rivonia, near Johannesburg. The trial of these leaders was called the Rivonia Trial and lasted from December 1963 to June 1964. Most of the leaders, including Mandela, were found guilty of treason and were sentenced to life imprisonment on Robben Island.

Nelson Mandela

The following extracts written by Mandela himself give a clearer insight into his life than any biographer could give. Some of these notes were written while Mandela was on trial in 1964 and were published in *A Healthy Grave* by James Kantor.

I was born in Umtata, Transkei, on July 18, 1918. My father, Chief Henry, was a polygamist with four wives. Neither he nor my mother ever went to school. My father died in 1930, after which David Dalindyebo, then acting Paramount Chief of the tribe, became my guardian.

I hold the degree of Bachelor of Arts from the University of South Africa, and am a qualified solicitor [lawyer]. I married Winnie, daughter of Columbus Madikizela, the present Minister of Agriculture in the Transkei, in 1958, whilst an accused in the Treason Trial. I have five children, three by a former marriage and two with Winnie.

My political interest was first aroused when I listened to elders of our tribe in my village as a youth. They spoke of the good old days before the arrival of the White Man. Our people lived peacefully under the democratic rule of their Kings and Counsellors and moved freely all over their country. Then the country was ours. We occupied the land, the forests and the rivers. We set up and operated our own Government; we controlled our own armies, and organised our own trade and commerce.

The Elders would tell us about the liberation and how it was fought by our ancestors in defence of our country, as well as the acts of valour performed by generals and soldiers during those epic days. I hoped, and vowed then, that amongst the pleasures that life might offer me, would be the opportunity to serve my people and make my own humble contribution to their struggle for freedom. At sixteen, as is our custom, I went to a circumcision school on the banks of the Bashee River, the place where many of my ancestors were circumcised. By the standards of my tribe, I was now a man ready to take part in the "parliament" of the tribe Imbizo.

The young Nelson Mandela talks to Nana Sita, President of the Transvaal Indian Congress in the 1950's. The Star, Johannesburg

Mandela then describes how, at the age of twenty-three, he went to seek work in the mines in Johannesburg. He worked in the mines for a short while.

I left the mines and worked for a year as an estate agent at £2 per month plus commission. It was the most difficult time in my life. In 1942 I was articled to a Johannesburg firm of Attorneys—Witkin, Sidelsky and Eidelman. To Mr. Sidelsky I will always be indebted.

In 1944 I joined the African National Congress. The movement grew and in 1952 I was elected President of the Transvaal branch. The same year I became Deputy National President. I was ordered to resign in 1953 by the Nationalist Government. In 1953 I was sentenced to a suspended sentence of nine months' imprisonment for my part in organising the campaign for the Defiance of Unjust Laws. Then in 1956 I was arrested on charges of high treason. The case lasted for five years and I was discharged in March 1961. Early in April 1961 I went underground to organise the May strike, and have never been home since. In January 1962 I toured Africa, visiting Tanganyika, Ethiopia, Sudan, Egypt, Libya, Tunisia, Algeria, Morocco, Mali, Senegal, Guinea, Sierra Leone, Liberia, Ghana and Nigeria. I also visited England. In all these countries I met the Heads of State or other senior government officials.

In July 1963 Nelson Mandela and several others were arrested. In October 1963 eleven men, including Mandela, appeared in court charged with sabotage. The state alleged that they had planned to overthrow the government by violent revolution. On April 20, 1964, Mandela delivered a powerful and courageous statement from the dock of the Pretoria Supreme Court. It ended with these words:

During my lifetime I have dedicated myself to this struggle of the African people. I have fought against white domination, and I have fought against black domination. I have cherished the ideal of a democratic and free society in which all persons live together in harmony and with equal opportunities. It is an ideal which I hope to live for and to achieve. But if needs be, it is an ideal for which I am prepared to die.

On 11 June 1964 Mandela and seven others were found guilty of sabotage and sentenced to life imprisonment. Mandela and some of the other accused were sent to Robben Island. There Mandela stayed until the mid-1980's, when he was transferred to Pollsmoor prison in Cape Town. In 1985 Prime Minister P. W. Botha offered to release Mandela on condition that he reject violence. This Mandela refused to do. The reasons were given in a speech made by his daughter Zindzi in Soweto:

Let Botha show that he is different from Malan, Strijdom and Verwoerd.
Let him renounce violence.
Let him say that he will dismantle apartheid.
Let him unban the people's organisation, the African National Congress.
Let him free all who have been imprisoned, banished or exiled for their opposition to apartheid.

And so Mandela remained in prison while the world and the majority of South Africans clamored for his release. In 1988 he was admitted to a clinic in Cape Town, where he was treated for tuberculosis. At the end of 1988 the Government announced that he would not be sent back to prison but would be given a house to live in adjacent to a prison farm near Paarl, a town about 35 miles (60 km.) from Cape Town. Here he could be visited by his wife, Winnie, and family. On February 11, 1990, Nelson Mandela was released from prison.

On September 6, 1966, Hendrik Verwoerd was assassinated in the Houses of Parliament in Cape Town. He was about to deliver a speech when he was attacked by a parliamentary messenger named Demetrio Tsafendas, who stabbed him several times with a knife. He was dead within two minutes. Tsafendas was sent to a mental institution and remains there today. Dr. Verwoerd, born in the Netherlands, had become more fanatical about the establishment of total apartheid in South Africa than many of his fellow Afrikaner Nationalists. He was a man of terrifying intellect and had an iron will. Some critics have argued that he was insane, others have said that he was evil, and yet others have claimed that he was both. We could say that he more than any other individual is responsible for the crisis that South Africa faces today. Soon after Verwoerd's death, his successor was appointed. He was Balthazar John Vorster, Verwoerd's former Minister of Justice.

In July 1967 Chief Albert Luthuli was knocked down and killed by a train on a narrow bridge near his home of Groutville on the Natal coast, north of Durban. At his funeral one of the main speakers, Chief Mangosuthu Buthelezi, in paying tribute to Luthuli, said the following:

He kindled a spark in men's hearts, he gave them the knowledge that God did not create second- or third-class human beings, and by doing so Chief Luthuli struck fear in the hearts of all those who dehumanise and degrade other human beings for no earthly reason except that they were born with a pigmentation of skin different from their own. For daring to stand for this he suffered the modern South African version of crucifixion.

Meanwhile the small but valiant Liberal Party continued to expose the injustices of apartheid. Many Liberals were watched closely by the Security Police, and some of them had their homes searched, their mail interfered with, and their telephones tapped. Peter Brown and Elliot Mngadi championed the cause of black farmers in northern Natal who were threatened with removal from their small farms and villages for no reason other than that they were surrounded by white farmers. (The black farms and villages were referred to as "black spots.") For their efforts both Brown and Mngadi were banned in 1964. The bans remained effective for several years. In 1968 the government passed the Prohibition of Political Interference Act, which made multiracial political parties illegal. It was impossible for the Liberal Party to continue, and it decided to disband. The Liberals had demonstrated the importance of cooperation and reconciliation, but most white South Africans refused to heed their advice or follow their example.

Steve Biko

Toward the end of the 1960's several new organizations were being formed by South African blacks. Most of these were linked to a new movement called Black Consciousness, which in turn was influenced by the black theology and Black Power movements in the United States. A dynamic new leader emerged as the chief proponent of Black Consciousness at this time. His name was Steve Biko. In 1968 a black student organization called the South African Students' Organization (SASO) was founded with Biko as President. In his book *I Write What I Like* Biko said the following about Black Consciousness: "Merely by describing yourself as black you have started on a road towards emancipation, you have committed yourself to fight against all forces that seek to use your blackness as a stamp that marks you out as a subservient being."

The Homelands

As criticisms of South Africa's apartheid policies continued to mount, the government tried to convince the world that the establishment of independent homelands for the various racial groups in South Africa was the ultimate solution to the country's problems. In 1970 the Bantu Homelands Citizenship Act was passed. Under this law all blacks were forced to become citizens of one of the "independent" or non-"independent" homelands regardless of whether they lived there—or had ever been there!—or not. Millions of black people were by then living in the "white" urban areas. They were not prepared to be told by the government that they belonged to a certain "homeland" when they were second- or third-generation city dwellers. On the other hand some of the homeland leaders willingly accepted the idea of self-government. They stood to become powerful and wealthy. It was only later, however, that the first of the homelands would ask for full independence.

In 1974 another all-white election took place. Again the National Party won an overwhelming number of seats. But the liberal Progressive Party managed to win seven seats in affluent, white, English-speaking areas. There appeared to be some stirrings of conscience about the worsening of race relations in the country from a small number of whites.

Resistance:
1976—1989

Wednesday, June 16, 1976, was another tragic day for South Africa. The black poet Gladys Thomas tells of the pain of that bloody day:

Soweto June 1976

The sun rose to give us light,
in Soweto.
We started our day like any other day,
in Soweto.
Starving, working, dying, slaving,
whoring, thieving, drinking
existing the way you want us to,
in Soweto.

But this day, unlike any other day,
our students came in silent protest and prayer:
"We will not speak your tongue,"
in Soweto.

You knew the fire
smouldering beneath our angry souls
in Soweto.
You should've stayed away that day
and left our students in protest and prayer,
in Soweto.

So with your guns you shot them down!
You started our fire,
let out our hatred and desire,
in Soweto.

This day is dark for us,
the flames'll grow higher;
and our people's bodies lay about.
You!
Thank your God for your dogs and guns.

And as we count our dead,
our courage, dignity and sorrow,
Your day is dark,
we don't forgive,
we don't forget!
Let the sun rise to light our to-morrows,
in Soweto.

On that fateful day several thousand black schoolchildren gathered at the Phefeni School in Orlando West, a suburb of Soweto. Like thousands of other black schoolchildren throughout the country, they were tired of the inferior school education meted out to blacks. In particular they objected to being compelled to study half of their high-school subjects in Afrikaans, which they regarded as the language of the oppressor. The pupils set off on an illegal protest march but were soon confronted by police. Tear gas was thrown by the police, and it is possible that stones were thrown in retaliation. Whether or not this was so, the police opened fire on the pupils, none of whom was armed. A thirteen-year-old student, Hector Pieterson, was shot dead. And by the end of the day many others had also been killed. Within a week 176 lives had been lost.

The news that schoolchildren had been killed by the police spread rapidly. Police vehicles were stoned and set alight, and raging mobs set fire to government offices in Soweto. Two white officials were beaten to death. The government closed all schools and sent an antiriot unit in armored vehicles into Soweto. These vehicles were soon labeled "hippos" by the local inhabitants because they looked like those lumbering animals. Within a few days hundreds of government buildings and vehicles in Soweto had been destroyed. And the violence spread rapidly to other parts of South Africa. Apart from government administration buildings the youthful mobs also destroyed schools and beer-halls. Over the next few months hundreds more were killed either in clashes with the police or in clashes between rival black organizations.

It is very difficult to say how many people died in the conflicts between June 1976 and the end of 1977. John Kane-Berman, in his book *Soweto: Black Revolt, White Reaction*, arrived at the figure of seven hundred deaths. Others have claimed well over one thousand deaths. Nearly all of the dead were black people. In addition thousands of

people were arrested or detained without trial. Many of the detainees were held under the Terrorism Act. Under this Act the police are under no obligation to release information about detainees.

The terrifying violence in Soweto and elsewhere caused shock waves throughout South Africa and in many parts of the world. In South Africa blacks were outraged, many embittered. Thousands of young black students left South Africa to seek military training abroad, much of it organized by the banned African National Congress.

Liberal whites were numbed. Some decided it was time to leave the country. Others decided it was time to move more to the left. They considered themselves "radical," no longer merely "liberal." Yet others held fast to their liberal principles.

Death of Steve Biko

Just over a year after the tragic events of June 16 there occurred another tragedy in South Africa. In August 1977 Steve Biko, leader of the Black Consciousness movement, was detained. He was held in solitary confinement in Security Police cells in Port Elizabeth. Here he was interrogated and badly beaten. In a critically ill condition and naked he was taken in a police vehicle to Pretoria, where he died on September 12. No one was ever punished for his death. When the Minister of Justice, J. T. Kruger, was informed of Biko's death, he remarked in Afrikaans: *"Dit laat my koud,"* meaning "It leaves me cold."

But many, in and out of South Africa, were outraged. Here is how poet Don Mattera responded, turning pain into pride:

A Soweto school pupil carries the body of thirteen-year-old Hector Pieterson, shot dead by police on June 16, 1976. Hector's grief-stricken sister walks alongside. The Star, Johannesburg

Steve Biko

how avidly we waited for your song
how tightly we held the sun to our hearts
refusing to let go
refusing to watch the white night triumph
over your beauty
and over our deepest dreams

we held back our tears
suspended our pain
but the blood burnt our eyes
and the sun slipped from our hands
taking away your fire
quenching what little light remained

and the darkness was deep

still we waited Steve
knowing you would emerge from your nakedness
and walk with our sons
singing from the graves
    a sons
      undying
      eternal . . .

although yesterday lies in the ashes
of spent emotions and unrealised dreams
and the wheat of black resistance
cracks under saracen heels
yet shall we eat of your wisdom,
warm our souls with your flame

Steve Biko died in police custody in 1977. The Star, Johannesburg

we defy your killers
and swear each day
shall see a sequence of our reprisal
for grief grows into anger,
anger into commitment

history owes us a debt

men still speak of those turbulent times
when we sang of life and liberty
inflaming the dark folk with a will
of stubborn pride giving beauty to blackness
and you, young Biko declared:

    BLACK IS . . .

                Don Mattera

Homelands

In spite of the turmoil of 1976 certain homelands areas in South Africa mistakenly thought that they were heading for prosperous futures. One of these areas was the Transkei. This homeland was granted "independence" in October 1976. At midnight on the October 25 at a ceremony in Umtata, the South African flag was lowered and the Transkei flag hoisted in its place. The only country present at the sham independence celebrations was South Africa. All Transkei citizens lost their South African citizenship at this time, including more than 1 million Transkeians who lived in the Republic of South Africa. The first President of the Transkei was Chief Kaizer Matanzima. In December 1977 the homeland of Bophuthatswana followed suit. Its first President was Chief Lucas Mangope. Venda became "independent" in 1979 and Ciskei in 1981.

But, sadly, the homelands have not enjoyed prosperity at all. The South African government's dream of creating separate, prosperous, independent countries for blacks has failed dismally.

Reform, Repression, Resistance

The situation in South Africa was becoming increasingly complex and confusing. In 1978 B. J. Vorster resigned, and a new Prime Minister was elected. He was P. W. Botha. Prime Minister Botha soon acknowledged that many things needed to be put right in South Africa and promised that he would begin a program of reform. He told the world that apartheid would be dismantled. The next few years were to see a compounding of the confusion in the country. Mr. Botha would introduce one or two reforms, his right wing would cry out that he was betraying the cause of Afrikaners, his opponents on the left would say that he was doing "too little, too late." Both violent and nonviolent resistance would break out, and this would often be followed by violent repression. One political commentator said that South Africa was a country where you "hoped on Monday but despaired on Tuesday." Another said that the government was taking "two steps forward and one step backward." But a third, more cynical, commentator remarked that it was more a case of "one step forward and two steps backward."

In the 1980's white right-wing attitudes hardened, as did some left-wing attitudes among a few whites and many blacks. The reader will see the attempts at reform coupled with violent resistance and harsh repression in the account of the 1980's.

A police armored vehicle called the "Ratel" moves across the rubble after the destruction of a squatter camp near Cape Town. Gideon Mendel, Afrapix

President P. W. Botha in a typical pose. In January 1989 he suffered a mild stroke and resigned as leader of the National Party. However, he continued in the office of State-President. The Star, Johannesburg

Soon after coming to power, P. W. Botha initiated some bold attempts in the direction of reform. A massive program of building new schools for blacks was put into action. The Department of Bantu Education, now very much hated throughout the country, changed its name to the Department of Education and Training (DET). But the change did little to change the image. At the same time certain black trade unions were legalized. One group of black unions that was allowed to register legally was called CUSA, the Council of Unions of South Africa. A more militant group of unions was formed under the influence of the Federation of South African Trade Unions (FOSATU). They employed well-trained leaders to fight for the interests of the workers in the marketplace. In December 1985 FOSATU and many other unions joined together in a giant federation known as the Congress of South African Trade Unions (COSATU).

By the early 1980's resistance to the apartheid policies of the South African government began to mount again in spite of P. W. Botha's attempts at reform. Thousands of young black people had left South Africa to receive military training; some of the training was given in various African countries, some in Cuba, and some in the Soviet Union. When the young people returned, they were sent to one of several ANC bases in countries such as Tanzania and Zambia. Some bases also existed in countries bordering on South Africa, such as Botswana and Mozambique. The South African Defence Force destroyed many of these in cross-border raids, and the South African government applied diplomatic and economic pressures on its poorer neighbors to expel all ANC supporters living in those countries. In recent times there have been many incidents of land-mine explosions on South African farms bordering on neighboring territories. Several farmers and workers, as well as members of their families, have been killed in these explosions. Members of the South African security forces have not hesitated to cross into neighboring countries to seek out the "terrorists" who have been responsible for planting the mines and destroy their bases. (Supporters of the white regime refer to the ANC forces as "terrorists" while the ANC calls them "freedom fighters." Some journalists use the neutral term "guerrillas.")

Most of the fighting involving South African armed forces in the 1980's took place in northern Namibia and southern Angola. (All South African white males have to undergo two years of military service.) Many South Africans were sent to fight against guerrillas from Namibia

Namibia and Angola

Namibia, until recently also known as South-West Africa, is a large territory on the Atlantic coast. It is mostly semiarid, but also includes a true desert, the fearsome Namib.

Despite its difficult climatic conditions, Namibia has considerable economic potential: It is a rich agricultural area, noted for its karakul sheep, whose wool is an important export, and its beef ranches. It is also richly endowed with minerals, particularly diamonds and platinum.

The total population of Namibia is a little more than one million. The country is sparsely populated, with few large towns, the most important of which is Windhoek, the capital. The majority of the people are black, from a diversity of ethnic groups including the Ovambos (nearly 50 percent of the total population), Hereros, Namas, and Damaras. The small white community includes Afrikaners, German speakers, and English speakers.

Namibia was colonized in the late nineteenth century by Germany, which pursued a harsh policy of repression and even wholesale slaughter of the indigenous peoples. When South Africa entered the First World War on the side of Britain and its allies, its forces invaded and took control of Namibia. After the War South Africa was given a mandate by the League of Nations to govern and administer the territory while preparing it for independence.

Despite many subsequent attempts by the United Nations to persuade South Africa to withdraw, Namibia was for many years effectively controlled by South Africa. A drawn-out guerrilla war was waged between the South African Defence Force and SWAPO (South-West African People's Organisation), which sought to gain control of Namibia as an independent country. The military wing of SWAPO operated from bases outside Namibia, particularly in

Angola. The South African government attempted to create an internal multiparty and multiracial government as an alternative to SWAPO, which it accused of being a Marxist puppet. While several important changes were introduced in Namibia, the continued refusal of the South African government to allow fully democratic elections and to dismantle the last vestiges of apartheid in the territory, led to an escalation of both the military and the political struggle.

This drew the neighboring state of Angola into the situation, since the South African Defence Force had pursued a policy of "hot pursuit," crossing the Angolan border to seek out and destroy SWAPO bases in that country. South Africa also gave support to the UNITA (National Union for the Total Independence of Angola) movement of Jonas Savimbi, which was engaged in a bitter military conflict with the MPLA (Popular Movement for the Liberation of Angola) party, which seized power when Angola became independent of Portugal in 1975. The MPLA was aided by the Cuban government at the time, and since then large numbers of Cuban troops assisted the MPLA. UNITA, on the other hand, received assistance from the United States as well as from South Africa. During 1988 the situation along the Angolan-Namibian border deteriorated sharply. South African forces invaded Angola, allegedly to eliminate "terrorist" bases, and clashed with a combined Cuban-Angolan force. Toward the end of 1988 a military stalemate was reached. Largely through American influence the opposing groups—Angolans, Cubans, and South Africans—met for a series of discussions that culminated in the signing of an agreement. As a result of this agreement South African troops were withdrawn from Angola, a phased withdrawal of Cuban troops began in January 1989, and Namibia started on the road to independence (according to the terms of United Nations Resolution 435) on April 1, 1989.

Young National Service conscripts beginning their two-year stint in the army. Photo Group/Link, Impact Visuals

struggling for the independence of their country. A large number of young white men have been reluctant to undertake military service that defends apartheid and have left the country. One or two have become conscientious objectors (people refusing to serve in the army on moral or religious grounds) and have been sentenced to long terms of imprisonment. An organization called the End Conscription Campaign has been severely restricted by the government.

Students at the University of Cape Town protest against the government's restriction of the End Conscription Campaign (E.C.C.). This organization fought for many years against the government's compulsory draft for white males. The E.C.C. was severely restricted by the government in 1988. Eric Miller, Impact Visuals

UNBAN ECC
LET CONSCRIPTS SPEAK
UNBAN ECC
VOTE
LET CONSCRIPTS SPEAK
UNBAN ECC

U.D.F. mourners at a funeral for seven ANC supporters shot by South African police. Those killed were allegedly planning to attack a police station. Orde Eliason, Impact Visuals

Some ANC activists have secretly made their way back into South Africa. Since 1980 the sabotage campaign aimed at toppling the apartheid regime has been stepped up. In 1980 the huge Sasolburg oil refinery was attacked by rocket fire. It was not destroyed, but a great deal of damage was caused. In 1983 a massive car bomb exploded in a main street of Pretoria near the Air Force headquarters. Nineteen people were killed and 217 were injured. Both blacks and whites were among the dead and injured. Since then bomb blasts of varying magnitude have occurred at frequent intervals in most of the urban areas of South Africa. Many more people were killed or injured. In some cases the ANC headquarters in Lusaka, Zambia, admitted responsibility for the blasts, in others responsibility was denied. And it is possible that some blasts were carried out by the PAC. Some of the saboteurs were tracked down and arrested. Those found guilty were sentenced to death or to long terms of imprisonment.

Unrest in the black townships of South Africa grew steadily in the 1980's. There were many strikes, both legal and illegal. Many consumer boycotts were organized. Blacks returning to the townships with parcels of goods purchased in white shops were assaulted by young black militants. Often the contents of the parcels were destroyed. In one instance an elderly woman was forced to drink fish oil and died.

In schools there was constant disruption of classes. Militant students in the black townships attempted to prevent other students from attending school and taking examinations. The army and the police force patrolled the townships. They arrested student protesters whom they called "troublemakers." They broke up gatherings of students by means of tear gas and rubber bullets. They surrounded and occupied schools. In defense of their actions they claimed that they were enforcing "law and order."

The Tricameral Parliament

In 1983 Prime Minister P. W. Botha attempted to show the world that South Africa was moving away from apartheid. He proudly announced to his critics at home and abroad that legislation would be passed allowing coloureds and Indians into the South African Parliament for the first time. And so a Tricameral Parliament was established. One house remained all white. A second house called the House of Representatives accommodated coloured members of Parliament, and a third house, the House of Delegates, was set aside exclusively for Indian members. It was decided that certain matters would be voted on separately, other matters would be discussed jointly. But in no way could the coloured and Indian members *overrule* decisions made by the white House of Parliament. Special elections were held in 1984 to elect

Religion in South Africa

Most the world's major faiths are represented in South Africa, which is a multireligious as well as multiracial and multilingual society. Christians, Jews, Muslims, and Hindus all help to make up the diversity of the country's population, and there is some influence from traditional African beliefs.

All the important Christian denominations are present, and a majority (72 percent) of the population claim to be Christian. The Jewish community, which numbered about 120,000 in 1988, is said to be one of the largest in the world. Islam is attracting a significant number of African converts, although it is still largely confined to South Africans of Asian descent. The Hindu community is the largest religious grouping among Indian South Africans, particularly in the province of Natal, where the Indians are concentrated.

The Christian churches can be roughly divided into three major groups. First, there are those that belong to the Dutch Reformed family, the largest being the *Nederduitse Gereformeerde Kerk*, to which just over 50 percent of the whites belong. It is the largest church among white Afrikaners, and has "daughter" churches for black and coloured followers. Second, there are the English-language churches such as the Catholic, Anglican (the Church of the Province of South Africa, the equivalent of the

coloured and Indian members of Parliament, but these were boycotted by two thirds of the voters. Under the new constitution the Prime Minister now became State-President.

Episcopal Church in the United States), and Methodist. Finally, there are the African independent churches, which now number more than three thousand and which represent attempts to create separate black churches such as the Church of Zion.

In general terms, the white Dutch Reformed churches have been supportive of the government's racial policies, although recently the *Nederduitse Gereformeerde Kerk* declared apartheid to be sinful. One result of this has been a breakaway by its own most conservative members to form a new all-white Afrikaans Protestant Church. The daughter churches have also been highly critical of apartheid.

The English-language churches are generally opposed to apartheid, and now have more black than white members. These churches, together with some of the African independent churches and the Dutch Reformed "daughter" churches, are grouped together in the South African Council of Churches, which is affiliated to the World Council of Churches. Over the years the SACC has become a major force in the antiapartheid movement in South Africa, and it is frequently subjected to pressure by the government. Some observers speak of a church-state clash in South Africa.

In the past decade several black South African theologians and clergymen have come to international prominence. They include Dr. Allan Boesak of the Dutch Reformed daughter church, Bishop Manas Buthelezi of the Lutheran Church, and Archbishop Desmond Tutu of the Anglican Church.

The opposition to the Tricameral Parliament from the coloured, Indian, and African communities was overwhelming. A powerful figure in this opposition was a prominent black (though classified as coloured) leader, Dr. Allan Boesak, who was elected President of the World Alliance of Reformed Churches at its conference in Ottawa. Dr. Boesak, an ordained minister, is a vociferous opponent of apartheid in the Dutch Reformed Church, to which he belongs. He was disgusted that the new Parliament of South Africa excluded the entire African population. He was instrumental in founding a new movement called the United Democratic Front (U.D.F.) at a mass rally in Cape Town in August 1983. The movement was also supported by Archbishop Desmond Tutu, leader of the Anglican Church in South Africa, who won the Nobel Peace Prize in 1984.

Patrick Mvemve is ordained as the new Catholic Auxiliary Bishop of Johannesburg in June 1986.   Santu Mofokeng, Afrapix, Impact Visuals

Archbishop Desmond Tutu

Desmond Mpilo Tutu was born in the small Transvaal town of
Klerksdorp on October 7, 1931. After attending mission schools
and the Johannesburg Bantu High School, he trained as a teacher
and taught for some years at a black school. As a result of the
introduction of Bantu Education as an inferior system of education
for blacks, he left teaching in order to train as a priest in the
Anglican Church and was ordained in 1961.

Between 1962 and 1966 Tutu served as a priest in Golders
Green in London before returning to southern Africa to teach
theology at a theological seminary and at Roma University in
Lesotho. In the early 1970's he moved to England again to work
for the World Council of Churches. In 1975 he returned to South
Africa as the Anglican Dean of Johannesburg, the first black
clergyman to fill this position. Thereafter his rise in the church's
hierarchy was rapid, and he was elected Bishop of Lesotho. Between
1978 and 1984 he was General Secretary of the South African
Council of Churches and began to speak out vigorously against
the apartheid policies of the government. He rapidly gained an
international reputation for his opposition to racial injustice, and in
1984 was awarded the Nobel Peace Prize, the second South African
to be so honored, the first being Chief Albert Luthuli.

In 1985 Tutu was elected Bishop of Johannesburg and the
following year the Archbishop of Cape Town, thus becoming the
head of the Anglican Church in South Africa, again the first black
person to fill these positions.

Archbishop Desmond Tutu, Anglican (Episcopal) Archbishop of Cape Town. The Star, Johannesburg

The U.D.F. was (and is, in spite of the severe restrictions placed on it in 1988) an umbrella movement uniting more than 500 organizations in a broad front against apartheid.

The U.D.F. stands clearly for nonracialism, in contrast to the Azanian People's Organisation (AZAPO), which denies a role to white organizations in the liberation struggle. AZAPO, which grew out of the Black Consciousness movement, has claimed that it is not antiwhite but pro-black. At the other end of the scale are the right-wing white parties, the National Party, the Conservative Party, and the ultra-right-wing Afrikaner Weerstandsbeweging. Needless to say, these latter organizations exclude black membership!

In the author's opinion the nonracial path, the path of collaboration, is the only hope for a peaceful future in South Africa. This is the path taken by the Mass Democratic Movement (M. D. M.), a movement that more or less replaced the restricted U.D.F. during 1989.

Black-on-Black Violence

Not all the violence taking place at this time was due to clashes between police and protesters. Certain militant groups of black students and adults took the law into their own hands. They set up special courts in

South African police making an arrest during demonstrations.   Jason Laure

the townships and acted as judges and executioners. Individuals were accused of providing information about revolutionary leaders to the police. If found guilty the accused person was forced to lie on his or her back and an automobile tire was placed around his or her neck. The tire was filled with gasoline and then set alight. This flaming tire was known as a "necklace" or "necklace of fire." While the victim was burning to death, the accusers sang and danced around the flaming body. Some necklacings took place without a "trial." For example, at a funeral in one of the townships (and with all the deaths there have been hundreds of these), an "informer" was spotted in the crowd. The victim was cornered and the necklacing followed shortly afterward.

In the past few years several hundred black people have died at the hands of rival black organizations. Regrettably, black-on-black violence has been one of the tragedies of the present-day South African situation. There has been evidence that in some cases the police have supported one black group in their clash with other black groups. Young militant blacks—often called "comrades"—have on many occasions clashed with older, more conservative groups of blacks called "vigilantes." It is likely that certain groups of vigilantes have been backed by the police. But perhaps the most terrible black-on-black violence has occurred in the Pietermaritzburg area of Natal. Since 1986 supporters of the U.D.F. movement have engaged in one bloody clash after another with Chief Mangosuthu Buthelezi's movement, Inkatha. Hundreds of supporters of both groups have died. Buthelezi's Inkatha enjoys considerable support from the Zulu population of Natal, though it has little support elsewhere. Clearly the growth of U.D.F. support in Natal has been seen as a threat by Inkatha.

A young relative at the funeral of four people allegedly killed by black policemen at the black township outside Grahamstown in 1987. Steve Hilton-Barber, Afrapix, Impact Visuals

The clashes between the U.D.F. and Inkatha reflect a pattern that is clearly recognizable in other areas of South African politics: those who envision a multiethnic, multicultural South Africa, versus those who are focused on defending a single group. Like the Afrikaner Nationalists, the Zulus in Inkatha are also concerned about preserving their language, culture, and identity. They fear, as do other organizations and groups in South Africa, that minority groups will lose their independence under a U.D.F. or ANC-type government. In fairness it should be pointed out that Chief Buthelezi has denied that Inkatha stands for Zulu nationalism. He has spoken out strongly in favor of nonracialism in South Africa and, through an organization called the Indaba, has been involved in discussions with various white leaders to establish a nonracial society in the areas of KwaZulu and Natal. He has also argued that the rights of minority groups should be protected under black rule.

State of Emergency

In spite of the violence and bloodshed sweeping the country, State-President P. W. Botha continued to press on with reforms. In 1985 he declared that blacks would no longer be forced to carry reference books. At the same time he called for law and order in the country and clamped down on press coverage of township violence. For a year or more the outside world had been appalled by the scenes of violence in South Africa, witnessed nightly on television. Suddenly South Africa faded out of the world spotlight. Yet the army and the police force remained in the townships. Detentions without trial continued, including those of many young people under the age of eighteen. The State of Emergency was renewed in 1986 and in 1987 and more restrictions were placed on the press. Again it was a case of hoping on one day and despairing on another.

Many critics of South Africa's policies have referred to a "right-wing" or "fascist dictatorship" in South Africa. What terms would these critics use for South Africa if the ultra-right neo-Nazi parties came to power? Incredible as it may seem, there are right-wing parties and organizations in South Africa who believe that the Nationalist government was far too liberal and is leading the country in the direction of a nonracial democracy! The least effective of these is the *Herstigte Nasionale* Party (Restored National Party, or HNP), which broke away from the National Party in 1969. Far more effective and threatening is the Conservative Party, founded in 1982. Its leader is an ex-Nationalist Cabinet Minister, Dr. Andries Treurnicht. This party believes in strict apartheid and would scrap many of Botha's reforms if it came to power. In the general election of May 1987 the Conservative Party won twenty-three seats and supplanted the Progressive Federal Party as the second largest group.

In October 1988 municipal (local) elections were held in South Africa. The Conservative Party candidates were successful in many areas, particularly in the Transvaal, where they took control of virtually every white town council outside the main cities. In Boksburg, a town near Johannesburg, the local Conservative Party council announced that they were reverting to "old-style" apartheid. The Boksburg Lake and other facilities in the town would in future be open to whites only. These announcements were followed by a huge outcry, particularly from the black community of Boksburg, who decided to boycott the white-owned shops in the town and to take their business elsewhere. There have been similar developments in many other Transvaal towns.

But most frightening of all is the *Afrikaner Weerstandsbeweging* (AWB) which in English means Afrikaner Resistance Movement. This is led by Eugene TerreBlanche, an ex-policeman and fanatically patriotic Afrikaner. His rhetoric is reminiscent of Hitler's, and his ranting

"Song of the Movement"
by Eugene Ney TerreBlanche

Hear the crunch,
hear the crunch of marching feet
Hear the din,
hear the din o'er distant fields
Fighters on the march
(With) fresh ideals contemptuous of pretence and
*   betrayal,*
(A) burning fire which tolerates no servitude.
But born of love and pain,
glowing resistance burns in our heart.
O, may God protect us with the drawing in of the
laager to protect our struggling country
We will work, we will grow, we will fight,
we will bleed for our Afrikaner land

speeches draw large crowds to his meetings. The insignia of his movement bears a striking resemblance to the swastika. While the AWB is
not a political party, there is no doubt that its members would vote for
the Conservative Party in an election. There is a clear link between the
slowing down of reforms and the growing support among whites, particularly among rural Afrikaners, of the Conservative Party.

Eugene TerreBlanche, leader of the Afrikaner Weerstandsbeweging (AWB), addresses a gathering of his supporters. The link between the insignia of the AWB and the Nazi swastika is obvious. The Star, Johannesburg

Right-Wing Terror

A campaign of right-wing terror has existed in South Africa for several years. Over one hundred opponents of apartheid have been assassinated in the last ten years, and the overwhelming majority of these murders has remained unsolved. One of the most recent victims of these assassinations was Dr. David Webster, a leading anthropologist from the University of the Witwatersrand. He was known as a warm and gentle man, and a fearless opponent of apartheid. But perhaps the most horrifying act of right-wing terror in recent times was carried out by Barend Strydom, a young former policeman. In November 1988 he cold-bloodedly shot dead eight black people in the streets of Pretoria and wounded several others. He claimed to belong to an organization known as the *Wit Wolwe* (White Wolves). During his trial in the Pretoria Supreme Court he was supported by members of the AWB. In May 1989 he was found guilty of eight charges of murder and sixteen charges of attempted murder. He was sentenced to death.

New Elections

In January 1989 President P. W. Botha suffered a mild stroke. He resigned from the leadership of the National Party but continued to hold the office of State President. Mr. F. W. de Klerk took over the leadership of the National Party, and became the State President in the General Election in September 1989. In May 1989 a new "liberal" party, the Democratic Party, came into being. The Progressive Federal Party (PFP) disbanded, and many former Progressives joined with other groups to the left of the government to form the new party. In the early stages the membership of the Democratic Party was predominantly white.

Revolution or Reconciliation?

Certain groups of South African whites—these more "liberally" inclined—have been appalled by the violence in the country. Some have emigrated in despair and settled in countries such as Australia, Great Britain, the United States, and Canada. They can see no hope for a peaceful solution to South Africa's problems. But some of those who have stayed have been working desperately for reconciliation. In the latter half of 1989 a significant number of whites supported the Mass Democratic Movement. And other whites have joined the new Democratic Party. On the whole it would be true to say that more whites seek reconciliation today than in the past two decades. This was foreseen by Alan Paton in his novel *Cry, the Beloved Country* (1946). But Paton also feared that by the time whites sought reconciliation, blacks would have lost patience and turned their backs on their white neighbors. His fears are expressed by a young black priest, Msimangu, who is talking to an older black priest, Kumalo. Msimangu says, "I have one great fear in my heart, that one day when they turn to loving they will find we are turned to hating."

And these prophetic words were written in 1946!

Economic Trends: 1948–1988

In the late 1940's, when the Western world became preoccupied with its economic revival after the Second World War, Britain came to regard South Africa as the "jewel in the Commonwealth crown." South Africa's position in the British Commonwealth was unquestioned: It owned the world's largest-known deposits of precious minerals—gold and diamonds in particular—and was undoubtedly the most prosperous nation in Africa and in the Commonwealth.

Even though the (Afrikaner) Nationalist government's rise to power in 1948 was accompanied by apartheid policies, the Western world smiled upon South Africa. By the late 1950's foreign investment in the country reached new highs. Surprisingly, when South Africa left the British Commonwealth in 1961, foreign investment continued. This resulted in the growth of South Africa's economy at one of the highest rates in the Western world during the 1960's. Investment in South Africa was so very profitable that the issue of apartheid could be ignored.

In the late 1960's, however, the Johannesburg Stock Exchange crashed. The economy had just recovered when the international oil crisis of 1973–1974 occurred. This marked the beginning of an economic crisis that has lasted until the present. In 1976 the Soweto riots caused investors to panic and take a large portion of their investments out of South Africa. Once again, just as things seemed to be improving, an economic recession occurred from 1980 to about 1984.

The economic recovery after this recession was brief. Not only was inflation in South Africa running at almost twenty percent, but the international community began to apply economic pressure on the Nationalist government to persuade it to scrap apartheid. This took the form of economic sanctions.

The South African economy is not in a healthy state today. The economic cost of keeping apartheid alive is so enormous that the government has insufficient funds to spend on health care or education, never mind the money it needs to spend in order to stimulate economic growth and job creation. Indeed, the South African economy may be described as being in a state of severe crisis.

The Present and the Future

The Present

South Africa has often been called "land of sunshine." A recent South African tourist calendar carries the caption "It's sunny today in South Africa" on one cover and "South Africa: A world in one country" on the other. The glossy color pictures depict a variety of beautiful scenes: the roaring surf on a Durban beach, attractive gardens in Pretoria, the majestic splendor of the Natal Drakensberg, a handsome lion in the Kruger Park. These scenes and many others were described in the first section of this book. Yes, South Africa *is* a world in one country and it *is* often sunny. But sadly, South Africa is one of the most unpopular countries in the world today. This is because its critics abroad are disgusted by many of the cruel practices of the apartheid government— residential segregation, removal of people from one area to another, censorship, detentions without trial, hangings, police brutality. No won-

A woman subsistence farmer threatened with removal from her home. Namaqualand, northwestern Cape. Dave Hartman, Afrapix, Impact Visuals

der more and more countries are applying economic sanctions against South Africa.

Apartheid is an abhorrent practice and deserves to be condemned. Yet many critics of apartheid in other parts of the world do not realize how complex the situation in South Africa is and how difficult it is to find solutions to the many problems that the country faces. Alan Paton once said: "South Africa is not a Nazi country but it is not a bad imitation of one."

There are many positive things that can be said about South Africa without in any way defending apartheid. In the appendix mention is made of South Africa's achievements in literature, theater, music, and sport. South Africa also has much to be proud of in the fields of scientific research and of medicine. The country has produced many

The last edition of the Cape Town newspaper South *before its temporary banning by the South African government during 1988.* Eric Miller, Impact Visuals

fine journalists and lawyers. Some critics, though, would suggest that a proud listing of achievements implies support for apartheid.

In what other ways can it be argued that South Africa is not a Nazi country? Though thousands have died in South Africa in the struggle against apartheid, the government has not sent millions of people to their deaths in concentration camps. Though there is severe restriction on press freedom in South Africa and though many newspapers have been forced to close down, a degree of criticism of government policy *is* allowed in the country. A newspaper like *The Weekly Mail* is outspokenly critical of the Nationalist government and has been so for several years. In Nazi Germany *The Weekly Mail* would have been banned after one week. In 1988 *The Weekly Mail* was banned for four weeks and then allowed to resume publication. It's possible that it will be banned again. Under the current State of Emergency all South African newspapers are severely restricted. And Emergency regulations also curtail the freedom of speech and the right of people to hold meetings wherever they wish. Nevertheless meetings *are* held where speakers condemn the actions of the government. Such meetings would not have been allowed to take place in Nazi Germany. But in our opinion, if a Conservative Party government were to come to power in South Africa, it would no longer be possible to argue that South Africa is not a Nazi country.

Yet there is no doubt that until recently, under Nationalist rule, South Africa was "not a bad imitation" of a Nazi country. A State of Emergency existed for many years, individuals were detained for lengthy periods—sometimes for one to two years—without charges being brought against them, many organizations critical of the government were banned or restricted, and the police and the army patrolled the townships. In 1988 another "treason trial" came to an end and U.D.F. leaders were sentenced to lengthy terms of imprisonment.

Government apologists have claimed that "apartheid is dead." Sadly, this is not true. Rigid segregation still exists in most areas of South Africa's cities. Blacks are not allowed to own property in areas set aside for whites. Black farming is more or less restricted to the homelands, though there are black workers on most white-owned farms. Education remains officially segregated. The primary and secondary education of each racial group is run by separate departments. Apartheid exists in all government schools. However, most private schools in South Africa admit pupils of all races.

One of the most negative aspects of South Africa today is the degree of capital punishment that still exists. More than one hundred individuals (mostly black) are hanged every year. In 1985 137 people were hanged and in 1987 the number of hangings was a record 166. Some of those who were hanged were "terrorists" found guilty of detonating bombs or mines that killed or injured many people. Others sentenced to death were political activists who were found guilty of murdering political rivals, government officials, spies, policemen, etc. Most of the individuals who were executed were sentenced to death for "nonpolitical" murders.

Degree of Support for Apartheid

The elections of September 1989 offered a faint glimmer of hope, in spite of the fact that blacks were again excluded from voting. The National Party lost votes to both left and right, but nevertheless came to power once again. In spite of an increased number of seats in Parliament gained by the Conservative Party, the "liberal" Democratic Party also gained many new seats. The new Nationalist State President, Mr. F. W. de Klerk, promised to work for reform. Soon after the elections he declared that many political prisoners, including Nelson Mandela, would soon be released. And he promised to work for the lifting of the State of Emergency. In the meanwhile many black militant leaders remained sceptical, remembering that Mr. P. W. Botha had also promised reform. Some of the black leaders vowed that never again would blacks allow elections to be held in South Africa that barred blacks from voting.

How many people in South Africa support apartheid? About 10 percent. How does 10 percent (nearly all white) of the total population stay in power? "Law and order" in South Africa is maintained by the South African police, an extremely powerful organization. Attempts to undermine the security of the state are closely watched by the South African Security Police (at one time referred to as "The Special Branch"). The armed and well-equipped uniformed force, both black and white, is at present able to contain most of the unrest that takes place in the townships, with some help from the army. Many black policemen play a leading part in quelling unrest. It is puzzling to many observers that black police have on many occasions shot or assaulted fellow blacks. How are security police kept so well informed about "subversive" plans by individuals and by groups? This is mainly due to an intricate network of spies that exists in South Africa. Thousands of informers, both black and white, are in the pay of the South African police. Information is gathered and is passed on to the police. Suddenly there is a large-scale crackdown. Hundreds are detained, some for very long periods. Some are charged on counts ranging from distributing subversive literature to acts of violence against the state. Some of the accused are fortunate enough to obtain the services of good lawyers and some are acquitted. Those found guilty are usually given stiff sentences.

In spite of the growing number of banned organizations, strong opposition to government policies continues. Many opponents of apartheid believe in nonviolent change. They work actively and courageously to achieve this. They are drawn from all walks of life and use a variety of platforms to promote their beliefs. The fight against apartheid is carried on in schools, universities, law courts, hospitals, newspapers, and factories. There are dedicated trade unionists who believe that worker power will eventually bring about change through strikes and boycotts. But there are also those activists who believe that the only way to put an end to the institutionalized violence of the government is by counterviolence, by armed struggle. Some of those who share this belief have joined liberation armies outside the borders of the country. Others have been involved in violent acts within the country. Hardly a month passed in South Africa in the late 1980's without a bomb blast occurring in one part of the country or another. Some of these blasts were on a massive scale, and many men, women, and children of all races were killed or injured. This violence was condemned by many, including those who were strong opponents of apartheid.

A Complex Land

The theme "beauty and tragedy" has been referred to on several occasions in this book. Though we ourselves have singled out this theme, we are well aware that it is a simplistic one. The beauty is there, the tragedy is there, but the situation in South Africa is much more complex than that. The courage shown by so many South Africans is remarkable. Sometimes this courage stems from a deeply held religious faith, sometimes from a fervently held political ideology. But there are also thousands, if not millions, of individuals who simply try to get on with daily living and who have little time to spend thinking of solutions to South Africa's complex problems. Like everyone else South Africans love and hate, shout and sing, cry and laugh. Yes, *laugh.* In this poem Dennis Brutus shows how.

Somehow We Survive

Somehow we survive
and tenderness, frustrated, does not wither.

Investigating searchlights rake
our naked unprotected contours;

over our heads the monolithic decalogue
of fascist prohibition glowers
and teeters for a catastrophic fall;

boots club the peeling door.

But somehow we survive
severance, deprivation, loss.

Patrols uncoil along the asphalt dark
hissing their menace to our lives,

most cruel, all our land is scarred with terror,
rendered unlovely and unlovable;
sundered are we and all our passionate surrender

but somehow tenderness survives.

Concerned critics abroad are rightly appalled by much that happens in South Africa. But some of them fail to understand that not all is gloom and doom. Laughter is often heard in this strange and beautiful land. Much of the laughter comes from the people who are the most oppressed. White observers are often taken aback by the ability of blacks to see the humorous side of apartheid. Many jokes about its absurdity are constantly being told by blacks, and in black theater there is a great deal of satire in which the absurdity of apartheid is exposed.

Nor are white opponents of apartheid a dour and serious lot. White satirists of apartheid exist particularly in the journalistic and theatrical worlds. Even in the strictly political arena humor is always present. In its fifteen years of existence the Liberal Party never failed at any of its meetings to inject some humor into the proceedings. One of the most courageous and humorous Liberals was the late Ernie Wentzel, leader of the Transvaal division of the party. On one occasion he was addressing a Liberal Party meeting in Durban. Present at the meeting were four members of the Special Branch (Security Police), two white and two Indian. Ernie Wentzel's speech opened like this:

Ladies and Gentlemen, please welcome the four members of the Special Branch. There they sit in the sixth row. Members of the Special Branch, my first remarks are addressed to you. For your benefit I am going to speak in

Sanctions: The news board announces the last South African Airlines flight to the United States; but, as the cigarette ad makes clear, some American products are still widely promoted. Catherine D. Smith.

words of one syllable. And in case you don't know what a syllable is, it's the bump in the middle of a word!

Sanctions

Many countries, including the United States, have argued that imposing sanctions and removing investments from South Africa are the only way to bring its proapartheid government to its knees. This view has been supported by leaders like Dr. Allan Boesak and Archbishop Desmond Tutu. On the other hand the late Alan Paton fiercely opposed sanctions and was appalled by the high rate of unemployment among black people, some of it directly attributable to the imposition of sanctions. Paton went on record as saying: "There is only one firm statement that I can make on disinvestment—I will have nothing to do with it. I will not, by any written or spoken word, give it any support whatsoever." This view was supported by Chief Mangosuthu Buthelezi, leader of the Inkatha movement.

The Future

What then, is the future of this beloved, beautiful, strife-torn country? How much longer will apartheid continue? Can a bloodbath be averted? Or will the beautiful South African landscape become one of the bloodiest battlefields that the world has seen this century? Will a new government be essentially pro-Communist or procapitalist or neither?

In considering South Africa's future, few analysts give sufficient attention to the population explosion that is taking place, particularly among South Africa's black population.

At present outnumbered five to one by blacks, whites will be outnumbered seventeen to one by the year 2040. It is obvious that any long-term solutions for South Africa's future will have to take this into account. It is also obvious that the days of apartheid are numbered.

Evolution or Revolution?

At one stage many people hoped that South Africa would become a nonracial democracy by means of peaceful evolutionary change. Regrettably that stage has passed. There has been a great deal of violence and bloodshed in the last two decades. Thousands have died. But will the violence escalate? No one knows.

There is no doubt that the ANC, in spite of the fact that it is a banned organization, has a large following in South Africa. Yet the government steadfastly refuses to talk to the exiled leaders of an organization that consists of "terrorists." On the other hand, several whites, including some leading businessmen, have openly held discussions with the ANC in various African countries. Organizations like the Conservative Party and the AWB have demanded that action should be taken against those who talk to the ANC.

Possible Solutions

The outlawed ANC is determined that it will become the future government of South Africa, and it would then introduce universal suffrage in a unitary state. While the ANC is not antiwhite—there is a small number of whites who belong to the organization—it does not support the view that "minority groups" should be protected in a future government. At the other end of the spectrum are the extreme right-wing nationalist groups. As has been pointed out, if they were to come to power, the chances of racial warfare in South Africa would be dramatically increased. They would attempt to reintroduce apartheid at every level and would stamp out any liberal or left-wing opposition in the country. But after the elections of September 1989 it seems unlikely that an extreme right-wing government will come to power in the foreseeable future. A great deal depends on the new leadership of the Nationalist government. It is possible that blacks will be given a say in a future Parliament. Yet there is no doubt that millions of blacks will refuse to vote for representatives to a Parliament that has not gone nearly far enough in dismantling apartheid.

Several "solutions" have been proposed to resolve South Africa's almost insoluble problems. Apart from the ANC's solution of one-person-one-vote in a single united state—which would mean whites would always be a minority vote—another possible solution is a federal system for the country. Let there be a central government (these sup-

Children at a Johannesburg kindergarten. Here apartheid does not exist. More and more private high schools in South Africa are also becoming integrated, but government schools remain strictly segregated along racial lines.   Ingrid Hudson

porters say) but let "minority groups" exercise their rights in local governments. There have been yet other arguments in favor of copying the government of Switzerland, which carefully balances local and national rights and responsibilities.

The world is clamoring for change in South Africa. Most South Africans want to see change. While thousands of South Africans have quit the country of their birth, the vast majority will not leave. For the 3.5 million Afrikaners there is "no further trek." South Africa is their home as much as it is the home of the millions of black South Africans as well as of coloured South Africans, many of them descended from Afrikaners and blacks. Indian South Africans and English-speaking South Africans have been in the country for well over a hundred years.

In our opinion the only peaceful solution to South Africa's problems is for leaders of *all* sections in the country to meet around the negotiating table without delay. Enormous courage is required from the new State President to announce to the world that finally discussions are to take place among all parties in South Africa, including the ANC. If this is not done, the bloodbath could well become a reality.

In a talk to the Foreign Policy Association in New York in 1986, Harry Oppenheimer, South African multimillionaire and former head of De Beers and the vast Anglo-American Corporation said the following:

South Africans, even white Africans, are not really worse than other people, they are just ordinary men and women who find themselves face to face with problems which require quite exceptional qualities of courage, magnanimity and faith for the solution. The hour may be late, but the way of peaceful change still deserves a chance.

The author would endorse this view in spite of the many atrocities that have been carried out by both embittered and frightened people in South Africa in recent times.

It is courage and faith that are required before South Africa's new dawn can begin. South Africans must be emancipated from the feelings of fear and hatred that still do exist in the hearts of many, as is suggested in the conclusion of Alan Paton's *Cry, the Beloved Country*:

Yes, it is the dawn that has come. The titihoya wakes from sleep, and goes about its work of forlorn crying. The sun tips with light the mountains of Ingeli and East Griqualand. The great valley of the Umzimkulu is still in darkness, but the light will come there. Ndotsheni is still in darkness, but the light will come there also. For it is the dawn that has come, as it has come for a thousand centuries, never failing. But when that dawn will come, of our emancipation, from the fear of bondage and the bondage of fear, why, that is a secret.

Appendix:
Literature, Drama, Music, and Sport in a Divided Nation

It is understandable that South Africa has been referred to as the "skunk of the world." Apartheid is largely to blame for that negative label. Some extreme antiapartheid critics refuse to have anything to do with *any* South African, black or white. Many talented black South Africans have been barred from sporting or cultural activities abroad for no other reason other than they *are* South Africans.

In this appendix four areas in which South Africans have received deserved international acclaim are discussed. These are in the fields of literature, drama, music, and sport.

Literature

South African writers have produced an impressively rich and varied body of literature in English, in the indigenous African languages, and in Afrikaans.

Most modern black South African authors choose to write in English, but several important figures stand out in the African languages.

One of these is Thomas Mofolo, whose novel *Chaka*, originally published in the 1920's in Sotho, has been translated into English and several other languages. It is a heroic epic, dealing with the rise to power of the legendary Zulu king Chaka (now usually spelled Shaka). Among Afrikaans writers N. P. van Wyk Louw, the poet, and Andre P. Brink, the novelist, have made major contributions to South African literature. Many modern writers in Afrikaans have begun to express their dissent from the policies of the South African state. The most notable of these is Breyten Breytenbach, who now lives in Paris and has decided to write in English in the future, as a protest against what he regards as the language of oppression in South Africa.

Early South African English writers were mostly settlers from England who brought with them the literary conventions of that country. They developed what is sometimes referred to, in rather derogatory terms, as the "veld-and-vlei" ("field-and-swamp") school of South African literature. They tended to write pastoral idylls, romanticizing the South African countryside using essentially foreign images. Thomas Pringle (1789–1834) is a typical example. Here are the first four lines of his sonnet "The Cape of Storms":

> *O Cape of Storms! although thy front be dark,*
> *And bleak thy naked cliffs and cheerless vales,*
> *And perilous thy fierce and faithless gales*
> *To staunchest mariner and stoutest bark . . .*

Until the recent past, one of the recurring themes in South African English writing has been the search for an authentic South African voice in the attempt to escape from the cultural domination of the "mother country," which is how England is often viewed. Many of the early writers were ambivalent about their South African identity and tended to follow the literary fashions of London.

The first major figure in South African English literature was Olive Schreiner, whose *Story of an African Farm* is quoted in Chapter IV. The book is both a powerful evocation of the harsh Karoo landscape and a profound psychological study of its inhabitants. Olive Schreiner was one of the first South African writers to challenge in forceful terms the racial and political attitudes of her fellow white South Africans.

Many of the earlier South African writers published their works in Britain and in fact spent most of their adult lives in Europe. They include poets William Plomer and Roy Campbell, who found the colonial mentality of the time to be stifling. Their attempts to satirize that mentality earned them considerable notoriety in their own country.

Here are two extracts from Roy Campbell's long poem "The Wayzgoose" (1928) in which he satirizes the way of life both in his native Natal and in South Africa as a whole:

> *Attend my fable if your ears be clean,*
> *In fair Banana Land we lay our scene—*
> *South Africa, renowned both far and wide*
> *For politics and little else beside . . .*
>
> *The 'garden colony' they call our land,*
> *And surely for a garden it was planned:*
> *What apter phrase with such a place could cope*
> *Where vegetation has so fine a scope,*
> *Where weeds in such variety are found*

And all the rarest parasites *abound,*
Where pumpkins to professors are promoted
And turnips into Parliament are voted?

A major event in South Africa's literary history was the publication in 1948 of Alan Paton's *Cry, the Beloved Country.* The book rapidly became an international best-seller. This moving novel tells the story of a Zulu priest's search for his son in the city of Johannesburg and is set against the background of the conflicts, fears, and prejudices of South Africa.

Alan Paton, author of Cry, the Beloved Country, *at a function in Johannesburg. He was born in Pietermaritzburg in 1903 and died at his home, near Durban, in 1988.*

In the same year that *Cry, the Beloved Country* was published, the Afrikaner-dominated National Party came into power and began to implement its apartheid policy. For the past forty years, English writing in South Africa has been characterized by dissent and protest against that policy. Nadine Gordimer, the novelist and short story writer, is one of the most notable examples. With Paton and, more recently, J. M. Coetzee, she is one of the few South African writers to achieve genuine international fame, and she has been nominated for the Nobel Prize for literature on more than one occasion.

A major theme in modern South African literature—explored by both Gordimer and Coetzee among others—is the painful transition to a postapartheid society, a transition marked by intense conflict. In *The Life and Times of Michael K*, Coetzee describes the desolation brought about by a bitter civil war, while in *July's People* Gordimer writes about the collapse of the lifestyle of privileged whites. These apocalyptic visions of the future of South Africa are echoed in much of the writing of modern black and Afrikaans authors.

The early 1970's saw a tremendous upsurge of writing by black South Africans. While older black writers such as Peter Abrahams, Es'kia Mphahlele, and Nat Nakasa had achieved considerable renown, their works were frequently banned in South Africa itself, and most black writers in the 1950's and 1960's were effectively silenced by the South African Government. Some liberalization of the censorship system occurred in the 1970's. This coincided with the emergence of black poets such as Oswald Mtshali, James Matthews, Sipho Sepamla, and Wally Mongane Serote, and with the establishment of a number of small independent publishing houses that were willing and even eager to publish their work. Serote's poem "Alexandra" is quoted in Chapter V.

The title of the collection of poems by James Matthews, *Cry Rage*, published by Ravan Press in 1972, summed up the feelings of protest expressed by this group of poets. James Matthews's poem quoted at the end of Chapter III is from this collection. In spite of the degree of liberalization in the censorship system, *Cry Rage* was eventually banned by the South African censors, but not before the first printing had sold out, evidence of the demand that existed for this kind of book. Oswald Mtshali's *Sounds of a Cowhide Drum* managed to escape banning. Copies of this collection of Mtshali's protest poetry achieved record sales. Mtshali's second collection—*Fireflames*, published in 1980—was immediately banned by the censors. Another protest poet to emerge in the 1970's was Don Mattera, several of whose poems appear in this book.

Two of the finest white poets in South Africa today are Jeremy Cronin, whose "To Learn How to Speak" appears in Chapter II, and Douglas Livingstone. Cronin's collection *Inside* was published soon after his release from prison in 1983. He was sent to prison in 1976 for having carried out underground work for the ANC, and the poems are about his prison experiences. Douglas Livingstone is a poet whose themes range widely and include poems about African animals as well as metaphysical love poetry. He is a superb craftsman and has won many prizes for his poetry both at home and abroad. His poem "The King" is quoted in Chapter VI.

Some of South Africa's best black writers live in exile and may not return to the country while the Nationalist government is in power. They include Dennis Brutus, whose "Somehow We Survive" can be found in Chapter XVIII, Mongane Serote, and Lewis Nkosi, all of whom are engaged in working for change in South Africa.

In more recent years black writers have turned increasingly to the theater.

Theater

A most vital theater movement, achieving both national and international recognition, has emerged in South Africa in the last three decades.

African storytelling, dance, song, mime, rhythmic chant, and traditional praise poetry have contributed greatly to the modern theater in South Africa. Today's theater is urban, multilingual, and multicultural, infused with a powerful energy of resistance to the status quo, yet full of humor and indestructible liveliness. It is a theater of the majority, locating its pulse in the heart of the racially segregated townships that surround every town and city in South Africa, but willing to benefit from a collaboration with liberal and progressive whites.

Robert Kavanagh, in his book *Theatre and Cultural Struggle in South Africa*, traces this township theater tradition to the 1920's, when Essau Mthethwa and his Lucky Stars toured South Africa with a repertoire of original comedies in Zulu. With the founding of the Bantu Men's Social Centre in 1924, a more literary tradition emerged. The plays of H.I.E. Dhlomo are associated with this center.

In the 1930's and 1940's a very popular form of culture and entertainment, known as Marabi, emerged in the slums of Doornfontein, to the east of the Johannesburg city center. This was primarily a form of African jazz, but included newly developing dance and song, which was to become very influential.

In 1948 the Afrikaner Nationalists came to power. The new ruling party met wave after wave of popular resistance in a rapidly transforming South Africa. The 1950's became known colloquially as the Decade of Defiance, and provided a major push to the developing theater tradition. Rapid urbanization and a deeply felt resistance to Afrikaner rule led to the development of a highly articulate group of black intellectuals and writers who were to set the creative tone for the next three decades. This was the decade of The Union of South African Artists, the popular and successful musical *King Kong*, the Drum school of

The Mamelodi Theater Group demonstrating prison life, October 1987. Eric Miller, Afrapix, Impact Visuals

· 262 ·

journalism (which developed a popular and witty form of black English), and the arrival on the scene of a young playwright named Athol Fugard.

Fugard, having recently arrived in Johannesburg, rapidly established contact with such notable figures as Nat Nakasa, Bloke Modisane, and Lewis Nkosi. His first major work, *No Good Friday*, emerged from these contacts. This production was rapidly followed by *Nongogo* and *The Blood Knot,* in which he played opposite Zakes Mokae. Fugard has now established a major world reputation as a playwright with such plays as *The Island*, *Sizwe Bansi Is Dead* (created in collaboration with the Tony award winners John Kani and Winston Ntshona), *"Master Harold" and the Boys*, and *The Road to Mecca.* In Fugard's own words, his plays attempt to "bear witness" and "break the conspiracy of silence" in the face of South African oppression.

With the rigid imposition of apartheid in the 1960's, it became almost impossible to have collaboration across the racial divide. This was not without its paradoxical rewards. Gibson Kente, now regarded as one of the most successful South African theater producers of all time, had originally attempted to find a creative outlet in The Union of South African Artists. Forced to set up a base in the segregated township of Soweto, he rapidly established a very large township audience for his musicals such as *Manana, the Jazz Prophet*; *Sikhalo*; *Lifa*; *Zwi*; and *Too Late.*

In the late 1960's and early 1970's Black Consciousness, under the leadership of Steve Biko, became a powerful force. This movement gave rise to many challenging theatrical works, including *Egoli*, written by Matsemela Manaka, and *The Hungry Earth* by Maishe Maponya.

The Black Consciousness movement of the 1970's, powerful as it was, did not have the monopoly on political plays. In 1971 a theater company called Workshop 71 began to create a series of significant works, including *Crossroads* and *Survival.* Workshop 71 provided a model for collaborative play creation by members of all racial groups under a democratic management. The very difficult question of language and cultural action in a multilingual country was tackled. Plays were to be constructed in the patois and "street language" of the majority, and were to make their audiences more politically aware. They would use familiar props and words to win over a new audience to a political vision of a democratic and nonracial future.

In 1976 Workshop 71 broke up. Many of its members went into exile. Three of the remaining members joined forces with members of Junction Avenue Theatre Company, until then an all-white student group based at the University of the Witwatersrand. Most of Junction Avenue Theatre Company's plays have dealt with what has become known as the "hidden history," the daily lives of those the government ignores. This company has had its major success with the play *Sophiatown*, which toured extensively on the international festival circuit in 1986, 1987, and 1988.

In 1979 the actors Mbongeni Ngema and Percy Mtwa, who were touring in Gibson Kente's *Mama and the Load*, decided to work on a play of their own. What if Jesus were to come to present-day South Africa? Would he not be jailed along with leaders such as Nelson Mandela? Barney Simon, artistic director of the newly formed Market Theatre, was invited to collaborate. The national and international success *Woza Albert!* was the result.

In the 1980's the Market Theatre, a converted fruit market in the center of the old section of Johannesburg, has dominated the scene. Play after play has originated there, and gone on to burst onto world consciousness. Plays such as *Bopha*, *Asinamali*, *Sophiatown*, *Black Dog*, *Born in the RSA*, and *Township Boy* have generated much critical and popular acclaim. Ngema's musical *Sarafina!*, dealing with the life of black schoolchildren under apartheid, has taken Broadway by storm. But it seems this phase of creative energy may have exhausted itself, and currently there is a hunt for new form and a new audience.

Two developments of significance must be noted. The first is a dissident Afrikaner cultural movement, which has taken to creating provocative cabarets, aiming sharp barbs at the ruling elite. Reminiscent of the political cabarets that emerged in the 1920's and 1930's in Germany, these performances are aimed at pricking the swollen and bloated self-righteousness of those in charge.

The second development of major significance is the emergence of a trade-union cultural movement, which includes the making of plays by workers for workers. In their stories, poems, and plays workers tell of the terrible conditions in the workplace and how they are exploited in terms of both race and class. The Natal area has generated two wonderful plays, both created by a workers' cooperative and assisted by the Durban Cultural Local. These plays, *The Long March* and *Bambatha's Children*, have been seen in union, community, and church halls across the country.

Music

"There is a richer mix of music in South Africa than exists in most areas of the world." So claims Billy Bergman in his book *African Pop*. The music of a land of such diversity of cultures exists in many forms, sometimes related, sometimes diametrically opposed. These social dynamics have resulted in both the flourishing of some musics and the struggle of others to survive.

Traditionally the music of the region was different from that of most of the rest of the continent. In contrast with the highly rhythmic instrumental music from central and west Africa, it has been vocal music that has dominated in South Africa. Under the influence of missionary-taught hymns, this took on the form of simple Western harmony. The style called *mbube* grew from these roots and is best exemplified by the internationally acclaimed vocal group Ladysmith Black Mambazo.

"The Merry Blackbirds" in the late 1930's.

After being driven by poverty into the mines or other industries, black workers from the country had to find new ways to express themselves in music. One such form developed in the *shebeen*, a kind of speakeasy in the slums where illicit liquor (called *skokiaan*) was sold and where dancing continued throughout the night. Out of this culture emerged *marabi*, a music using guitars, pianos, concertinas, and homemade percussion. This repetitive music was created for relaxation and dance and developed into archetypal South African music, in a similar way to the blues in the United States.

Young Zulu women dancing during a competition held in Durban.   Jason Laure

In the 1940's U.S. culture strongly influenced South African black society, and several big bands emerged, such as the Merry Blackbirds and the Harlem Swingsters. A synthesis of big band and *marabi* styles was apparent in bands like the Jazz Maniacs (led by Solomon "Zulu Boy" Cele), and this formed the basis for new styles created by leaders in the South African jazz field such as Hugh Masekela, Jonas Gwangwa and the late Kippie Moeketsi, all of whom emerged in the 1950's. But those blacks with more middle-class aspirations looked down upon the *marabi* influences and settled rather for imitations of Duke Ellington, Count Basie, and the Mills Brothers.

Another offshoot of *marabi* is the music known as *mbaqanga*, a guitar- and, currently, synthesizer-dominated, repetitive popular music that has been the most commercially successful form of South African music for several decades. Groups such as the Soul Brothers exemplify *mbaqanga* (which means "corn bread").

Perhaps the best way to understand South African music is to examine the effects that separation has had on it. One main division that has existed is the obvious black-white one, but the urban-rural division is also significant. Ethnic identity is encouraged by the government-controlled South African Broadcasting Corporation (SABC). The Corporation has a policy of separate broadcasting stations for ten or so language groups. Thus the idea of a strong, unified black culture is kept in check. Unfortunately, the record companies have been largely compliant with these policies, and so the divisions have been perpetuated.

But many individual musicians have aspired to do the very opposite—to produce music across the barriers. Indeed, the most famous

In a backyard in Soweto children practice the gumboot dance. The dance was originated by the Zulus when they worked in the sugarcane fields near the Indian Ocean. Jason Laure

South African musicians, such as singer Miriam Makeba, Hugh Masekela, and pianist Dollar Brand (Abdullah Ibrahim), have maintained strongly political stances in opposition to apartheid. And the now-famous Johnny Clegg pioneered the way into "crossover" music in his collaboration with Sipho Mchunu (a guitarist-singer-dancer from KwaZulu). Their group, Juluka, performed in the late 1970's and early 1980's. Clegg today has achieved international success with his group Savuka (meaning "we have awoken").

Most whites, however, remain unaware of the dynamics of change and listen to European and American music. State funding for music goes mostly to so-called "serious" or European classical music, in a strange attempt to assert European roots. The official education system does little to encourage the emergence of indigenous, traditional, or contemporary styles.

Boycotts

Many South Africans of all races have had to pay a penalty for living in apartheid-ruled South Africa. Aside from the implementation of fierce economic sanctions against the country, strong sporting and cultural boycotts have also been put into operation. South African playwrights, actors, and musicians have had to struggle to get their work performed in countries outside the Republic. Many of the world's leading performers have refused to perform in South Africa. Some actors and directors, such as Woody Allen, will not allow their films to be screened in the country. Some authors refuse to let their books be sold there. Some of the world's best television programs never get to the Republic. Paul Simon was rebuked by the African National Congress for coming to South Africa to look for material for his *Graceland* record. Nevertheless, the black groups Ladysmith Black Mambazo and Stimela became famous as a result of their participation in the Simon record.

Sport

But it is in the field of sport that South Africans, black and white, have been made to suffer most. Until the 1950's most of South Africa's sports teams were open to whites only. Visiting black sportsmen and sportswomen were not welcome in South Africa. The All Black (their name relates to the color of their uniforms, not to their skin color) rugby team from New Zealand used to leave their Maori players behind when they toured South Africa. Thus the All Blacks who toured South Africa were in fact all whites! In later years Maori players *were* accepted in South Africa, but in recent times all official tours have come to an end. White South Africans, particularly Afrikaans-speaking South Africans, are fanatical about rugby football. The Springboks were for many years world champions in international rugby and, if allowed back into the international arena, would probably be champions again.

In the 1960's the pressure to isolate South African sport was growing. South African exiles such as Dennis Brutus in the United States and Peter Hain (whose parents were both members of the South African Liberal Party and banned by the government) in Britain were leaders in this campaign. The boycott was intensified in 1968 when Prime Minister John Vorster refused to allow England's cricket team to tour the country because they had included in their team an ex-South African coloured cricketer, Basil d'Oliviera.

By the 1970's the boycott movement against South African players had grown very powerful. Long excluded from the Olympic Games, South Africans now experienced isolation in many other sports events. Proposed tours by Springbok rugby and cricket squads were canceled one after another or else severely disrupted by militant demonstrators.

Particularly disastrous was the Springbok rugby tour of New Zealand in 1981, when violence broke out at nearly every match. Sadly, New Zealand became a divided society as a result of the tour.

So great was the pressure on South Africa to eliminate apartheid in sport that many sports administrators embarked on a policy of rapid integration. The government also changed its stance. Apartheid signs began to disappear at various stadiums, and in sports such as gymnastics and soccer integration took place in many of the leagues. Soccer is perhaps the most integrated sport today and is certainly the most popular sport in the black community.

In spite of the changes—and still many more need to be made—South Africa has not managed to make its way back into the international sporting arena. Golfers such as Gary Player have not been affected by sports boycotts, but in other sports South Africans have been frustrated. In favor of South Africa's continued isolation is the South African Council of Sport (SACOS). A SACOS representative has stated: "The only way sport will function in a normal way here in South Africa is if apartheid is removed." Those who favor South Africa's continued isolation maintain that there can be "no normal sport in an abnormal society." Black athletes such as Sydney Maree and Mark Plaatjies found that in South Africa SACOS frowned on their participation in South African competitions, and they were not allowed to compete abroad because they were South Africans. Both athletes have taken up residence in the United States.

Other leading South African sportspersons, such as the tennis player Kevin Curren, have decided to pursue their sporting careers outside South Africa. The young runner Afrikaans-speaking Zola Budd managed to secure British citizenship and ran for Britain. But she refused to condemn apartheid, and as a result was eventually forced out of competitive athletics. She returned to her home in the Orange Free State.

Several leading sports administrators, such as rugby bosses Danie Craven and Louis Luyt, have traveled outside South Africa to consult

A soccer match at a stadium in Johannesburg. Soccer is one of the most integrated sports in South Africa today.   Santu Mofokeng, Afrapix

with the African National Congress in an attempt to bring South Africa's sporting isolation to an end. But these visits have been frowned upon by the South African government and by conservative sports administrators.

One day, when apartheid has eventually been totally eradicated, South Africa will become a truly great sporting nation.

Bibliography

South Africa—Geography

Robertson, T. C. *South African Mosaic.* Cape Town: C. Struik Publishers, 1978. Impressionistic photographs and informed text combine to give the reader brilliant insights into South Africa's environment and variety of cultures.

South Africa—History

Callinicos, Luli. *Workers on the Rand: Factories, Townships and Popular Culture, 1886–1942.* Athens, Ohio: Ohio University Press. Deals with lifestyles and occupations of working-class people and also tells the story of men and women who played a major role in the country's industrial revolution. The book contains fine historical photographs. Two other books by the author, *Gold and Workers 1886–1924* and *Working Life 1886–1940*, are also available from Ohio University Press.

De Villiers, Marc. *White Tribe Dreaming: Apartheid's Bitter Roots as Witnessed by Eight Generations of an Afrikaner Family.* New York: Viking, 1987. An eighth-generation Afrikaner now living in Canada tells the story of his ancestors since their arrival in South Africa in 1688. An impeccably researched study of "apartheid's bitter roots."

Elphick, Richard. *Khoikhoi and the Founding of White South Africa.* Athens, Ohio: Ohio University Press, 1986. A history of the Khoikhoi people and of their confrontation with the Dutch. For specialized research.

Morris, Donald R. *The Washing of the Spears: The Rise and Fall of the Zulu Nation.* New York: Simon & Schuster, 1986. A detailed and absorbing account of the rise and fall of the Zulu nation.

Pakenham, Thomas. *The Boer War.* New York: Random House, 1979. The first full-length account of the history of the Anglo-Boer War since 1910. Perhaps *the* definitive history of the war. For advanced readers.

Parsons, Neil. *A New History of Southern Africa.* New York: Holmes and Meier, 1983. A comprehensive history of Southern Africa with numerous illustrations and quotations from contemporary documents. For advanced readers.

Peires, J. B. *The House of Phalo: A History of the Xhosa People in the Days of Their Independence.* Berkeley, California: University of California Press, 1982.

Stanley, Diane, and Peter Vennema. *Shaka: King of the Zulus.* New York: Morrow, 1988. A picture book about the mighty King of the Zulus.

South Africa—Contemporary Commentary

Biko, Steve. *I Write What I Like.* New York: Harper & Row, 1986. A collection of essays on Black Consciousness by the late Steve Biko. They were first published the year after his death.

Leach, Graham. *South Africa: No Easy Path to Peace.* New York: Routledge, Chapman and Hall, 1987. A lively and incisive account of South Africa's recent history by the BBC's Southern Africa Radio Correspondent.

Paton, Alan. *Save the Beloved Country.* Johannesburg: Hans Strydom Publishers, 1987. A collection of Alan Paton's articles and speeches written since 1965. This collection was published shortly before his death in 1988.

South Africa—Miscellaneous

Bergman, Billy. *Goodtime Kings: Emerging African Pop.* New York: Morrow, 1985. A lively and informative book about various pop styles in sub-Saharan Africa.

Branford, Jean. *A Dictionary of South African English*, rev. ed. New York: Oxford University Press, 1987. An excellent and entertaining dictionary covering a wide range of South African English, with many examples quoted from literary texts and newspapers.

Coplan, David B. *In Township Tonight.* New York: Longmans, 1986. Traces the fascinating diversity of music in South Africa, including its links with that of the United States.

South African Literature

(By no means an exhaustive or even a representative list. Rather, a few suggestions for curious readers.)

Novels

Brink, Andre. *A Dry White Season.* New York: Penguin, 1984.

———. *Rumours of Rain.* New York: Penguin, 1984.

Coetzee, J. M. *Waiting for the Barbarians.* New York: Penguin, 1982.

———. *Life and Times of Michael K.* New York: Penguin, 1985.

Dikobe, Modikwe. *The Marabi Dance.* London: Heinemann, 1973.

Gordimer, Nadine. *Burger's Daughter.* New York: Viking, 1979.

———. *July's People.* New York: Viking, 1981.

Paton, Alan. *Cry, the Beloved Country.* New York: Scribner, 1961.

———. *Too Late the Phalarope.* New York: Scribner, 1985.

Plaatje, Solomon T. *Mhudi.* Washington: Three Continents, 1975. First published by the Lovedale Press in 1930. A beautiful edition with illustrations by Cecil Skotnes was published by the Quagga Press in Johannesburg in 1975.

Schreiner, Olive. *The Story of an African Farm.* Various publishers. First published in Great Britain in 1883, it has recently been released in a beautifully bound, illustrated edition by Century Hutchinson, London.

Autobiography

Abrahams, Peter. *Tell Freedom.* Winchester, Ma.: Faber, 1982.

Mphahlele, Es'kia. *Afrika My Music.* Athens, Ohio: Ohio University Press, 1986.

————. *Down Second Avenue.* Winchester, Ma.: Faber, 1985.

Tell the story of Es'kia Mphahlele's life from his birth in 1919 until 1983.

Paton, Alan. *Towards the Mountain.* New York: Scribner, 1987.

————. *Journey Continued: An Autobiography.* New York: Scribner, 1988.

In *Towards the Mountain* Alan Paton tells his life story from his birth in 1903 until 1948. In *Journey Continued* he tells the rest of the story. This book was published two weeks after his death in April 1988.

Short Stories

Gordimer, Nadine. *A Soldier's Embrace.* New York: Penguin, 1982.

Ndebele, Njabulo. *Fools and Other Stories.* New York: Reader's International, 1986.

Paton, Alan. *Tales from a Troubled Land.* New York: Scribner, 1961.

Other Prose

Patel, Essop, ed. *The World of Nat Nakasa..* Athens, Ohio: Ohio University Press, 1985. This book contains selected writings from one of South Africa's top journalists, Nat Nakasa, who committed suicide while exiled in New York in 1965.

Children's Writing

Two Dogs and Freedom was jointly published by Ravan Press and the Open School in 1986. It is subtitled *Children of the Townships Speak Out.* The book contains drawings and commentary by Soweto children who were responding to the presence of police and army in their townships. The title comes from the contribution of Moagi, aged 8: "When I am old I would like to have a wife and to children a boy and a girl and a big house and to dogs and freedom my friends and I would like to meat together and tok."

Drama (Theater)

Fugard, Athol. *Boesman and Lena.* New York: Oxford University Press, 1978.

————. *"Master Harold" and the Boys.* New York: Knopf, 1982.

Junction Avenue Theatre Company: *Sophiatown.* David Philip: Cape Town, 1988. First performed in 1986. Contains an introduction by Malcolm Purkey, who directed the play.

Mtwa, Perey; Mbongeni Ngema; and Barney Simon. *Woza Albert!* New York: Methuen, 1983. First performed in 1981.

Poetry

Brutus, Dennis. *Stubborn Hope: Poems.* Washington: Three Continents, 1978.

————. *Letters to Martha.* London: Heinemann, 1968.

Campbell, Roy (Peter Alexander, ed.) *Selected Poems.* New York: Oxford University Press, 1982.

Levenson, Marcia, and Jonathan Paton, eds. *Voices of the Land.* Johannesburg: Ad. Donker, 1985.

Novels and Story Collections for Younger Readers

Naidoo, Beverley. *Journey to Jo'Burg: A South African Story.* New York: Lippincott, 1986.

————. *Chain of Fire.* New York: Lippincott, 1990.

Rochman, Hazel, ed. *Somehow Tenderness Survives: Stories of Southern Africa.* New York: Harper & Row, 1988.

Discography

The following is a sampler of contemporary South African music available in the United States.

The Boyoyo Boys, *Back in Town* (Rounder 5026)
Johnny Clegg, *Third World Child* (MINC 1146)
Johnny Dyani, *African Bass* (Red VPA 149)
Abdulla Ibrahim (Dollar Brand), *Echoes from Africa* (Inner City 3019)
Ladysmith Black Mambazo, *Ulwandle Oluncgwele* (Shanachie 43030)
Dudu Pukwana, *In the Townships* (Virgin 90884–1)
Philip Tabane/Malombo, *Malombo* (Kaya 300)
Rhythms of Resistance (Shanachie 43018)
The Indestructible Beat of Soweto (Shanachie 43033)

Filmography

The following is a sampler of films, their distributors, and other clearinghouses for South African movies.

Art Against Apartheid. Distributed by Not-for-Profit TV, 180 Claremont Avenue, #32, New York, NY 10027.

Fight Where We Stand, an excellent filmstrip on the movement of black families from the country to the city, is available through the American Social History Project, Graduate Center, CUNY, 33 West 42 Street, New York, NY 10036.

Mining Centre: Johannesburg; *The Turning Point*; *Rock Art Treasures*; *Images of South Africa*; *South African Drama*; *Alan Paton: Profile of a Critic*; and *The Story of an African Farm* are just some of the movies available from the University of the Witwatersrand's extensive collection, though they may be difficult to obtain. Write: University of the Witwatersrand, Johannesburg, P.O. Wits, 2050 South Africa.

South Africa: The White Laager. Distributed by Pennsylvania State University, AV Services, Special Services Building, University Park, PA 16082. Also available from the University of Illinois/Champaign Film Center, 1325 South Oak Street, Champaign, IL 61820.

Girls Apart; *Children of Apartheid*; and *Generations of Resistance* are among the films that can be obtained through the Southern Africa Media Center, California Newsreel, 630 Natoma Street, San Francisco, CA 94103.

Media Network's *Guide to Films on Apartheid and the African Region* is a useful guide to additional films about South Africa, and is available from Media Network, 208 West 13 Street, New York, NY 10011.

Index

Numbers in *italics* refer to illustrations.